THE MATCHMAKER WORE MARS YELLOW

MYSTERIOUS DEVICES BOOK 3

SHELLEY ADINA

Moonshell
Books

This is a work of fantasy and science fiction. Names, characters, places, and incidents are a product of the author's imagination. Locales and public names are sometimes used for atmospheric purposes. Any resemblance to actual people, living or dead, or to businesses, companies, events, institutions, or locales is completely coincidental.

Cover art by Seedlings Online, images used under license.

ISBN-13: 978-1-939087-97-3

The Matchmaker Wore Mars Yellow / Shelley Adina—1st ed.

❀ Created with Vellum

INTRODUCTION

Book three of the Mysterious Devices series of clockwork cozies set in the Magnificent Devices world!

Daisy and Frederica Linden have tracked their missing father to Bodie, the most dangerous town in the Wild West, where bad men murder without guilt and single ladies are as rare and valuable as gold. Here they must depend upon the help of the society of absent friends, that secret network of boarding-house keepers who know everyone's business—and make secrets their stock in trade.

But some secrets are fatal, and when the local matchmaker pays the price with her life on the night of the Autumn Ball, the ladies of the society beg Daisy and Freddie to help them find the killer of their fallen sister. Aided by Miss Peony Churchill, an intrepid family of aeronauts, and a Rocky Mountain Detective, the Linden sisters must see justice done and unmask a deadly conspiracy. But in a town where murder is more common than spiked absinthe, will they find themselves in the killer's sights instead?

"This ... continues much of what I always loved about the *Magnificent Devices* series—an involved world, and some excellent, intelligent, capable, flawed but growing female characters with excellent relationships between them." — Fangs for the Fantasy, on *The Bride Wore Constant White*

Visit Shelley's website, www.shelleyadina.com, where you can sign up for her newsletter and be the first to know of new releases and special promotions. You'll also receive a free short story set in the Magnificent Devices world just for subscribing!

"An immensely fun book in an immensely fun series with some excellent anti-sexist messages, a wonderful main character (one of my favourites in the genre) and a great sense of Victorian style and language that's both fun and beautiful to read."

For Leyton and Cindy Howard
and for Jeff, always,
with gratitude

THE MATCHMAKER WORE
MARS YELLOW

CHAPTER 1

SEPTEMBER 1895

The Texican Territories

*B*y the second day of their journey west from Santa Fe, Daisy Linden was beginning to feel that everyone she met was trying to talk her out of traveling to Bodie.

Well, perhaps not *everyone*. But enough concerned souls had spoken up to give her qualms about whether she ought to be taking her younger sister Freddie to "the wickedest place in the Wild West" on the next stage of their search for Papa.

There had been two such souls on the airship on which they had sailed from Santa Fe to Reno, for instance.

"What is Bodie like?" repeated a well-to-do gentleman down the length of his nose. "Well, I say two young ladies from Bath have no business going there." His considerable bulk appeared to be laced into a man's brocade corset—possibly in protest at his destination, for he was bound for Bodie, too. "But I will tell you this—it is a gold-mining town. The richest in the Texican Territory. The Bodie Consolidated

Mine produces hundreds of thousands of dollars in gold every year."

"It's a confounded hellacious death trap," put in a grizzled individual who might have been a miner, or a cowboy, or a journalist, come to that. He had been leaning on the rail of the viewing platform at the stern of the ship, and joined the conversation uninvited. "It ain't no place for young ladies, though I hear wimmin like ye are goin' for a premium these days. Ye'll be married by Friday to some buck who's struck it rich, see if you ain't."

Daisy had shuddered in horror, and she and Freddie had left the viewing platform shortly thereafter.

It was no different on the passenger train, which ran south from Reno on the branch rail line built by the late Josiah Comstock.

"Bodie is the home of the devil," a man in a black suit and a cleric's collar had intoned when he joined them in their second-class compartment. "With twenty thousand sinners under his rule, seeking their own damnation with desert flowers, in opium dens and saloons, in murder, betrayal, and theft. One can almost believe that God turns a blind eye to the place when the most frequent inquiry each morning is whether there has been a man for breakfast."

Meaning has someone been shot, Daisy heard William Barnicott's warm voice say in her memory. But that thought sent a pang through her, and if she allowed another, she would overflow into tears.

"Do you minister to these poor people, sir?" Freddie was ready to see nobility in anyone at first meeting.

A spasm passed over the man's face, like a catspaw of wind on calm water. "No indeed, young lady. I minister to the saved, that they may stand firm against the onslaught of the enemy." Seeing that Freddie had been silenced, he went on, "I hope we will welcome you in church. The Methodist Church is the only building with a steeple in the entire town. I myself am not a Methodist, so I will be hiring a hall in which to bring my message of hope to the Christians there."

By the third day of their journey, it was clear the Linden sisters had not yet been deterred from their quest—or perhaps people had simply turned once again to their own business. The train pulled into a tiny station on the hillside on the Monday afternoon following the day they had left Santa Fe, puffing great clouds of steam into the air.

The sign on the platform said BODIE. Daisy and Freddie peered out of the lowered windows, fixed in their seats by the panorama below them.

"This ... is not a town, Daisy," Freddie managed at last. "It is a ..." But she could not finish, and Daisy did not blame her, for how could one describe Bodie when one could hardly take it in?

Now that they had reached their destination, the vicar was one of the first to the doors. The train gave one last huge belch of steam and three quick hoots to signal it was safe to disembark.

Daisy gathered her reticule. "We had best collect our things."

"But where will we even begin our search?"

Daisy could not say. For in the valley below lay what seemed to be two miles of streets, houses, shacks, saloons, and hotels, laid out higgledy-piggledy as though by the hand of a drunken civil engineer ... or by no hand at all. In the huge bowl in the mountains in which the town was cupped, there was not a tree to be seen from horizon to horizon, only scrub and grass, as though the land itself would murder anything that dared raise its head.

And high on the hill west of town was a series of large buildings, smokestacks, and conveyor belts that must be the mine. It dominated the landscape, reminding everyone below what their purpose was in being here.

Gold.

She doubted she had enough sticks of charcoal with her to sketch that monstrosity, even if she were tempted to commit the sight to one of the precious sheets of paper in her sketchbook.

Oh, Papa, what possessed you to come here?

But she already knew. A mistake.

For from the mists of his memory, abused by men and time and unfortunate circumstance, had surfaced a name. It was their tragedy that Bodey was not the name of this town, but of a man. The president of the university in Victoria in the Canadas who had offered him the deanship of the engineering department last year. Heaven only knew whether Dr. Bodey had given up on ever seeing Dr. Rudolf Linden, R.S.E. Having heard nothing in months and months, he had probably awarded the post to someone else.

But that was not Daisy and Freddie's affair. Finding their father was, and had been since their arrival in the Texican Territories from England in July.

And now it was September, and while they had accomplished a number of things, finding their father had not been one of them. They were no closer than they had been when they stepped off the transatlantic airship *Persephone* in New York.

"Daisy, here. I will pull the traveling trunk, and you must take both valises. It seems we will have to walk down the hill into town."

Freddie's powers of observation, however, proved to be incorrect. For waiting outside the station was a twelve-mule team pulling an enormous wagon. Even the strait-laced man from the Reno airship had perforce to hoist himself up, trunk, valises, and all. Daisy grasped the handle of the wheeled traveling closet that had belonged to Emma Makepeace before her untimely death, and heaved it up to Freddie, who sat upon it, leaving one of the last seats on the bench for Daisy.

In the course of their quest, with each arrival in a new town, they were becoming familiar with what must be done. Find somewhere to sleep. Find a meal. Then, find someone who might have seen Papa. A simple formula.

Twenty thousand people lived—and tended to die, apparently—here in Bodie. Any one of those thousands might have seen him. Daisy refused to let the prospect cow her further. After all, she and Freddie had found clues to Papa's whereabouts in Santa Fe, and that city held easily that number. It was simply a matter of applying logic and narrowing the field.

The road into town was wide, but pitted with rocks and potholes. The iron wheels of the wagon found every one. A young man on a steam-powered velocipede sailed past them, goggles over his eyes, a kerchief over his nose to keep out the dust, his valise tied to the handlebars. He wore a Harris tweed belted jacket that combined dark gray and green in an appealing mix. Daisy felt a moment of envy at his freedom even as she wondered where she had seen that jacket before. On the airship from Reno, perhaps? Was everyone en route to Bodie, then?

"What a good idea," Freddie said with some admiration, watching the sturdy figure sail down the hill. "In the absence of a horse or a landau, that is the very thing. For there is certainly nothing in this landscape to prevent one from going anywhere one wishes. Nothing except rocks."

Minutes later, the mules lurched to a halt outside the livery stable, and all the passengers disembarked. In the relative silence empty of the sounds of the train or the wagon, Daisy felt a subtle vibration in the ground. Not only that, the sound of thunder, muted, yet continuous, was an undercurrent below more homely sounds. Not like natural thunder at all.

She and Freddie exchanged a glance. No one else seemed to be alarmed by the sound. How very strange.

Daisy approached the clergyman, who might best be able to help them, before he strode away with his valises.

"Excuse me, Vicar, but could you direct my sister and I to a respectable boarding-house? I should have inquired before, but I am afraid we were overwhelmed by our arrival."

"Certainly, young lady." He put one valise on the ground and pointed to the left. "You are standing on Green Street. You will find several down there, clearly marked. And in the opposite direction—" His arm swung like a weathervane, pointing west. "—you will turn left up there on Main Street, where you may find any number of hotels, the best being the U.S. Hotel or the Occidental." He looked down upon them with a forbidding expression. "On no account must you venture down Main Street as far as King Street, for beyond that lies Maiden Lane, and I will not sully my tongue further on that subject."

Daisy could guess the trade being plied in Maiden Lane.

There was no need for such a disdainful tone, though. She and Freddie had found—and lost—good and brave hearts in the flower houses of other towns. But he would not appreciate her pointing this out. So she said merely, "Thank you, sir."

He strode away in the direction of the Methodist Church before she could ask him about the subtle thunder in the air. Never mind. First things first. Daisy fished the tiny enamel zinnia out of her reticule and affixed it to the collar of her walking suit. "Come, Freddie. Let us see where this takes us."

For in the language of flowers, the zinnia meant *thoughts of absent friends*, and was the emblem of the sisterhood of boarding-house keepers in the Wild West. In Santa Fe, they had been fortunate enough to meet one of that sharp-eyed band, and in thanks for services rendered, Daisy had been given the brooch.

There were five boarding-houses on this end of Green Street alone, with neat painted signs beside their doors.

CASA GALLINA—6 ROOMS, $5 PER NIGHT AND FOUND.
SIERRA AZUL—12 ROOMS, HOT WATER, BREAKFAST TWICE DAILY, $6 PER NIGHT.
SUNRISE HOUSE—8 ROOMS, HOT WATER AND 3 MEALS, $5 PER NIGHT.

"Dear me," Daisy said at last, when they had perused all the signs and seen varying measures of neatness and cleanliness about yards and fences. "How does one choose?"

"I vote for the velocipede," Freddie said firmly. "It is around the side of Casa Gallina. If a forward-thinking gentleman of some technical knowledge chooses this one, then it is good enough for me."

In the absence of any other way to differentiate, Daisy nodded, and they knocked on the door.

It was opened with a flourish by one of the most beautiful women Daisy had ever seen.

Her hair was blonde and piled up on her head in a fetching concoction of curls, one of which dangled down to lie upon her shoulder. She wore a form-fitting bodice of tawny silk—Mars Yellow, Daisy would swear to it—with huge puffed sleeves, and a skirt of the same color embellished at the hem by whorls of soutache braid. Her eyes were as blue as a September sky, fringed with long lashes, and her lips were soft and smiling with welcome.

Daisy's gaze went to the lady's throat, where a red zinnia reposed. "Good aft—" she began.

"Why, you are absent friends as well!" the lady exclaimed, and the smile took on such delight that it was dazzling. "Oh, this is a happy occasion. Come in, come in. You must be exhausted. I am Mrs. Clarissa Moss, the proprietress here."

They barely had time to set their bags down in the hall when Mrs. Moss said, "How far did you come today?"

Heavens, how cordial she was. Had Mrs. Alvarez written from Santa Fe to let the sisterhood know they were coming?

"We have been two days on the train from Reno," Freddie said shyly. "We would have been here sooner, but there was a landslide."

Mrs. Moss *tsk*ed. "Such a bore. I make the journey as seldom as possible. But the day is coming soon when airships will fly here directly, now that the Royal Kingdom will not be shooting them out of the sky. They must certainly build a proper airfield, with mooring masts. The absence of trees means they must build them of iron, and they simply have not got around to it yet. They would be quicker to build them of gold." She laughed. "Come upstairs, do, and I will show you your rooms."

Rooms, plural?

"We are quite used to sharing a room, ma'am," Daisy said. "I am afraid our pocketbooks are not up to the expense of two."

"Sharing a room?" The lady ushered them into a large room that held two beds, overlooking the velocipede and the side yard. "Are the two of you acquainted?"

"Why, yes," Freddie said. "We are sisters."

"Sisters!" Mrs. Moss clasped her hands. "I knew you were traveling together, but I did not know you were actually related. Well, you will be quite the belles of the ball, and if we are successful, you will not need to be parted."

"Successful, ma'am?" Daisy was battling a feeling of confusion, as though she had been caught up in a whirlwind. Or was listening through a door to someone else's conversation.

"Parted?" Freddie echoed, clearly feeling the same way.

But Mrs. Moss was fluffing the pillows, and did not seem to hear. "You must tell me where you came by your pin. Does your mother keep a boarding-house?"

"No, indeed," Daisy said. Here at least was a fact to settle on. "It was a gift from Mrs. Alvarez, of Santa Fe. When she heard we were coming to Bodie, she felt it might pave a path to friendships we might not otherwise be so fortunate as to cultivate."

"Eileen Alvarez!" Mrs. Moss said in delight. "I know her well. Any friend of Eileen's is a friend of mine, and now you shall have your clothes laundered at no charge." She beamed at them. "You will find that is no small gift here. The dust is terrible."

"It seems rather ... barren," Freddie ventured. "Thank you very much. And please, could you tell me what that thundering sound is? I can feel it in the very soles of my feet."

Mrs. Moss made a moue of distaste. "Yes, it is the first thing you notice when you come to Bodie—after the dust. It is the automatons, you know. Up at the mine." When Daisy and Freddie both looked blank, she went on, "The ore must be broken up into small pieces to get the gold out. Enormous automatons stamp them to bits. It is quite horrible. A man dies at least once a week from sheer carelessness, the life crushed out of him under their feet."

"Good heavens." Daisy's throat felt dry.

Mrs. Moss waved a hand, as though to erase such unpleasantness. "Never mind. We will talk of happier things. Settle in now, and we will have some tea. Downstairs in the parlor, say in half an hour?"

Tea sounded wonderful. So wonderful that they presented themselves in the parlor in twenty minutes, hands and faces washed and hair taken down, brushed, and repinned in presentable order.

The owner of the velocipede—and the Harris tweed jacket —turned as they entered. His eyes widened.

Freddie's did, too. In her astonishment, Daisy opened her mouth to greet him, but he shook his head urgently.

"Allow me to introduce you," said Mrs. Moss, bustling in with the tea tray. "Miss Hannah Harding and Miss June LeVesque—have I pronounced that correctly?—may I present Mr. David Carnegey of St. Louis."

Daisy was no more capable of speech than of walking on

the ceiling. For at least three of the four people in the room were not who they were supposed to be. In the silence of shock, she could do only one thing.

She offered her hand.

He shook it with grave solemnity. When she lifted her gaze to meet his, the message in his eyes was clear.

Say nothing, and later I will explain.

"Miss Harding," said Barnaby Hayes, Rocky Mountain Detective. "How do you do?"

CHAPTER 2

MONDAY, SEPTEMBER 2, 1895

4:20 p.m.

*M*iss Harding. Dear me. This cannot be allowed to go on.

"Mrs. Moss," Daisy said, "I am afraid there has been a small misunderstanding. My sister and I are not Miss Harding and Miss Levesque. We are the Misses Linden, from Bath. I am Daisy, and this is Frederica."

In the act of pouring the tea, Mrs. Moss stared, then dropped her gaze to concentrate upon filling the cup. A delicate pleat formed between her fine brows. When she handed the cup and saucer to Daisy, she said, "You are not Miss Harding, of Philadelphia?"

"No, ma'am. I do apologize for not correcting you before, but we did not realize … I mean to say, it never occurred to us that you might be expecting two altogether different young ladies. I simply thought that Mrs. Alvarez had written to her acquaintance here to say we were coming."

"She has not." Mrs. Moss seemed to be rapidly re-evaluating their situation. Daisy hoped it would not affect her promise of laundered clothes at no charge. "My goodness. I do apologize for making such an assumption."

"Young ladies are few and far between in these parts, I understand," Detective Hayes—rather, Mr. Carnegey, said. "Imagine the joy when the male population discovers there are to be four, not two."

"That is certainly something to be considered, from my point of view." Fully recovered now, Mrs. Moss gave Daisy and Freddie sunny smiles. "I am the town's matchmaker, you see. Miss Harding and Miss Levesque will likely be on tomorrow's train. I have been corresponding with them in order to match them as closely as possible with the most eligible bachelors in town." She twinkled at Detective Hayes. "You must tell me if you wish to be included in that number, Mr. Carnegey. For with you, that will make two journalists in residence here at Casa Gallina. Should you fall in love and settle down, perhaps you and Mr. Pender might start a paper together. Goodness knows we could use a more respectable rag than the *Bodie Barker*. If I wish to read the latest in the *Tales of a Medicine Man* by An Educated Gentleman, I must have a paper sent on the train from Bridgeport. That is our county seat, you know."

She handed Freddie her cup of tea, then poured one for Detective Hayes.

"Let us begin again, Miss Linden. For you must have thought me quite mad." She gave a trill of laughter.

"Indeed, we could not help but think you were a most hospitable and welcoming hostess," Freddie said eagerly. "And since we have not signed a register, it is easy to see how the error might be made."

"All in good time. Tea first." Mrs. Moss handed around a plate of biscuits, then sat back to enjoy her tea. "If I have not corresponded with the people to whom I let rooms, then I depend upon recommendations and word of mouth from members of the sisterhood, such as the excellent Mrs. Alvarez." She lifted her teacup in Daisy's direction. "And of course, anyone wearing the zinnia is instantly welcomed, with no questions asked."

"The zinnia?" Detective Hayes inquired with some interest.

Daisy explained the significance of her little brooch.

"An excellent notion," he said, admiring the piece. "For what could be more useful than a network of persons in the same line of business throughout the Wild West? One has at once friends to count on, a place to sleep, and news communicated that may not come by any other means."

"How perceptive of you, sir." Mrs. Moss said.

He thinks like a detective, Daisy thought. But he was quite right. She and Freddie had discussed those very advantages on their way here, and had found comfort in them.

"You must tell me about yourselves," Mrs. Moss urged. Then she glanced at Detective Hayes. "That is, unless the young ladies would prefer we do so in private."

If she only knew how well acquainted they were!

"Indeed not," Daisy said. "There is nothing about us that may not be generally known." Well, with the exception of the events of Georgetown and Santa Fe. And of Freddie's unusual gift ... which even the detective did not know about. "We are from Bath, as I said. We are in the Wild West in search of our father, Professor Rudolf Linden, who was impressed into the engineering crews of the Royal Kingdom of Spain and the Californias last year."

The cheerful countenance of Detective Hayes became grave. Clearly, he was remembering the man he knew as Dutch, and experiences so terrible he had declined to share them with Daisy in Georgetown.

"Following the Rose Rebellion, it seems he made his way back to Santa Fe, the last place he remembers seeing his family."

"Remembers?" Mrs. Moss repeated.

"We have since discovered that he suffers from loss of memory, likely the result of a blow to the head during his ordeal," Freddie said. "He remembers only fragments of his life. Of himself. His own name has only recently been recalled to him. He knows that he had a family, but not what we are called. He can recognize certain pieces of music. His own distant past. But only fragments, from what we understand."

"Gracious me," Mrs. Moss murmured. "The poor man."

"We received information that he intended to come to Bodie," Daisy went on with a glance at Detective Hayes, to whom this was new information. "But what he did not know was that the Bodey in his mind is not a town, but a person— the president of the university where we were bound last year, before all this happened. He was to take up a post in Victoria, in the Canadas."

"I see," said Mrs. Moss. "Do you think he might still be here in town?"

"It would be wonderful if he were," Freddie said with feeling. "But it has been two weeks at least since he left Santa Fe. We must brace ourselves to learn that he has moved on, while remaining hopeful that he has not, and that we have a chance to find him."

"Of course you will find him." Mrs. Moss laid a sympathetic hand upon Freddie's, and gave it a squeeze. "You may count on the help of the absent friends. We have quilting bees, glees, and tea together at least once a week, to exchange news, embroidery and knitting patterns, recipes ... that sort of thing. We meet on Thursday. If you come with me, we will tell your story to the ladies. If your dear papa is still here, depend upon it, someone among their connections will have seen or heard of him. If not, we will see that the word gets out."

"Oh, thank you, ma'am." Tears welled in Daisy's eyes at the prospect of such help, offered quite without strings attached. "Bless the sisterhood. We are so grateful."

"I am happy to render whatever assistance I may here, also," Detective Hayes said in a casual tone that belied its true meaning. "In my profession, I have the advantage of being able to go where ladies may not. No one finds it odd that a journalist asks questions." Or a professional detective.

"You must be careful, sir," Mrs. Moss warned him. "There are places here where neither drover nor miner is safe—an educated man from away even less. I need not advise you to keep a close watch upon your pocketbook, to say nothing of any drink you are given. In some of the establishments at the lower end of town, one is as likely to receive belladonna as absinthe in one's glass."

"Thank you for the warning, ma'am," he said. "I will take precautions."

A thump of boots on the steps up to the wraparound porch sounded. "Ah, perhaps this is Mr. Pender, our other journalist in residence." Mrs. Moss set her tea on a table at her elbow and had half risen when the front door opened with such energy it banged off the wall.

"Clarissa!"

Mrs. Moss gasped as a man filled the doorway into the parlor. Daisy's eyes widened in recognition, for it was the tall, beefy man in the brocade corset from the airship. The one who had made her feel so stupid and young.

He glared at Mrs. Moss as though he had caught her in a compromising position with a gentleman. "I've finally found you. How long did you think you were going to hide from me, woman?"

Mrs. Moss stood as though turned to stone, one hand at her throat. Slowly, it clenched into a fist.

"Well? What have you to say?"

"Mr. Moss." Her throat sounded dry. "This is a surprise."

This man was her husband? Daisy could hardly imagine the beautiful, delicate Clarissa Moss locked in the bonds of matrimony with a man who looked like a prizefighter gone to seed. Though if she had been tempted to paint him, she might have given a hint or two at past glory, past handsomeness. Hints which were rapidly fading under the influence of too much rich food and a choleric temper.

"A surprise? I'll say, you silly fool. It was a surprise to me when you up and left five years ago. It was a surprise when the Pinkerton man I hired last year finally had something to show for the money I paid him." He took another step into the room.

Detective Hayes rose slowly to his feet.

"But it's no surprise at all to find you running a flower house in the wickedest town in all the Territory." Mr. Moss spat with unerring aim into the heart of a rose woven into the carpet, and glared at Detective Hayes. "You her new fancy man?" The glare swung to scorch Daisy's face, and she flinched. "What does she charge for your services, whore?"

"That's enough!" Detective Hayes roared. "Apologize at once to these ladies. This is a respectable boarding establishment, which you would know if you had eyes and a brain in your head."

"Says who?" Daisy shrank back into the depths of the wing chair as the man bent his knees and assumed the stance of a pugilist, his fists up. "Come on, fancy man, tell me."

"Oh, for heaven's sake, Cyril," Mrs. Moss snapped. "There will be no fighting in my parlor."

"Fine." He bounced on the soles of his feet. "We'll take it outside, fancy man. You'll pay for your share of my wife's favors."

This time Detective Hayes did not bother with a reply. Faster than Daisy had ever seen anyone move, he landed two blows to the man's head and a kick to the ribs. Cyril Moss swayed, gaping stupidly at the younger man. Then his eyes rolled up and he toppled backward like a fallen tree. The teacups jumped in their saucers. A petit point embroidery of a bouquet of yellow zinnias fell off the wall.

In the sudden silence, Detective Hayes bent to rescue the zinnias. He handed the small, oval frame to Mrs. Moss. "I am very sorry. I hope it is not damaged."

She took it, as blankly as an automaton might, and gazed from him to the man on the floor. "Did you just kill him?"

"No indeed. I placed the blows carefully, so as not to cause permanent injury. But he will have a headache when he wakes up."

"What am I to do with him, Mr. Carnegey? For I certainly

do not want him waking up in my house. He is likely to cause considerable damage." She looked down at the zinnias as though she had only just noticed she was holding them, and moved behind the detective's chair to hang them from their hook. "That was the final straw, you see. What finally made me leave him. Because after the destruction of vases and furniture, I knew I should be next."

"A wise choice." Detective Hayes looked about him. "If you ladies will assist me, we can move him out to the street."

It took all three of them to drag and roll the unconscious form out the door, down the steps, and into the scrub grass bordering Green Street, which had not even a boardwalk or a sweep of gravel to glorify it. It was simply dirt, running straight up the hill to the mine. Detective Hayes dropped the man's torso into a rabbit bush without much ceremony, and dusted off his hands.

"It is likely he will return," he said to Mrs. Moss. "How do you propose to protect yourself?"

"I will make a report to the constable."

"There are policemen here?" Daisy said in some surprise. The policing force must not be very effective, if men died each night and were drugged and robbed in saloons.

"Not policemen. One policeman." Mrs. Moss frowned at her husband. "For twenty thousand lawless inhabitants. My report will likely be filed and forgotten. And then I suppose I must carry a gun again. So inconvenient. Half my dresses do not have pockets."

Feeling rather sick inside, Daisy and Freddie encouraged their landlady to go upstairs and lie down. They washed and dried the tea things, and then reconvened in the parlor, where Detective Hayes had dabbed the rug clean of insult, locked the front door, and was standing at the parlor window, watching a small crowd of boys gather about the still recumbent form in the street.

"Is there somewhere we may speak in private?" Daisy asked the detective in a low tone.

"We cannot use one of our rooms, for propriety's sake, and I hesitate to take a walk and leave Mrs. Moss alone in the house," he said. "Perhaps we might speak here, if we keep our voices down."

"Very well." Freddie joined them at the window. "It is very good to see you again, Detec—I mean, Mr. Carnegey."

"Today is certainly a day of surprises, Miss Freddie," he responded with a smile. "This is the last place on the continent I would have expected to meet the two of you again."

"We follow Papa's trail, wherever it may lead," Daisy said. "When we left Georgetown for Santa Fe, we hardly dared hope we might find a clue to his whereabouts."

"But we did—a young lady known to our family. It was she who told us he was heading here," Freddie said. She gazed out of the window, to the mix of homes and boarding-houses opposite, and the sere golden hills beyond. "We are fortunate in the sisterhood of absent friends. At least they have given us a place to start. Otherwise I should lose hope at the outset."

"Very fortunate," he agreed. He took a quick breath as outside, Cyril Moss stirred, rolled over, and slowly pushed himself to his knees, then to his feet. He took a half-hearted swing at one of the little boys, then lumbered away down Green Street, not to another boarding-house, but in the direction of Main Street.

"I think we may be seated," Daisy suggested. "He is in no condition to return."

"With any luck he will get into a fight with someone meaner than he is," Detective Hayes remarked, taking a chair close to them so that they could speak in an undertone.

"I think he already has." Freddie raised her brows rather pointedly. "Are you able to tell us, Mr. ... Carnegey ... what brings you to Bodie?"

"I am not," he confessed. "But I do appreciate your willingness to go along with my subterfuges. Suffice it to say that I am posing as a journalist for an English paper, which, as I said, will allow me to ask questions. I would tell you more, but my employer demands the strictest confidence."

"We understand," Daisy said. "I must say, I feel safe when you are here. Since—" She broke off.

"And Mr. Barnicott and the children?" he asked after a moment, as though he had divined the rest of her sentence. "Are they here, too?"

If he had delivered one of those punches she had just witnessed, Daisy could not have felt more winded. While she tried to catch her breath at a pain in her very being she would never have suspected at the sound of William's name, Freddie spoke.

"No, they are not. Mr. Barnicott needed to make some improvements to his conveyance in Santa Fe."

"Ah, so he did follow you there." The detective sat back. "I thought he might." He glanced at Daisy, but had the delicacy to say no more. After a moment, he rose. "If you will excuse me, I believe I will go to the telegraph office. I must let my— er, the newspaper know that I have arrived. May I perform some errand for you while I am out?"

Daisy took a deep breath to shake herself out of her abstraction. "May we accompany you? I must confess I am very nearly terrified to go out of doors in this place. And yet, we must orient ourselves, in case the inquiries of the sister-hood result in our needing to locate people and speak with them."

"It would be my great pleasure. I believe our hostess is safe for the time being, and I do not expect we will be long."

Daisy and Freddie fetched their hats, and Daisy took a firm grip upon her reticule, wherein reposed her sketchbook and her slender pocketbook. Then each took a proffered arm, and sallied forth into the wickedest town in the Territory.

CHAPTER 3

TUESDAY, SEPTEMBER 3, 1895

3:45 p.m.

*P*eony Churchill was, in the schoolgirl vernacular she had once employed at St. Cecilia's Academy for Young Ladies, as cross as two sticks, and no mistake.

For she had been led a merry chase across the width of the wretched continent, and if she did not locate her quarry soon, she would give the whole thing up as a bad job and go back to London. What fate might await her there, she had no idea. Some chinless heir to a dukedom, presumably. Or possibly the rather dashing clerk, Lewis Protheroe, who had unaccountably become her dear friend Lady Claire Malvern's financial advisor. A man skilled in the making of money was not to be sneezed at, no matter his lack of family or breeding.

But her present search had nothing to do with men. Well, yes, it did, but only in the sense that she needed information about one man in particular. Her mind and heart must be set at rest, or she would go mad.

The two young ladies who possessed this information

23

were supposed to have been in Georgetown, to the west of Denver. But they had not been there. Instead, her informant had said that they had moved on to Santa Fe, the capital of the Texican Territory. Peony had been there before, with her redoubtable mother, who had been lobbying on the behalf of some nation or other. Mama, thank heavens, was in Africa at the moment, shrieking at Sir Cecil Rhodes about diamonds, but at least she had been useful in that she had thawed Peony's bank account to the point where funds might safely be withdrawn once more.

Her mother had frozen them when Peony had made the mistake of confiding in her about her plans to marry Sydney Meriwether-Astor. The man Peony had loved with such abandon that she had very nearly put herself beyond the pale by flying to join him in Egypt. Had it not been for the true heart and the unexpected intervention of Lady Claire, Peony might at this moment be a social pariah, penniless, alone, and unable to return to London ever again.

That fate had been averted by friendship. The next step in her journey had been facilitated by friendship. In fact, Peony was coming to understand that without friendship, a woman could not function very well in the world at all. So here she was, with an airship and crew of her very own, sailing in to what had to be the most peculiar hodgepodge of a town anyone had ever seen, in the hopes that friendship would once again come to her aid.

Bodie (such an unprepossessing name) did not appear to possess an airfield, though through the viewing port Peony could see the railroad, which terminated in a depot a little distance up the hill from the town itself.

Not only was there no airfield, there were no trees to

which an airship might be moored. There was not even a mooring mast fixed on any flat spot. In fact, other than the fantastical jumble of shacks, houses, and hotels, and an enormous and rather terrifying edifice up on the hill, there did not appear to be many marks of civilization here at all.

"Captain Boyle," she said, "Can you see where we might land?"

"Only the entire valley, miss. It is as bare as a monkey's rump. Begging your pardon, miss."

While Captain Alturas Boyle had not exactly come with her ship, he had come highly recommended by Stanford Fremont, Gloria Meriwether-Astor's handsome railroad baron of a husband. Peony had stayed with her former schoolmate in Philadelphia following her disembarkation from *Persephone* in New York. Gloria and Stanford had taken her to their airship works to see if she might find something suitable for chasing people about the country. Peony had taken one look at the sleek elongated shape and beautifully worked gondola of *Iris*—named for the goddess of sea and sky—and fallen fathoms deep in love. Love was expensive, but she handed over the rather shocking sum to Gloria without a qualm, then had to provision and crew her, too.

Captain Boyle was of that far-seeing and taciturn persuasion that some might associate with the sailors of old. His skin and eyes told her he was of Nubian descent, a trait shared by many of the aeronauts of the Royal Aeronautic Corps at home. The proud tilt of his head told her he was not to be argued with in his domain of air. His person was both substantial and immaculate, his head bald under his airman's cap and goggles, and when he spoke, it was in a basso tone that one could practically feel in one's bones.

His wife Persis acted as cook, and without fanfare or waste of time—or consulting his ship's new owner—the eldest Boyle son Timothy had been hired on as navigator, and his niece Dinah as engineer. Dinah's younger brother was midshipman and the two youngest Boyles, Luke and Rebecca, who were as skilled with firearms as their siblings despite the fact they were only ten, were assigned to fuselage and rigging.

Peony hoped that there would be no call for firearms, but experience had taught her it was better to be prepared. Which was why she had been wise enough to accept the lightning pistol Claire had built for her before she'd left London.

When she had asked Captain Boyle with excessive civility if there were any other members of his family he would like aboard, he had shaken his head in the negative. "They have been my crew since they discovered which part of an airship suited them best," he had said. "We travel as a family on long hauls, or not at all. My brother and his wife are dead, and I am responsible for seeing his children have a trade. If that doesn't suit, miss, we will take no more of your time."

Peony was no fool. For what ship could be flown and defended better than one where every member of its crew did so out of love and loyalty? Claire had taught her that. Claire, who had acted *in loco parentis* to any number of street sparrows who, once they had done saving her and each other's lives, were now making their own way in the world with astonishing success.

"I am afraid we must choose a spot," Captain Boyle said now, his intense gaze upon the ground. "In the absence of moorage, we must cast anchor. Middy!" he shouted.

"Sir!" Twelve-year-old Samuel—"Call me Scooter, miss, everyone does"—appeared out of nowhere.

"Man the winch. We shall drop anchor presently."

"Yes, sir."

He leaned into the speaking horn. "Engineer, aft!"

"Sir!" Dinah responded promptly.

"Cut back main engines, vanes vertical. We are about to drop anchor."

"Yes, sir."

But where? *Iris* sank lower and lower, on a long, cautious approach. "There." Peony pointed. "I see a church steeple, so that must be the respectable end of town. The buildings are painted, at least. Let us find some level land close by."

"Aye, miss."

"Captain, don't you find it rather odd that in all this expanse, there are no airships?"

"I do, miss. I cannot account for it at all."

"We are still in the Texican Territory, are we not?"

Timothy, the navigator, looked up from his table, the protractor glinting in his nimble fingers. "We are, miss. But it does not signify. Remember Mrs. Fremont said that the Royal Kingdom has opened the borders to airships. So if we cross the Sierra Nevada, we will not be shot down for flying in the face of God. But Mrs. Fremont did not know if the Royal Kingdom had airships of its own yet, that might be visible in the skies here."

Every Boyle aboard *Iris* seemed to treat Mrs. Fremont's slightest word as coming direct from Olympus itself. How wonderful it would be, Peony thought with the smallest of sighs, to command that kind of respect and love.

Well, there was still hope for her. If determination and courage were a beginning, then at least she had that much.

4:05 p.m.

After a tiring and fruitless morning of inquiries after Papa in the town, on the afternoon following their arrival Detective Hayes was kind enough to escort Daisy and Freddie in an exploration of the delights of the dry goods store, the milliner, and a number of suppliers of stationery, footwear, and food-stuffs. Their purses were too slender to admit an indulgence at any of these shops, especially since, in the case of the milliner at least, one saw at a glance that the fashions in hats were at least a year behind.

"I feel quite in the *avant garde*," Freddie confided, touching her second-best hat, which was the only one she had brought with her when she stowed away back in July.

Once outside, Daisy did not release the arm of the detective. For if she had, she and Freddie might have been swept away in the seething tide of miners, speculators, newspaper men, and ladies in very showy dresses who thronged the streets. Half the population seemed to be drunk, the other half wishing to be. And it was barely four o'clock. She had thought Georgetown's miners to be uproarious, Santa Fe's streets to be crowded, but those places were positively bucolic in comparison to Bodie.

"Is it always like this?" Daisy wondered aloud.

"The mine has three shifts," Detective Hayes explained, "and the saloons never close. So yes, I suppose it is always like this. I have been here a time or two before, and it has been no different."

"I think I should like to go back to the Casa Gallina," Freddie said faintly, clinging with both hands to his other arm. "It is all too much."

28

They made the turn off Main into Green Street, only to practically run face first into a gentleman in a beautifully tailored waistcoat and a caramel-brown overcoat. "My word, Mr. Carnegey," he said, looking in amazement between Daisy and her sister. "What is this?"

"Not what you think, sir," the detective said with a smile. "Ladies, may I present Mr. Richard Pender, who occupies one of the rooms at Casa Gallina. He apparently dined out last night, so you did not meet him. Sir, this is Miss Linden and her sister Miss Frederica, likewise staying at Mrs. Moss's establishment, on the ladies' floor."

The gentleman bowed as they dipped curtsies. "I do apologize, ladies," he said, his cheeks ruddy with embarrassment. "Clearly I have been away from polite society far too long. Are you on your way back?"

"We are," Daisy said. "My sister finds the streets too raucous, and I must agree they do not exactly lend themselves to sightseeing."

"You will likely find more sights than you signed up for," he agreed, offering her his arm. "Shall we?"

No one cared, apparently, if one took a gentleman's arm on five seconds' acquaintance. Fortunately, Daisy heard her Aunt Jane's disapproving voice in her head much less often these days. So she took Mr. Pender's arm in the spirit in which it was offered, and thanked Providence that at least it would prevent her being pushed off the boardwalk and into the street by a crowd of inebriated miners.

Mr. Pender had a very nice arm, in any case. He was a bit older than she, in his early thirties, perhaps. His hair, instead of being flattened into obedience by macassar oil, was curly but neatly trimmed. His face held more character than beauty, with a wide mouth, direct blue eyes, and a chin that meant business. Exactly the kind of face that she would like to paint. Perhaps after one or two days they would have become well enough acquainted over the breakfast table that she might ask his permission to do so.

"Goodness me," Freddie said suddenly behind them. "Look at that!"

For sailing in on a long approach was the loveliest airship that Daisy had seen since she and Freddie had left England. In the Texican Territories, ships tended to be of the freight and passenger variety, out of necessity. Distances between settlements and cities were long, the weather sometimes hostile, with an ever-present danger of air pirates.

But this ship seemed as little concerned with danger as a lady of quality concerned herself with street sparrows. Her fuselage, a tawny golden yellow, was elongated for speed. Below it clung a sleek gondola of brass and some hardwood, decorated with vines and whorls that incorporated its propellers and other mechanics in sheer artistry.

"*Iris*," she said, reading the name painted on the bow. "What is she doing here?"

"And who is flying her?" Mr. Pender glanced at Detective Hayes. "I smell a story, don't you?"

"Come along, ladies." The detective picked up his pace. "There is time to find out before dinner."

Past the Methodist church, and beyond the end of Green Street where the road turned to climb to the cemetery, there was a rise in the ground. It was a conical sort of hill, flat enough on the top to serve as a landing field, if one did not object to sagebrush and rocks. *Iris* slowed, her vanes vertical, and the propellers reversed their direction. The anchor lowered, ratcheting out on its chain. Neat as you please, the ship settled about six feet off the ground.

The gangway lowered, and a pair of children scampered down with stakes and mallets, and proceeded to stake and secure the ship's ropes as though they had done it a hundred times before. What they might not have done so often was attract the kind of crowd that was surging up the street to view the spectacle.

"Have they never seen an airship before?" Freddie wondered aloud, glancing behind and skipping every few steps to keep up with Detective Hayes's rapid pace. "How is that possible?"

"Private vessels are not so common in these parts," the detective said. "Those as pretty as this, even less."

"Someone either very rich or very famous may be visiting our fair town," Mr. Pender said with a glance full of smiling challenge over his shoulder. "It remains to be seen which reporter will be first to the *Bodie Barker* with the account."

But the detective only laughed. Since he was not actually a journalist, Daisy had the feeling he would not be competing very hard with Mr. Pender for the honor. But journalistic curiosity aside, it was hard not to be interested in the beautiful ship and its occupants.

"We cannot exactly dash up to them and demand to know their business," Daisy said, beginning to lose her breath on the slope. "Mr. Pender, you must go on ahead. I am not so anxious to intrude on these people that I must run."

"I am sorry." He slowed enough for Freddie and Detective Hayes to catch up. "You will think I am quite the boor. I promise you I do know how to behave like a gentleman. It is only that—ah."

For as they crested the hill, they could see the occupants of the ship coming down the gangway. A tall, muscular man with cocoa skin and a captain's wings upon his collar led the way, with a younger man and woman behind him who must be relations, if their bearing and bone structure were any indication.

Behind the pair came a young lady in a burgundy velvet walking dress, vandyked all along the hem in black silk, her bodice similarly embellished, with the addition of large brass buttons. Her auburn hair was done up in the Pompadour style, and upon it rested the prettiest little hat, a confection of straw, burgundy silk pleats, and black and gold ribbons.

"Oh, her hat," Daisy sighed in envy.

"That dress," Freddie moaned.

"Dear heaven," Detective Hayes said blankly. "If that is not Miss Peony Churchill, you may truss me up and call me a Christmas goose."

CHAPTER 4

4:15 p.m.

*A*nd who is Miss Peony Churchill?" Mr. Pender asked, his voice filled with laughter. "An old flame, is it? I say, Carnegey, I had no idea you were so popular among the ladies of England that they must follow you here."

Daisy was glad he had asked, for she did not want to appear ignorant to a man to whom she and Freddie owed so much. Even if the remarks were rather personal.

"Heavens, no." Detective Hayes did not seem overly bothered by such misplaced humor. "I have merely seen her image in the newspapers in connection with her famous mother. For of course a newspaper man like yourself will have heard of Isobel Churchill."

"Indeed I have." Mr. Pender gazed at the approaching party with new interest. "So this is the daughter? Is she as terrifying and troublesome to governments and men of power as her parent?"

"It seems we are about to find out," Freddie murmured.

"Good evening," the young lady called.

Daisy and Freddie curtseyed, and the gentlemen bowed. The man in the captain's wings stood at the young lady's right hand, and inclined his head.

Detective Hayes stepped forward, a hand outstretched, and both the young lady and the captain shook it. "My name is David Carnegey. And if I am not mistaken, you are Miss Peony Churchill?"

The young lady looked gobsmacked. "How on earth...?"

"I am a newspaper man, Miss Churchill. We possess all kinds of useful knowledge. And yours is a face that, once seen, is not soon forgotten."

She hardly seemed to hear this pleasantry. Or at least, chose not to acknowledge it. "Upon my word, it is not often I have reason to thank my mother, but I suppose in this case I must. Mr. Carnegey, this is Captain Boyle, of *Iris*, and Mrs. Boyle. My navigator Timothy Boyle, and First Engineer Dinah Boyle."

Detective Hayes shook hands, then indicated Daisy, Freddie, and Mr. Pender. "Allow me to introduce my friends Miss Linden, Miss Frederica Linden, and Mr. Richard Pender."

Miss Churchill gasped, her wide eyes fixed on Daisy. "Not Daisy Linden?"

After a moment, Daisy was able to control her sagging jaw long enough to say, "Yes. You—you have the advantage of me, Miss Churchill."

"What are the odds?" Miss Churchill turned to Captain Boyle in some excitement. "Captain, these are the very young ladies I have come all this way to find." Lifting gloved hands in the direction of heaven, she said, "After such a journey, who would believe they would be the first ones I would meet upon mooring?" She seized Daisy's hand, and Freddie's, too. "I cannot tell you how glad I am to meet you!"

"I—why—but why—" Daisy gave it up. That a young lady of some wealth and reputation should practically fall from the sky was one thing, but a young lady looking for her and Freddie? That was beyond everything.

"It is quite clear that she thinks me mad," Miss Churchill said in an audible aside to Captain Boyle.

"Can't say as I blame her, miss," he said dryly.

"Why don't we return to *Iris*?" Mrs. Boyle suggested. "I can have a meal ready in two shakes."

"Would that be all right?" Miss Churchill looked from Daisy to her sister. "Do come, and I will attempt to be more clear in my communications."

"Oh, but—that is, we are expected to dinner ourselves, elsewhere." Daisy found her wits. Goodness, she could not waltz aboard a strange airship with someone she had only just met—and someone with a story so wild it might be called mad at that. "Perhaps we might meet in the morning, Miss Churchill? We are staying at Casa Gallina." She pointed down the slope. "Just there, the three-story building painted white with green trim."

Miss Churchill covered reddening cheeks with her hands. "You are quite right. What a featherbrain you must think me. May I say only this before you go—are you acquainted with Lady Claire Malvern?"

"No, not at all," Daisy said. "But the name is not unfamiliar to me."

"I am acquainted with her," Freddie said hesitantly, with a glance sideways at Daisy, as if to beg forgiveness for getting them in too deeply with this odd young person. "I was at school with her ward, Maggie Polgarth."

Miss Churchill beamed. "There, you see? This is not as strange as you might think. For I know Maggie well, and have done for some years. Lady Claire is one of my dearest friends, and in fact, it was she who agreed that I ought to speak with you personally on—" She glanced at Detective Hayes and Mr. Pender and flushed becomingly once again. "On a private matter."

"That lets us out of the frolic, old man." Mr. Pender clapped a hand on Detective Hayes's shoulder. Then, to Miss Churchill, he said, "Is there any service I might perform for you and your crew, Miss Churchill? Bodie can be both strange and dangerous to newcomers ... though I truly believe any danger will be to the hearts of all the eligible bachelors in town once they realize that you are the owner of that beautiful ship."

For indeed, the crowd had crested the hill now, and were pointing up at the lettering on the bow. Children were hopping up and down, trying to get a glimpse of someone who might be its owner and loudly speculating about that person's identity.

Mr. Pender nodded at a man setting up a daguerreotype box on wooden legs. "And there is the photographer from the *Bodie Barker*, if I am not mistaken. Miss Churchill, you are about to become front-page news."

The young lady made a face. "If I had not already found the people I was looking for, I would have been happy to hear it. As it is ... oh dear, such a nuisance."

"If you would vouchsafe me five minutes," he said, "at least you may be assured that the copy will be respectable."

"Are you a journalist, sir?"

"I am. But that is not why I came." He indicated the rest of their party. "We are all staying at Casa Gallina, and are on the way to becoming fast friends."

Her face cleared. "Then I shall trust in friendship," she said merrily. "Five minutes. Mr. Pender, do tell me, is it all right if we moor here?"

"I hardly think anyone will object." He folded her hand over his arm. "I doubt this hill belongs to anyone but you. But if it is, and the owners are not honored by the privilege, their neighbors will certainly overrule them."

"Tomorrow morning, then, Miss Linden," Miss Churchill called over her shoulder as she and the detective strolled away in the direction of the photographer. "Eleven o'clock?"

"We will look forward to it," Daisy called back.

What an extraordinary beginning to an acquaintance!

Captain Boyle turned to Daisy, his brow furrowed in a frown under the bill of his airman's cap. "You will not blame me for asking if the young lady is in safe company, miss?"

"No, indeed," Daisy responded. "I admire you for your concern. I confess I have only known Mr. Pender for a very short time, however."

"Half at hour at most," Freddie put in.

At the captain's alarm, Daisy hastened to reassure him. "But as to the other gentleman, you may rest assured that Miss Churchill can be in no safer hands than those of Mr. Carnegey."

Captain Boyle gazed at her, his dark eyes searching her face.

"In fact," Daisy went on steadily, "I would trust him with my life."

"Let us hope it does not come to that, miss." The captain bowed, gathered his family, and headed off down the slope to town.

∽

FROM THE BODIE BARKER, morning edition
Wednesday, September 4, 1895

ADVOCATE'S DAUGHTER PAYS UNEXPECTED VISIT
by R. M. Pender

Townspeople who happened to look up into the sky last evening were treated to an unusual sight—not a comet, not a meteor shower, but the airship *Iris* on a long approach to our fair town. Built by the Meriwether-Astor Manufacturing Works, she is a Class 3 touring ship captained by Alturas Boyle, a retired member of the Royal Aeronautic Corps. *Iris* is owned by none other than the lovely and brave Miss Peony Churchill, who disembarked upon mooring, and was met by a cheering delegation of townsfolk enchanted by the unusual sight.

The Churchill name strikes the more cosmopolitan members of our populace with awe, and rightfully so. Miss Churchill is the daughter of none other than Mrs. Isobel Churchill, world famous activist and advocate on behalf of the national underdog intent on protecting itself from large and rapacious entities who would seek to steal said dog's bones for themselves. At this writing Mrs. Churchill is in

Africa fighting on the side of the kingdoms there who quite naturally wish to trade their own diamonds and minerals, rather than being forced to mine them for the benefit of rich men from a foreign country.

But during her visit, Miss Churchill is not burdened with affairs of state. In fact, this reporter may venture to say that for this young lady, any affairs ought to be of a much more congenial and numerous nature. She is visiting friends, and we very much suspect that she will be the chief ornament of the Autumn Ball on Saturday, should she be convinced to stay.

Miss Churchill's arrival brings into embarrassing focus the urgent need for an official airfield to serve Bodie and the Consolidated Mine. When a personage of such renown as this is forced to land on a hilltop with neither mooring mast nor so much as a tree, what does it say of our town's pretensions to industry, to say nothing of gentility?

Now that the Royal Kingdom of Spain and the Californias has opened the neighboring skies, there is no sense whatsoever in continuing to blackball airship traffic. Let us be blunt: Josiah Comstock is dead. Why, then, must we continue to put up with his monopoly on transportation, to use only his rails? The Comstock Spur Line can be one of many routes that visitors, miners, and speculators alike may take to find their way to Bodie.

We, after all, welcome anyone with a will to work and to make his own fortune.

MEN WANTED

Four men are needed to man the stamp engines, performing maintenance on the automatons and clearing rock from under their feet. Training provided. Good benefits. Doctor on site. Recent reductions in staff have resulted in these openings. Apply to Vincent Selkirk, director.

CHAPTER 5

WEDNESDAY, SEPTEMBER 4, 1895

10:45 a.m.

*B*y a quarter of eleven the next morning, both Daisy and Freddie found themselves hovering at the parlor window, though Daisy could have sworn she and her sister had come in to sketch and to write letters, respectively, to pass the hours between breakfast and the arrival of their guest. But both sketchbook and writing table lay abandoned as they watched Miss Churchill's distant figure, escorted by that of Captain Boyle, make its way down the slope of the hill.

Mrs. Moss brought in a tea tray laden with teapot, cups, and a three-armed cake stand that, when placed upon the tea table, slowly revolved to offer teacakes, sandwiches, and fruit. Its clockwork mechanism was housed in the base of the stand, and as it operated, it made a kind of whispering music. "I know you had breakfast only three hours ago, but let this be your luncheon as well," she said.

"Thank you so much," Daisy said. "We had not expected this."

Mrs. Moss smoothed her skirts—today a very pretty blue linen, with a bodice trimmed in Brussels lace. "It is not every day that the daughter of Isobel Churchill visits one's house. This will show all those old tabbies at the Ladies' Aid that they have greatly underestimated me… and my guests. Perhaps the long-awaited invitation to join their ranks will be forthcoming now."

The words were no sooner out of her mouth than a knock came at the door, and she bustled out to admit her celebrated visitor and introduce herself. When she showed Peony in, her eyes were shining with delight—or perhaps it was simply admiration for Peony's walking costume. It was made of sky blue gabardine, with a deep border of crystal pleated ruffles at the hem and a smaller frill forming the collar of the jacket. Her hat was an airy confection of blue feathers and black ribbon, with a jaunty cockade of the same pleated silk.

Daisy gave a silent sigh of helpless envy.

Peony practically bounded into the room and shook Daisy's and Freddie's hands. "Well met again," she said gaily. "What a lovely house. And my goodness, luncheon! Mrs. Moss, what a wonder you are. All this for me?"

"Indeed it is," Mrs. Moss said, clearly pleased that the care she had taken was appreciated. "We may be in the back of beyond here, but at least we have brought some aspects of civilization with us." She turned to the gentleman in the hall. "Captain Boyle, will you stay also, and have some lunch?"

He inclined his head. "I have errands in the town, madam, but I thank you." To Peony, he said, "Will an hour be sufficient, miss?"

"Yes, thank you, Captain."

He bowed and went out, and Mrs. Moss hovered in the entryway. "If you need anything, I will just be in my room, along the passage here."

"Thank you, Mrs. Moss." Daisy found her voice. "But I cannot imagine that anything could be added to this delightful lunch. It is perfection."

"Let us eat it at once," Peony said. "I did have breakfast, but there must be something in the air up here. I am famished."

Mrs. Moss pulled the pocket doors closed behind her, leaving them in privacy. Daisy heaped three plates with delicacies while Freddie poured the tea into fragile cups painted with sprigs of blue rosemary entwined with ribbons. Peony examined hers before taking a sip of her tea. "Rosemary for remembrance," she said. "How very appropriate, for I have come all the way from England to ask you to remember."

"Have you indeed?" Freddie said. "I do not know whether to feel honored ... or frightened."

Peony smiled. "Neither, I hope. You would not think, would you, that in traveling so far it would be possible to remain in a state of paralysis. But that, I fear, is what I suffer. And only you can cure me by giving me the information I seek."

"Information that will free you of your paralysis?" Daisy could hardly conceive what this could be.

"I hope it will."

"Then please ask us anything you like," she said earnestly. "For since we have never met before last evening, I cannot imagine that a single moment of our lives could have any significance to you. We spent an hour before bed last night, trying to puzzle it out."

Peony swallowed half her tiny teacake. "Then let me begin by asking what you know of Sydney Meriwether-Astor."

It was as though the name fell from a great height into a well, where it landed after a moment with a splash of astonishment.

"Sydney Meriwether-Astor?" Freddie repeated.

Daisy felt rather like doing the same, like a parrot, for the subject made no sense at all. But she must say something. "Why—why, nothing at all. We have never met him in our lives."

"But you know of him," Peony persisted, leaning a little forward. "Through a young lady of your acquaintance. A young lady who I am told is recently passed away."

"Miss Makepeace?" Freddie blurted. "Do you refer to Emma Makepeace?"

"I do."

"Miss Churchill," Daisy said, trying to get a grip on the conversation, "you must forgive us. But my sister and I are both quite at sea. Were you acquainted with Miss Makepeace?"

"We were on speaking terms, at various balls and things in London, but that was all," Peony said. "I understand that she was acquainted with—no, had a relationship with—oh, dear, one can hardly speak ill of the dead, but—" She stopped. Then took a breath. "I am in quite the dither. Claire would be ashamed of me. Let me begin again."

She took a sandwich for sustenance, while Daisy gulped a teacake down with her tea. It really was delicious. Thank goodness teacakes always made sense, no matter what the rest of the world was up to.

"Last spring, as the snowdrops were coming up in Paris, I

met Mr. Meriwether-Astor," Peony said. "It was not long before I fell in love, and when he confided to me that he felt the same, it was as though I suddenly realized the purpose of my life—it had led me straight to that moment."

Daisy nodded in understanding. One's life led to a series of moments—or rather, one's moments created a life. But now was perhaps not the time to debate which was the better philosophy.

"We returned to London to join in all the entertainments of the season," Peony went on. "I first saw Miss Makepeace at a ball that I attended with Sydney. I do not even remember whose house it was, only that there were baskets of spring flowers. I remember thinking what an enormous expense it must have been, for it was March and the crocuses were hardly up in Hyde Park."

"And … that was where Mr. Meriwether-Astor met Emma?" Daisy asked.

"It was. And yet I did not notice, for I was laughing with my friends and dancing with him, secure in the thought that even though he was among the gentlemen who danced with her, it was I whom he would escort home afterward. She was quite the belle, you know." Peony gazed into memory. "Her gown on one particular occasion was a pink so pale you could hardly see the tint. It made her skin look like porcelain."

"She was the loveliest woman I ever saw," Freddie said. "Daisy sketched her portrait as a wedding gift for the man she was to marry in Georgetown."

"I left it with him," Daisy said sadly. "Otherwise I might show it to you."

"I am not likely to forget her," Peony said. "She was the

toast of the season. It was only later that things began to look decidedly odd."

"Her father," Freddie said wisely.

Peony's eyebrows rose. "Was he the cause? I suppose he must have been, for no gentlemen were permitted to call, and all flowers were returned, I heard."

"All quite true," Daisy said. "But somehow Sydney and she managed to meet, for when she departed for Georgetown, she was—" Oh, dear. How could she say this to a young woman who had no reason to love Emma, and who might use this sad story as a weapon to disgrace her memory?

"She was...?" Peony prompted.

"She was corresponding with a respectable man in Georgetown, and came out to him as a mail-order bride," Freddie said, when it became clear Daisy could not speak. "We met on *Persephone* and became friends. We were to be bridesmaids at her wedding, for she had no other friends to support her."

Peony gazed at them. "Claire said— She told me that—" She took a sip of tea. "Is it true that she was expecting Sydney Meriwether-Astor's child?"

This was the question that Miss Peony Churchill, possessor of all that one could wish with the lift of a finger, had come all this way to ask?

Daisy's mouth trembled. "She has nothing left," she whispered. "Not even her life. Do not take the frail remains of her honor from her, too."

"I shall not," Peony said, her voice cracking on the final word. "Not a word of this conversation will ever pass my lips. But I must know, or I cannot let him go."

Daisy's lashes were wet as they flicked upward to gaze at

her. "You must let him go, for he is entirely unworthy of you or any other respectable woman. Yes, he was the father of her child. And there is a man who loved her, in Georgetown, who would have brought up that child as his own, for her sake. Sydney Meriwether-Astor is not fit to be mud on Mr. Hansen's shoe."

At Daisy's fierce words, Peony released a long breath, and her spine sagged as though something within her had irretrievably fled, leaving her limp. A full minute passed, broken only by the clink of cup into saucer, before Peony came back from whatever dark place her thoughts had taken her.

"I knew, somehow, that it was true," she said at last. "But I could not bring myself to believe it. For what does that say about me, that I could be so easily duped and taken in?"

"It says that you have a warm heart, and a brave one, too, to offer it to another," Freddie said. "There is nothing to be ashamed of in that."

"My mother would beg to differ," Peony told her with an edge to her voice. "You may not know that Sydney fled to Egypt as a result of these events. When I would have flown to be with him, she froze my bank account so that I could not go. Clearly she believes that one's brain must be as stout as one's heart, and I fell short on that side."

"The good thing about the brain is that it is constantly learning," Daisy said. "Next time you will apply both brain and heart, and it will be in service of someone worthy of you."

"How wise you are." Peony smiled. "Have you ever been in love?"

"I—I—" She glanced at Freddie, who was looking a little startled. "I do not know."

"Then you have not," Peony said with the firmness of

conviction. "For if you ever had been, you would know it, and it would have changed you irrevocably."

"Has it changed you?" Freddie asked, when Daisy was silent.

"Oh, yes." Peony sighed. "I cannot say it is an improvement, but at least there is hope. After all, I am not merely fluttering about the capitals of Europe any longer, looking for amusement. I am here, the mistress of my own ship, with a purpose." She gazed at them. "I want to press you for details of your acquaintance with Miss Makepeace, to weasel out of you all the many reasons why he chose her and not me, but I will spare you that pain. For I see that you mourn her loss."

"We do," Daisy managed. "Still. And we only knew her for a few weeks—the length of time it took to cross the ocean and fly to Denver with Captain and Lady Hollys, and spend a night or two in Georgetown."

"What—you came to the Territories with Alice and Ian?"

Daisy gaped at her. "You know them?"

"I do indeed. Goodness me. Next you will be telling me you know Queen Victoria, and I swear I will not even be surprised."

"Sadly, we do not," Freddie said with a smile. "Though I am but one degree removed—Maggie has been presented."

"So she has, and I too, but I cannot say I can claim an acquaintance with Her Majesty. My mother, on the other hand, may."

Imagine one's mother being acquainted with the Queen! Daisy would be content if her own mother were acquainted with no one but the dustman, if she could but see her one more time.

"Are you telling me, then, that the Hollyses frequent the

shipping lanes on this side of the sea?" Peony asked, taking another sandwich.

"They must," Freddie said, "for we took passage with them in New York. Though I believe the voyage was only part of a longer journey."

"Lady Hollys was attending her mother's wedding, we understand," Daisy put in. "But we have no way to know where they are now, of course."

"At least friends may be found if one were to look." Peony was clearly attempting to look on the bright side of some argument going on in her own mind. "The Hollyses, the Dunsmuirs, my friend Gloria Fremont." She sighed. "She is Sydney's cousin, you know. Needless to say, I did not vouchsafe my sad tale to her. I do not think their relationship was a happy one, and I did not want to set myself on the side of one she despises."

"Gloria Fremont?" Daisy asked.

"Née Meriwether-Astor. Surely you have heard the name."

Goodness. Daisy certainly had. But under circumstances that must not be revealed if Detective Hayes were to maintain his disguise. "I may have, in one newspaper or another," she murmured.

A knock came at the door and Peony glanced toward it. "That will be Captain Boyle, come to collect me."

But it was not. When Mrs. Moss answered the door, a male voice could be heard through the pocket doors. "She has left me, you wretched woman. Left me in the lurch, and gone home to her father. I demand satisfaction."

"Mr. Parsons, as a married man, the only satisfaction you will get is in the conjugal bosom. Now, remove yourself from my porch before the neighbors begin looking out of their windows."

"I will not. I paid you a thousand dollars in gold for a wife, and now I don't have one. How are you going to make good on what you sold me—other than a false bill of goods?"

"If you do not have a wife, it is your own fault, and none of mine. I made the match, and at the time you were pleased. If you are no longer pleased, you must take it up with the lady and not with me, sir."

"How can I take it up with her when she is not here?" the unseen Mr. Parsons demanded, his voice rising.

Daisy had a glimmer of intuition as to why Mrs. Parsons had not been happy.

Mrs. Moss said, "You do what many men before you have done—you go a-courting with your hat in one hand and a bouquet of flowers in the other. Now good day to you, Mr. Parsons. I have an important guest and I do not wish her to be disturbed."

"Does she know what a swindler you are?" Mr. Parsons was clearly not going to be brushed off so easily. "Does she have any idea of the callous nature of your character?"

"That is quite enough, sir," came the calm bass voice of Captain Boyle. "The lady has asked you to leave, so you had best do so."

"And who are you? Another poor dupe to be taken in by this woman and those substitutes for womanhood that she peddles to unsuspecting respectable men?"

"No," Captain Boyle said, apparently unmoved. "Who I am is none of your business. Your business is to remove yourself from this verandah so that I may carry out mine. Now, if you please."

With a torrent of invective, Mr. Parsons took his leave. Daisy glanced out the window to see a man in his early thirties stamping up the road, his coat flying out behind him, swatting shrubs and wildflowers alike with his hat, as though their destruction were the only thing that could improve his mood.

"My goodness," Peony said. "Somehow I cannot blame the estimable Mrs. Parsons for returning to her father, if *that* is what comes through the door at night."

The pocket door slid back to reveal Captain Boyle, impassively polite, and Mrs. Moss, whose cheeks were flying scarlet flags of embarrassment and temper.

Her gaze went to Peony at once. "I do apologize for that appalling intrusion, Miss Churchill. I hope it will not prevent you from returning to visit with your friends."

"Not at all, Mrs. Moss." She smiled at the captain. "Thank you, Captain, for coming to our hostess's rescue."

"All in a day's work, miss," he said. "Are you ready to take your leave?"

"I am, but I am not." Daisy was surprised and gratified to have her hand seized. "Do say you will come to dinner aboard *Iris*," Peony begged. "I cannot say good-bye quite yet. Name a day."

"Any day but Saturday," Mrs. Moss trilled before Daisy could get out a word. "It is the Autumn Ball—quite the event of the year. Miss Churchill, you must honor us with your presence. It will be talked of for years to come, I declare it will!"

Peony's fine brows rose before she turned to Daisy. "Are you going, Miss Linden?"

"Well, I had not thought precisely— I mean to say—"

"Of course she is going," Mrs. Moss exclaimed.

"But ma'am, we have not been invited." Freddie came straight to the point.

"Goodness me." Mrs. Moss made a motion in the air as if batting away a troublesome fly. "You are a respectable female. That is the only entree you need to have three or four gentlemen clamoring for every dance. In fact, you must all three resign yourselves to splitting each dance at least once. You will make quite the sensation."

"Gracious!" Freddie said with a disbelieving laugh. "A ball—are we truly to attend a ball?"

"I suppose we are," Peony said with a nod. "Captain, you and Mrs. Boyle must certainly come, too, and Dinah and Timothy."

"I would be honored, miss," he said, inclining his head in a way that included Mrs. Moss as the joint source of the invitation. "We shall see you young ladies there. Perhaps we might even eat supper together, as a party?"

"I should like that of all things," Daisy said impulsively, to be rewarded with a wide smile from Peony.

"It is settled, then." She clapped her hands. "Who would have thought I would be treated to such a social whirl here in Bodie?"

"You will find that, and much more besides," Mrs. Moss assured her, and smiling, Peony and the captain made their farewells.

FROM THE BODIE BARKER, EVENING EDITION

Wednesday, September 4, 1895

She Must Go Back, Says Mine Officer
by E.M. Cookson

Not two months have passed since the July wedding of John Parsons and Emily Coogan, a couple matched by Mrs. Clarissa Moss and married in what many considered to be the wedding of the year. At a cost of nearly two thousand dollars, railroad engineer Joshua Coogan could not be blamed for wishing his investment in his daughter to have lasted a little longer, or at least until a bundle of joy might have brought him some return.

However, with the failure of his marriage and his bride's return to her father's house, Mr. Parsons has brought suit against Mrs. Moss before a judge at the county courthouse in Bridgeport, stating that the marriage was contracted under false pretenses.

"I cannot live with that woman," he said outside the courtroom this afternoon. "She was presented to me as biddable and good-tempered, and so she appeared to be until two minutes after the ring was on her finger. Then she turned into a demanding, shrieking termagant who was never satisfied with what she knew perfectly well I could provide. I hold Mrs. Moss responsible. She has duped me and heaven only knows how many other respectable men, squirreling her outrageous fees away into her own pocket."

Mrs. Moss, a familiar sight in the parlors and civic spaces of Bodie, dismisses such claims this evening with airy disdain. "It is amazing what a childish fuss a man can put up the moment a woman expects a roof over her head instead of flattened coffee cans. Or perhaps a cupboard filled with dry goods instead of vermin. I fear that Mrs. Parsons is the one to be pitied here. Put quite simply, Mr. Parsons is an expert and convincing liar. Dear Emily got a pig in a poke, to be sure, and her neighbors are willing to testify to it."

The next hearing will be in Bridgeport in late September, when the circuit judge arrives from Reno.

CHAPTER 6

THURSDAY, SEPTEMBER 5, 1895

From the Bodie Barker, morning edition

NINTH ANNUAL AUTUMN BALL
by D. Carnegey

The annual Autumn Ball, the highlight of the social season, will take place Saturday evening at the Miners' Union Hall on Main Street. In this humble reporter's opinion, the Ladies' Aid Society has outdone itself this time, turning the largest indoor public space in Bodie into a veritable wonderland of wheat sheaves and cornucopias.

Mrs. Lavallee, President of the Ladies' Aid, says, "We have been working for two weeks on the decorations. It would have been finished much sooner had *some* people been more willing to volunteer. Consequently, we regret that the meeting of the Miners' Union had to be moved to the Methodist Church last Wednesday. But that is what comes of depending on the undependable."

Hitches in the planning aside, the residents of our fair

town look forward once again to hearing the sweet strains of waltz and polka performed by the Volunteer Firemen's Orchestra, ably aided by the seventh grade class of the Bodie School, who will perform a set dance during the first interval.

During the second interval, per prevailing custom, there will be a cake walk. The organizers encourage gentlemen attending to arrive early to bid on these wonders of the culinary arts. Winners of each cake will partner the fair baker for a full, uninterrupted dance of the lady's choice.

Gentlemen are advised to abide by this rule, or risk censure and even ejection.

The ball will be opened as usual by Miss Elizabeth Selkirk, daughter of Bodie Consolidated managing director Vincent Selkirk, at eight p.m. sharp. A raffle will take place to determine her fortunate partner. All proceeds from the raffle will go to benefit children who have lost their fathers in mine accidents during the course of the this year. Last year's raffle, you may remember, netted over ten thousand dollars for these sad cases.

Since it is likely that gentlemen will outnumber the ladies, Mrs. Clarissa Moss encourages all to enter the partner lottery for the opening dance, where Lady Luck will determine a lady's partner rather than crowds or brute force. "We do not wish fisticuffs to mar our ball," she warned. "Remember that despite so much good fortune in one place, a gentleman may be both rich and courteous."

The doors open at half past seven. Formal dress required. Any gentleman or lady not appropriately attired will be turned away, and Constable Lynch will be in attendance to ensure the safety of the assembly.

1:30 p.m.

The house seemed strangely empty and quiet without the prospect of a call from Peony Churchill, though the two young ladies were expected on the afternoon train. Daisy was beginning to think that Miss Harding and Miss LeVesque were figments of everyone's imagination. They were able to use speculation about them as a handy distraction, though, as they cleared away the luncheon dishes and helped Mrs. Moss to tidy the parlor while Mrs. Boswell, the cook, did the dishes in the kitchen. For Mrs. Moss was still interested in Miss Churchill, from the provenance of her frock to the purpose of her visit yesterday to their own guesses as to how long the young lady might stay in Bodie, and whether she might be interested in marriage.

Finally Mrs. Moss gave in, or else tired of Daisy and Freddie's lack of information on all these subjects. "You will remember my saying that this afternoon I meet with the society of absent friends," she said. "I would very much like you to join me."

"Oh, yes," Daisy exclaimed. "I should like to give the ladies as much information as I can, and perhaps we may be fortunate enough to receive a few crumbs ourselves."

"For my part," Freddie put in shyly, "I should like to be acquainted with as many of the ladies as we might. One never knows where or when we might meet another such, and find the delicate chains of acquaintance a help in time of need."

"Exactly one of the reasons that we decided to form an unofficial society," Mrs. Moss said, clearly pleased that on this subject, at least, her guests showed no shortage of interest.

"Life is uncertain enough, and a friend is a welcome sight in any circumstance. We leave promptly at one thirty."

Daisy and Freddie presented themselves in the foyer at the designated hour, hats pinned on neatly and reticules in hand. Detective Hayes came along the walk just as they sallied forth, and Daisy made free to tell him where they were going.

"Just there," Mrs. Moss said, pointing at the blue house with white trim across the street. "We shall return at four."

"Enjoy yourselves, ladies." He bowed and went into Casa Gallina.

How strange it was, Daisy thought, that she felt safer if the detective knew where they were. If she had been in Bath, and obliged to tell her aunt that she was walking up to the shops, or paying a call, or some other less than noteworthy errand, it would have made her cross.

The boarding-house ladies squealed with delight upon learning they had guests, and a babel of introductions ensued as soon as the little orange zinnia upon Daisy's lapel caused them to realize they arrived under the auspices of not one, but two of their sisterhood.

Mrs. Calvert was their hostess. "Formerly of Savannah, mind you, but not ashamed to call Bodie my home for all that."

Two sisters, Alvira Manning and Muriel Porter, owned identical houses next to one another. "Our husbands were miners during the rush of forty-nine," said the former.

"And when they died in a collapse, we sold the workings and came here," said the latter. "I don't mind telling you there is more money to be had in housing miners than in being married to them."

The ladies laughed merrily, and the last of them shook

Daisy's hand. "I am Selena Chang. I have the oxblood-colored house at the bottom of the hill where the airship is moored. I am still married, but my husband chooses to live in his own house, up on Mine Hill."

"Isn't it scandalous?" Mrs. Moss elbowed her friend.

"The truth of it is that I cannot abide the thunder of the automatons' stamping," Mrs. Chang confessed. "I live as far from it as I may, and still be in town."

"I cannot blame you," Daisy said sincerely. "The vibrations make me feel anxious, as though there were a storm perpetually brewing."

The ladies nodded in sympathy, before their hostess said, "Come and sit. Clarissa tells us that you young ladies have something you wish to discuss with us."

Daisy and Freddie seated themselves on a sofa that was a little threadbare, but which one hardly noticed because it was covered with a quilt of such complexity and beauty. Daisy forgot her manners so far as to turn over one corner like a teacup, to see what was on the back.

"Do you like my quilt?" Mrs. Calvert said. "Dear Selena made it for me."

"It is the loveliest piece of handwork I have ever seen," Daisy told them, looking from one to the other. "I cannot possibly continue to sit upon it."

"Of course you can," Mrs. Chang said with a smile. "A beautiful thing may be useful, too, may it not?"

"Indeed. Though I am guilty of making things for beauty's sake, and forgetting function altogether."

"My sister is a painter," Freddie said by way of explanation.

Whereupon the sketchbook in her reticule must be

produced and exclaimed over—even the paintings of teacups that acted to soothe upsets in Daisy's soul.

"Why, I recognize this very garden," Mrs. Moss exclaimed in delight. "It belongs to Eileen Alvarez. My goodness, how talented you must be that I could place it immediately."

"It is how I remember the places we have been and the people we have met," Daisy said, a flush staining her cheeks as she realized she had never painted the series of cheerful triangles that was William Barnicott's face. And now she might never see him again to make right that omission.

"Who is this?" Selena Chang pointed to the portrait of Lin.

"That is a young friend of ours," Freddie said. "We met in Georgetown, but she was with us in Santa Fe also."

"She is very pretty," Mrs. Chang said thoughtfully. "She reminds me very much of someone I knew as a girl, back in San Francisco."

"She is in search of someone, too," Daisy said. "Her aunt, who I believe lived in San Francisco at one time."

Mrs. Chang's dark gaze rested on Daisy's face. "Do you remember her aunt's name?"

"I am sorry to say I do not," Daisy said, suddenly regretting every moment that she and Lin had been at odds with one another. For if they had not, she might have been able to make a connection to aid the girl in finding her own family.

"And the girl's name?" Mrs. Chang persisted. "One never knows when one might meet someone who is likewise looking for this young lady."

Which was quite true, if unlikely.

"Her name is Lin," Freddie told her. "I understand that the Canton custom is to begin an introduction with the surname. Hers is Yang."

Mrs. Chang nodded. "Yang is a common name, but it may still be useful. Now, do make yourselves comfortable, and tell us of yourselves and whom you seek."

Daisy began, at first hesitantly and then with more fluency, with the account of their family's first foray into the Texican Territories the year before, the kidnapping of their father to help build the dam in the Royal Kingdom of Spain and the Californias, and their mother's fruitless search and subsequent death. Freddie told them of their voyage in July, skipping over the events of Georgetown and dwelling at slightly more length on those of Santa Fe. Daisy picked up the story with their arrival in Bodie and their faint hope of having any word of their father in this uproar of a town.

This account took the space of a cup of tea, and when they were finished, Daisy felt the need of another.

"Let me, dear," Mrs. Calvert said, her eyes filled with sympathy as she poured. Then she passed a plate of raisin tarts to them, as though after such a tale they both might need a homely restorative.

It was the kindness more than the tarts that restored Daisy's spirits, the interest and concern in the eyes of the ladies as they knit briskly or hemstitched linen. In the bosom of this feminine circle, she almost felt as though she had come home to a bevy of aunts who did not feel she was a burden at all; on the contrary, it was as though she brought a sense of adventure with her in which they were only too eager to participate.

"Have any of you seen or heard news of Professor Linden?" Mrs. Moss asked, bringing the discussion back to the main point. "Apparently he was last seen wearing a greatcoat of Prussian blue wool—military grade, you understand—and he speaks with a slight Prussian accent."

"He stands about six feet, and has a stocky build," Freddie put in. "His eyes are blue, his hair once dark but is now going gray at the temples and forehead."

One by one, the ladies shook their heads. "No one answering that description has stayed at my establishment," Mrs. Chang said, "but that does not signify. He may have stayed at one of the hotels on Main Street, or even bought time in a miner's bunk. There is a flourishing trade in that, I understand."

When Daisy and Freddie both looked blank and slightly horrified, she went on, "A man who works the morning shift does not need his bed. So the man coming off night shift sleeps there, and gives way in his turn to the man coming in off afternoon shift."

"The thing to do is to check with Mr. O'Hara, the proprietor of the Palace Hotel," Mrs. Manning said with a decided nod. "Many get off the stage from the train there, and he may have seen a man in a military coat."

Daisy made a note on the back page of her sketchbook, next to her list of those who could have been responsible for Emma Makepeace's death. This at least was a more appealing direction than checking the cabins of miners.

"In the meanwhile," said Mrs. Porter, "we will put the word out among our acquaintance in town—the shopkeepers, the more respectable saloons. All you girls need do is wait while we cast our bread upon the waters, and see what comes back to us."

"I do not know how to thank you," Daisy said. "Such kindness and help—it is almost too much to believe."

"You will find that, out here, kindness and help mean the difference between survival and death ... or a fate worse than," Mrs. Moss told her quietly.

"But the inconvenience—" Freddie began.

Mrs. Calvert was already shaking her head. "There is no inconvenience. We have our errands in the town, and it is no trouble at all to put a word in a friend's ear and ask that it be passed on."

"You wear the zinnia of an absent friend," Mrs. Chang said as though that clinched the matter. "We help our own—for if we do not, who will?"

Who, indeed. "I cannot imagine taking on Bodie in search of him without your help," Daisy said honestly. "It would be frightening."

"There are always Mr. Pender and Mr. Carnegey," Mrs. Moss said with an arch of one eyebrow. "I am sure you could count on those gentlemen for assistance, if you asked."

"Ooh, do tell." Mrs. Calvert leaned forward in her seat. "Is there romance in the air?"

The artless question surprised a laugh out of Daisy at the very idea. "I am sorry to disappoint you, but no. We have known both gentlemen for the sum total of four days."

"It took fewer than that for me to fall in love with my Edmund," Mrs. Manning told her with a reminiscent sigh. "Do not discount love at first sight, my dear."

Unbidden, William's face flashed before Daisy, and just as quickly, she shook it away. Watching a man be thrown out of a house to measure his length on the grass at one's feet did not exactly qualify as love at first sight.

"But mention of our scribbling friends has made me think of something," Freddie said. "Could we not ask one of them to place an article in the *Bodie Barker*? That would cast quite a number of crumbs upon the waters, and possibly in places where you ladies would not care to be seen getting your hems wet."

"An excellent idea." Mrs. Moss looked positively delighted. "I shall ask one or the other on your behalf. Possibly Mr. Pender, for his is a more official position at the paper. Mr. Carnegey seems to content himself with the society news."

"Rather too much, to my mind," Mrs Porter muttered. "Too much time spent with that insufferable Sarah Lavallee—to say nothing of the number of his treks to the Selkirk house."

"Elizabeth Selkirk would never accept the suit of a newspaper man," Mrs. Moss said firmly. "Her father's eyes are set much higher."

Daisy exchanged a glance with her sister. Detective Hayes was courting—or pretending to court—the foremost young lady in the town? That was certainly news. Perhaps it was connected with the hush-hush matter that had brought him here.

"But Mr. Pender is altogether an odd duck." Mrs. Moss was not finished with her male boarders yet. "Imagine coming to a place like Bodie with nothing but a pearl-handled waist-coat pistol to defend yourself with!"

"Really?" Mrs. Chang looked puzzled. "Had he not heard of Bodie's reputation before he came? Why, even I have my trusty Winchester Trapper should there be trouble."

"Is that a rifle or a person?" A Winchester Trapper sounded like it would mean business either way. When Mrs. Chang indicated it was the first, she said, "You do not take such a thing to town for protection, surely?"

Mrs. Chang laughed merrily, as did Mrs. Moss. "Dear me, no. Not to town. The Trapper is far too heavy, despite its short barrel, and too difficult to disguise as a parasol." The ladies laughed again, as though this were a standing joke. "It is, however, quite sufficient to cow a rowdy boarder, and with nine rounds, can warn off a party of drunken miners should they reach this end of town."

"And Mr. Pender has no such protection?" Mrs. Manning asked.

"The pistol he has is a darling little thing," Mrs. Moss confided. "I should love to carry it myself. With its pearl handle and all the brass engraving, it seems much more suited to my reticule than the waistcoat of a man."

Daisy rather thought that a man's sidearms were his own business, and not to be gossiped about by the town's ladies. But what did she know of polite customs in this place? The discussion of rifles and pistols over tea was astonishing enough.

"What firearms do you carry, dear?" Mrs. Porter asked her on the heels of this thought.

"Why … none," Daisy said a little blankly. "One does not, you know, in England. And the thought has not occurred to either of us."

"Best see them outfitted," Mrs. Calvert advised Mrs. Moss. "Among our circle, there ought to be something suitable."

"Dear me, no." Daisy set down her cup and pushed this idea away with both hands. They spoke of guns as though they were overshoes! "We could not possibly. You have already been so kind that we can never repay you."

"Stuff and nonsense," said Mrs. Manning. "I've had two boarders killed over the last year, and both left their pistols with no one to claim them. I'll look them over and see if something might suit."

"Thank you, but—"

"No buts, young lady." Mrs. Manning looked fierce. "You may not yet have been in a position to need a gun, but you are in Bodie now. All previous rules of society do not apply here."

"Good heavens," Freddie said faintly as Daisy simultaneously whispered, "Yes, ma'am."

There was being outnumbered—and there was being completely outgunned. Her estimation of the capabilities of the society of absent friends was undergoing a radical change.

CHAPTER 7

SATURDAY, SEPTEMBER 7, 1895

7:45 p.m.

ome along, my dears, or we shall be late." Clarissa Moss, resplendent in a gown of dusky green that recalled her name, shrugged on a velvet wrap. "Miss Harding and Miss Levesque, I am afraid, are once again elsewhere. We can wait no longer."

For the young ladies had not been on today's train, either.

"I suspect they have cold feet, and have given up their matches," Freddie whispered. "Oh Daisy, what if no one asks me to dance?"

"Mr—Mr. Carnegey certainly will, and Mr. Pender, too. Truly, Freddie, you look very pretty."

"And the trimming that Simone Colfax added to your dinner gown in Santa Fe has stood up surprisingly well to travel." Freddie touched her braided chignon as though it might have fallen down on the way downstairs. "Do you think it will matter that we have no cakes for the cake walk?"

But Mrs. Moss had heard. "Never fear, dears. I asked Mrs.

Boswell to make a cake for each of you. They are already over at the Union Hall. Now, do come along. We must on no account miss the welcome and the opening dance."

The newspaper men joined them at the gate, and they sailed down Green Street, turned right on Main, and there was the Miners' Union Hall lit up as though the Queen herself were expected.

"Mr. Carnegey, your article in the *Bodie Barker* did not exaggerate," Daisy told him, awestruck, as they passed through the wide front doors into the hall. "It is a fairyland."

It was not the Assembly Rooms at Bath, to be sure, but for the Wild West the high-ceilinged room possessed a kind of elegance as it welcomed them. Tiny moonglobes on strings festooned walls and ceilings. The promised cornucopias were arranged on the tables, and paintings of them hung on the walls for the occasion. Sheaves of wheat competed with bouquets of autumn flowers that had clearly been imported, for no flowers grew in the valley save for a few coddled roses in sheltered gardens.

Suddenly Freddie clutched Daisy's gloved wrist. "Oh my goodness, look at her *dress!*"

There was Peony Churchill, laughing and surrounded by gentlemen, dressed in a silk gown that was the very height of fashion. No pastels or a debutante's white for Miss Churchill, oh no. Her gown was of royal blue silk, the skirt split down the back to reveal a froth of pale blue chiffon ruffles that would show beautifully as she danced. The neckline was daringly low and trimmed with poufs of chiffon, the sleeves likewise split and filled. Her shoulders were becomingly revealed, her bodice a marvel of boning that showed her small waist to perfection. Two peacock feathers danced in her hair, which was dressed high to show off her elegant neck. Her gloves reached nearly to her puffed sleeves, and she wore no jewelry but gold earrings.

"Why can't I look like that?" Freddie moaned. "I look like a spinster hoping for tea."

"Nonsense," Mrs. Moss said. "Buck up, Miss Frederica. You will be in as much demand as Miss Churchill, never fear, for there are so few ladies that you will never be allowed to sit down."

Daisy felt that she might have left off that last bit, for Freddie did not look comforted.

Detective Hayes rose to the occasion. "Miss Frederica, perhaps you might bypass the lottery and allow me the privilege of the first dance?"

"Mr. Carnegey!" Mrs. Moss exclaimed. "What will Miss Selkirk say?"

"Thank you, sir," Freddie said in grateful tones, for Miss Selkirk must have resources far exceeding theirs. "I accept."

Having had one young lady elude her, Mrs. Moss was not about to allow another to do so. Even as Mr. Pender was opening his mouth, she raised a hand. "That is *not* how we do it here. Your youth may excuse you this once, Miss Frederica, but your sister must not follow your example. Mr. Pender, you will enter the lottery like every other gentleman here, and I'll hear no more."

"Yes, ma'am," he said, looking crestfallen. He stole a glance at Daisy as though they had been frustrated in their plans together, but she did not share in it by looking at him. Detective Hayes and Captain Boyle were the only men in the room with whom she felt the freedom to really enjoy herself.

In the next moment, Peony Churchill had caught sight of

them, and with a glad greeting she swept them into the circle of her acquaintances, making introductions with the aplomb of a society hostess.

"Oh, how well the two of you look," she said at last, when the gentlemen had gone to enter their names in the lottery and they had a minute to speak alone. "I am so glad to see friends among the company."

"You did not look as though you needed friends," Freddie said. "You are a belle already."

But Peony waved a dismissive hand. "If I have any social graces, it is thanks to my mother's tutelage and not my own inclination. I had far rather enjoy an evening with a few close friends than any number of insincere swains."

"I am quite certain they are sincere," Daisy pointed out. "There are so few ladies. Look, is that the famous Miss Selkirk?"

"That dress is from Worth or I am an automaton," Peony said in the flat tones of surprise.

Daisy promptly lost her breath at the beauty of the white confection, its folds and embroidery a work of art that, unfortunately, turned its wearer into nothing more than a mannequin on which it might be displayed.

"She looks miserable," Freddie said with that keen observation that Daisy had often envied—not the observation of surroundings and surfaces to which she herself was prone, but of what lay beneath them.

A well-upholstered woman in black silk called the young lady's name, confirming their guess that this was indeed Miss Selkirk as she hurried forward to intercept her progression into the room on her father's arm. Miss Selkirk nodded and smiled, but under her carefully dressed blond hair, her face was white as porcelain, her brown eyes dark with misery. Her gaze, when it was not politely directed to someone greeting her, swept the room, coming to rest at last upon Detective Hayes.

When the detective joined the Lindens' party, she took them all in and spoke briefly to her father. Moments later, the lady in black looked affronted as the pair left her and crossed the room.

"Mr. Carnegey," Mr. Selkirk said in tones that indicated he was performing this service at his daughter's request, and for no other reason. "Good evening, sir."

"Mr. Selkirk. Miss Selkirk, you are looking very well. That dress becomes you."

"White becomes no one but a bride, but I thank you for your kindness," the girl said, every word appearing to push past an internal barrier.

Suddenly Daisy realized that the girl was all but paralyzed with shyness, the rapid pulse beating in her throat betraying that the poor thing wanted nothing more than to flee. Her own sense of being overwhelmed in such a crowd melted away. Peony caught her eye, and between the two of them flashed a moment of understanding. Miss Selkirk, despite all her wealth and standing, needed friends more than anything this evening—and it should be themselves.

"You will be a bride by Christmas, Elizabeth, or I will know the reason why," her father boomed. He was as thin as a lath, so where that volume of voice came from was a mystery. His moustache was waxed into a marvel of immobility, and his starched collar seemed to hold up his chin in a way that forced him to look down his nose at his company. Though perhaps that was more the fault of his tailor than any actual inclination.

Daisy thought Miss Selkirk might buckle at the knees with the embarrassment this perfectly audible announcement caused her.

As smoothly as though he had not heard it, Detective Hayes said, "May I introduce my friends? Mr. Selkirk, Miss Selkirk, I would like to present Miss Margrethe Linden and Miss Frederica Linden of Bath, England, and Miss Peony Churchill of London."

Daisy curtsied to the father and took the gloved hand offered by the daughter. "I am delighted to meet you." She squeezed the trembling fingers. "Truly. Nothing enriches a journey so much as finding a friend. My friends call me Daisy."

Her eyes widened a moment under her curled blond fringe at being thus included in this number, before she turned to Freddie, shook hands, and then looked up at Peony.

"How do you do? Your dress is lovely."

"Thank you." Peony leaned in to whisper. "Do not tell a soul that I have already put my heel through the hem of my train. Honestly, a greater scapegrace than I am I have yet to meet."

Unbidden, a smile wavered into being on the pale lips, and Daisy saw the ghost of who this girl might become, given half a chance.

"I promise I won't tell," Miss Selkirk said. "No one will notice, anyway—the rest of your ensemble is so beautiful."

"You are a darling, and I love you for saying so. Come, let us take over the ladies' powder room. One of us must have a pin and can help me repair the tear."

"I do," Daisy said. She linked arms with Freddie and Miss Selkirk, and they promptly abstracted her out from under her father's astonished moustache.

"The opening remarks—" he managed to say to their trains.

"Back in a moment, dear sir," Peony called merrily over her shoulder.

Peony was the sort of woman for whom an entire company would wait, and tonight Daisy was glad of it. They had the powder room to themselves, and the moment Daisy's pin had closed the tiny tear in a chiffon ruffle, Peony had dug into her beaded evening bag for her rouge.

"You are terrified, aren't you?" she asked Miss Selkirk.

"Does it show?" the girl asked bitterly.

"May we call you Elizabeth? Or even better, Beth. You look quite like a Beth."

"You will have the distinction of being the only people in town to call me so. I hate this dress. I wanted a chestnut brown shot silk with birds embroidered on it in gold thread, but Papa would have none of it. It was this or nothing, solely because it was the most expensive."

"With your eyes, chestnut brown would suit you exactly. Now, hold still." Peony dabbed a bit of rouge on her lips, and a tiny amount on her cheekbones. "Blend that in. It will help disguise your feelings."

"Is that what rouge is for?" Freddie asked. "I always thought it was to disguise the effects of the night before."

"I have never had a night before," Beth said. "Days are exercises in dullness, and evenings in futility." But she obediently removed her glove and did as she was told with one dainty finger. She gazed at herself in the mirror, judging the effect, then turned to her companions. "Who are you, exactly?"

"That would be a very long story," Peony said with a laugh.

"My sister and I are in town searching for our father, who has lost his memory," Daisy told her. "He was said to have made his way here in the last few weeks. We arrived Monday, and are staying with Mrs. Moss at Casa Gallina."

"And how do you know David?"

David? Goodness. On a first-name basis, are we?

"We became acquainted with Mr. Carnegey during the course of our search." Daisy glanced at Freddie. "Newspaper men seem to turn up in the most unexpected places. But we are always glad to see him. He can be depended on in a pinch."

"It doesn't hurt that he is easy on the eyes," Peony said slyly.

A blush that had nothing to do with rouge spread over Beth's cheeks ... chin ... forehead. It engulfed her in a wave and then receded just as quickly. "He is not courting me, if that is what you are implying," she said hoarsely. "Though gossip has had us on the point of an engagement since his last visit."

"Mr. Carnegey does not strike me as the kind of man who would mislead a young lady in that way," Daisy said gently. "I believe you. Would I be wrong in saying that he makes a most satisfactory friend?"

"You would not." Beth raised her head, the brown eyes soft and starred with long lashes. "He is helping me. In a kind of deception. The happy result is that for the time being, the parade of men through our parlor is much decreased."

"Why would you need such a deception?" Peony asked. "A

parade of men through the parlor sounds delightful, as long as they wipe their boots."

"I—I have no desire to be married." Again the color blossomed in her cheeks. "Unfortunately, it is my father's chief object. I am his only child, you see. I am nearly twenty-one, but he says no child of his should be on the shelf past eighteen. It seems I disgrace him in every unmarried moment I spend on this earth."

"We have had some experience with fathers set on the same course," Freddie said. "You have our sympathy. A woman should be able to choose her own path in life."

Beth's face took on some animation, and again Daisy had that fleeting sensation of seeing a different woman living a different life, through a mist of possibility and potential. "Exactly. I wish to write. For the papers if I must, but novels if I can. Mr. Carnegey has been most useful in helping me. Those articles in the *Bodie Barker* under his byline are actually mine."

Daisy was impressed. "You must cease that practice at once, and have your own byline. Build your own reputation."

Beth shook her head. "Papa would burn the *Barker*'s offices to the ground before he allowed that. But I come into my money later this month, and then I shall be independent."

A pair of ladies came in on the heels of this interesting declaration, and they were forced to make their way back into the ballroom. "Miss Selkirk—Beth—may we call tomorrow, after church?" Daisy said hurriedly, before they were parted. "I hope we might continue our acquaintance—and our conversation."

"I would welcome it." She flashed a smile at them, then

waved at Mrs. Lavallee and hastened toward that lady and her father, who were waiting impatiently to begin.

Due to the heaving impatience of the crowd, the opening remarks were blessedly brief. The orchestra struck up some preparatory chords, after which Mrs. Lavallee stepped up on a box with a list in her hand. The name of each eligible lady present was called, beginning with Miss Elizabeth Selkirk, and paired with that of a man.

"Miss Daisy Linden will take the floor for the first dance with Mr. Alonso Gabriel."

A young man materialized in front of Daisy and bowed. "Miss Linden?" She curtseyed as Freddie's name was called and Detective Hayes claimed her. They took their places in the set of a country dance, with Elizabeth and her partner leading off, and with a fanfare, the ball began.

The figures were close together and involved several holds and clasps, which Daisy had no doubt was intentional on the part of the Ladies' Aid, who had organized the event. Mr. Gabriel lost no time in striking up conversation. This and the cake dance were the only ones not to be split, so the next few minutes were his exclusively.

"Miss Linden, you look very lovely this evening."

"Thank you, sir." Daisy could not help a blush, for truly, his gaze was ardent, as though they had been courting and he had been waiting hours to see her. It was most disconcerting.

"I have never seen so pleasing an aspect. Are you long in town?"

"We arrived Monday, and are seeking our father, who has lost his memory and must be found."

"Your father?" The mask of the swain slipped and real

concern took its place. "Then you are unprotected here in Bodie?"

"I would not say tha—"

"Miss Linden, I am overcome. You must allow me to express what is in my heart."

"Why—what—?"

The turn took him around another lady, but before she could catch her breath she was in his arms again, twirling between the two lines of dancers. "I consider it a welcome duty to make myself your protector. Miss Linden, would you do me the honor of becoming my wife?"

CHAPTER 8

8:20 p.m.

$\mathcal{D}$aisy lost the step and nearly stumbled. If it had not been for the man waiting to sweep her into the hands-four she might have stopped dead altogether to gape at Mr. Gabriel, and consequently disgraced herself.

"Miss Linden?" Mr. Gabriel reappeared for the next figure and held her far more closely than propriety dictated. "I would make you a good husband. Gold has made me well off, and I can build you a house in any city of your choosing."

"I—I—have no doubt of that, sir, but you must see that this is ridiculous."

"It is not. I must secure your affections before every other man in Bodie realizes your situation."

Good heavens. Mrs. Moss had tried to tell them, but Daisy had not believed it. She could hardly believe what she was hearing now. Did Elizabeth Selkirk have to endure this nonsense in her parlor every single day? "I am very sorry, but I must decline."

"Miss Linden, please." The expression in his eyes was painful to see. "Please accept me. You must accept me."

"I disagree, sir."

"You need protection—you have said so yourself."

"I said no such thing. You interrupted me in a most ungentlemanly way. I have friends here. I am in no need of protection—yours or any other man's."

"You may regret this." His hold had become rigid, his face fixed as he attempted to master what Daisy assumed to be his disappointment.

"Let us talk of something else," she suggested.

But it seemed that Mr. Gabriel's only purpose in dancing with her had been to propose. And as the dance ended and the next began, she distinctly heard him declare his devotion to his next partner.

But her ordeal was not yet over. Her new partner was a burly individual who had clearly been buttoned into his best bib and tucker for the occasion. "Miss Linden, allow me to make you the offer of my hand—"

"I thank you, sir, but no."

"I am rich. Name your heart's desire and I can provide it."

Was every single man in town wealthy? Not that it meant a thing. "No."

"A house in Reno? An airship of your own?" Sweat had broken out on his forehead. "Diamonds and pearls? Any or all will be yours if you will only say yes."

"I am sorry to disappoint you, sir, but no."

A tall, weedy man in his middle years did not even make it through the first sixteen measures of the waltz. Nor did he bother with pleasantries. "It will be worth your while if you marry me. I have a wasting disease and won't last long. You'll be a rich woman."

This time she kept her head and did not miss a step. "That does not hold the appeal you may think it does, sir."

A young man barely older than Freddie said, "Miss, I would be forever honored if you would—"

"No."

"But I have not said—"

"I have said no, sir."

It was quite a relief when Mr. Pender cut in and the poor young man was forced to withdraw. Her fellow boarder cocked an eyebrow as he looked into Daisy's face. "Having a good time?"

"I cannot say so. I am glad you have rescued me." Thank goodness he, at least, did not seem inclined to propose. "Mr. Pender, I have had several partners and nearly as many proposals of marriage. Are the men in this town mad?"

He smiled and changed the waltz hold for a skater's hold, so that she might catch her breath as they circled the room. "Not mad. Only desperate for a good woman's company. Many of them have struck it rich and want a home and family. You cannot blame them for that."

"Perhaps not ... but proposing on the spot is no way to secure one's happiness. It is rather like—what is that expression I have heard here in the Territories? Taking a pig in a poke."

She had made him laugh, and two dozen men glared from the sides of the room. But then it was his turn to yield to another, and as he turned away, he tapped the underside of his chin with the back of one finger.

Keep your chin up.

So she would. How refreshing even a few minutes with a friend could be! It lasted through the first interval, and through the exhausting hour of unrelenting dancing after that.

Daisy kept one eye on Freddie lest she lose her head at receiving a similar tidal flood of proposals. Until she saw Mr. Gabriel cut in on her for the second time that evening, his face flushed and a look of determination in his eye. "Miss Frederica, I am overcome. You must allow me to express what is in my heart."

At which point Daisy lost her composure. And possibly her temper.

She abandoned her partner with no explanation and marched across the dance floor. "Mr. Gabriel, I forbid you to dance with my sister again."

"The young lady may make up her own mind," he told her, both eyebrows raised as though judging her and finding her insufferably rude. "I flatter myself that I have found more favor with her than with you. No doubt your *age* and *greater experience* have worked against me."

"Mr. Gabriel!" Freddie exclaimed. "Do not speak to my sister that way."

"Is there some difficulty, dears?" Mrs. Moss rustled up and ushered all three of them over to the side, where a potted palm gave them the illusion of privacy. "Mr. Gabriel, I thought I warned you about this kind of behavior. No woman present will believe you sincere if you go through them like a dose of salts, proposing right and left."

"But I must have a wife or I lose all!"

"I understand your family situation—and may I say you might have availed yourself of my services earlier and spared us all this scene. Despite their cruel situations, there are any number of decent women in Maiden Lane who will accommodate you, and gladly, for a chance to better themselves."

"I cannot bring a desert flower or even a laundress home to my grandparents, madam."

"Then you are overlooking a great many good women," Mrs. Moss said. "They are not all as wicked as many think."

"Your definition of *good*, madam, differs from mine, I am afraid. Now, please allow me to return to my partner."

But Freddie stepped behind Mrs. Moss's silk skirts, as though for protection. Mrs. Moss's lips thinned. "You are causing distress to this and several other young ladies, sir. You will leave our ball at once."

"Do you know what this could mean to me?" His voice was quiet. "You cannot insist, madam."

"No, but Constable Lynch will." And on the heels of this smug announcement, a man built like a bear, with a black handlebar moustache and the smell of liquor surrounding him like a cloud, seized his arm.

"Causing trouble, sir? Can't have that in the presence of ladies. 'Specially not this one. She walks in beauty like the night." Weaving slightly, he frog-walked Mr. Gabriel out through a side door, where a gale of male laughter resulted at his ignominious exit.

"Thank you, Constable," Mrs. Moss said to him on his return.

"Your servant, madam." He bowed and mimed tipping one of the town's ubiquitous Stetson hats to her, though he must have left the actual article in the cloakroom. The action nearly caused him to tip forward along with his imaginary hat. He righted himself and walked away with the firm step of a man who does not believe himself to be drunk.

"Are you all right, dears?" Mrs. Moss asked, looking Daisy and Freddie up and down as though seeking evidence of torn clothes.

Ragged composure was Daisy's only complaint, but she would not say so. "Yes," she said. "Thank you."

Freddie added, "Mrs. Moss, I should very much like to go home."

"Oh, my dear, I hope you will not. Take your Miss Churchill as your example."

Indeed, Peony seemed able to laugh off proposals as though they were no more amusing than a joke well told, and somehow her partners were not offended, but merely determined to try again.

"I do not think I can," Freddie said. "I have never experienced such behavior in the whole of my life."

"Perhaps you might repair to the buffet to regain your spirits," Mrs. Moss suggested, her tone hopeful. "I must just run a quick errand, but I will not be long. The cake walk is next and you must not miss that."

The buffet was a crush, though, and what was more, between the salads and the cold roast of beef, they were each proposed to no fewer than three times. A dash to the powder room and the comforting presence of ladies seemed their only course.

"Bother," Freddie said when the door closed behind them. "I had hoped Mrs. Moss might be in here. At this rate we will be hanging from her skirts like children, seeking her protection."

"Perhaps she is with the other absent friends," Daisy

suggested. "Let us see. No one will bother us behind a phalanx of respectable ladies."

But she was not among the group of absent friends happily making personal remarks about the dancers from behind a screen of potted palms, and worse, Mrs. Lavallee spotted them and descended upon them like an overfed turkey vulture. "You are the Miss Lindens, are you not? Staying at Casa Gallina? You must tell me at once where Clarissa is hiding."

Daisy called upon her courage, and did not take a step back, though it was rather like facing down a gale. "We are in search of her ourselves. She said she had a quick errand."

"What errand? She is to announce the cake walk!"

Over Mrs. Lavallee's shoulder, Daisy caught a glimpse of the man in the brocade corset—their landlady's erstwhile husband—pomaded and starched to within an inch of his life. Never mind the cake walk—Mrs. Moss had probably done what any sensible woman would do and slipped away as soon as she saw him, so as not to attract his notice and risk a scene.

Mrs. Lavallee glared at Daisy, clearly incensed by this momentary lapse in attention. "You will find her at once, or I will know the reason why. I will not have my ball spoiled by her flirtations."

"I doubt she is flirting, ma'am," Daisy said, lifting her chin. "A woman as lovely as she has no need."

Mrs. Lavallee seemed to take this as a personal insult. "You mind your manners, missy, and do as I say."

"Miss Linden," said Detective Hayes, materializing at her side, "may I have the honor, if you are not otherwise engaged?"

"You may not, sir, at this moment," Mrs. Lavallee snapped.

"Miss Linden *is* engaged ... on a commission from me. Mrs. Moss must be found at once, before this polka ends. Think of the cake walk!"

If he had difficulty doing so, he did not show it. "Then allow me to assist you in locating her." And before Daisy could say a word, he had folded Daisy's hand over his arm while Freddie was simultaneously commandeered by a partner.

"She is not at the buffet, or in the ladies' powder room," Daisy said to him in a low tone as they made their way toward the side door. "But Mr. Moss is here, and were I she, I should have dashed out the back to avoid a scene."

"Mrs. Moss, in my experience, does not back down from a scene."

"You may be right, but there is a difference between a scene in one's parlor and a scene in public, at the biggest event of the year."

"Too true." He inclined his head. "But I must tell you that I did see her near this side door not five minutes ago. She may have slipped out into the street for a breath of air."

But when they looked, threading through the chattering, mostly male crowd who were drinking as liberally in public as they might have in the hall itself, they could not see her. A smaller group of men were pushing and shoving, and voices rose.

Daisy and her escort turned in the opposite direction. "Could she have gone home on her errand?" she asked, perplexed. "This does not seem like her, to neglect a social duty. She and Mrs. Lavallee do not get along, but she would not give that lady a chance to criticize her for anything."

"The polka is half over." He glanced through the open

door, from whence the music could be clearly heard. "Let us be quick, then. If she has gone home, then we will fetch her. If not, then at least we will have two minutes of quiet together. I do not like the look of the scrum brewing over there."

"But Freddie—"

"Freddie has Miss Churchill if need be. Come. Let us be quick."

She matched his rapid pace up the street and around the corner. "Mrs. Moss will be very angry that we left the ball for her sake."

"No one will even notice the absence of a man," he said frankly. "But the loss of a young lady will likely cause a riot. Which is why I am setting such a pace. I must get you back to the company as soon as may be."

She felt her cheeks heating as she lengthened her stride to keep up. "I am not the sort whose absence is missed. If I were Miss Churchill, now ... we would not be on this errand at all. The crush would prevent our even reaching the door."

He laughed. "Do not sell yourself short, Daisy. I know what you are capable of. As for Miss Churchill—" But he stopped and would not finish. Or perhaps it was just that they had arrived at Casa Gallina and must carry out their errand with dispatch.

The door was unlocked. "Mrs. Moss?" Daisy called from the front hallway. "Are you here? Mrs. Lavallee is all in a swivet. The cake walk is about to begin."

The silence of an empty house was her only answer.

"Check upstairs," she suggested to Detective Hayes. "I will see if she is in her room."

"It doesn't feel as though anyone is home, but all right." He bounded up the staircase and she could hear his shoes on the floorboards of the hall.

"Ma'am?" She tapped on the bedroom door, which swung open. No one was inside.

Perhaps the cook was in the kitchen, and could tell them if her mistress had been here.

But the kitchen was empty, save for a cast-iron pan upside-down on the white linoleum. Goodness. Perhaps she had better reconsider her eggs for breakfast, if this was how the pans were treated. Daisy picked up the heavy pan and rounded the corner of the worktable, intending to put it on the stove.

On the floor, a flood of green silk skirts fetched up against the woodbox.

Blond hair spilled on the linoleum. Pins lay everywhere.

And blood. An ocean of it. On the floor, on the white walls, even on the ceiling.

Daisy screamed—a ragged sound that was abruptly cut off. She dropped the frying pan and was violently sick into the sink.

CHAPTER 9

11:15 p.m.

"We must summon the police," Daisy croaked in the safety of her room.

Detective Hayes, ignoring the rules of propriety as though he had never heard of them, dipped his handkerchief in the basin, wrung it out, and handed it to her.

While she cleaned up her face and rinsed her mouth, he said, "There are no police here. There is only Constable Lynch and a man who acts as night watchman at the gaol."

"Two men? For a town of twenty thousand?" Her voice cracked. His unhappy eyes confirmed it. How could that be possible? "The constable seems—seemed—on good terms with Mrs. Moss. Fetch him."

"I will, if he is not already busy. It is quite likely there has been a murder outside the union hall already. Apparently there were three during last year's event."

She stared at him, hardly able to believe that something so callous would come out of the detective's mouth.

He met her gaze soberly, without flinching, as he leaned a shoulder on Freddie's bedpost. "Daisy, I'm very much afraid that we may be on our own with this."

"But that is ridiculous! We are not the law—the constable is!"

"Constable Lynch's ability to solve a case, I have observed, is directly inverse to the amount of liquor he has taken in. He is overworked and overwhelmed by his duty, so I can hardly blame him for taking to drink. It is my belief that if anyone is going to find out who did this horrible thing, it will be ourselves."

"No!" The contents of Daisy's stomach threatened to come up again, though there could hardly be anything left. "I refuse to believe that. Constable Lynch must do his job and find who did this, and I must do mine and find my father." She leaned both hands on the wash stand, her voice trembling. "I cannot bear any more inquiries of this kind. Not after Emma. I cannot." Tears overflowed her eyes and trickled down her cheeks. She straightened, angry with herself, and swiped at them with the wet handkerchief.

He seemed to be struggling within himself, too, as though he weighed her tears against the likelihood of the constable's being able to help. "Very well. I will bear this burden, then, and fetch the constable if it will make you feel better."

"Thank you," she whispered.

"You will be all right alone in the house? With—with her?"

She had seen the dead before, but not under such brutal circumstances. So immediate. Why, the perpetrator must have slipped out the back door even as they were coming up the front walk. Her stomach heaved again, and she fought it down by force of will. "Yes."

He clattered down the stairs and a moment later the front door closed behind him.

Daisy would have given anything for a cup of tea. But both tea and cups were in the kitchen, which would mean going down there, and she could not. She felt paralyzed with horror, as though opening the kitchen door would make it all happen again.

There was nothing she could do. Others would shoulder this burden, leaving her and Freddie with their own.

And yet—

Mrs. Moss had been so alive! So vibrant and lovely. Only half an hour ago she had been kindness itself, wading in to protect the two of them from Mr. Gabriel unasked. And yesterday, making certain they knew the other absent friends. Creating a welcome atmosphere of home at breakfast and dinner among such disparate guests as she and Freddie, Mr. Pender, and Detective Hayes.

And now? Now she lay there, the victim of someone's hatred and rage.

Mr. Gabriel? Surely not. Being chased away from a marriage prospect was no reason to murder.

Mr. Moss? Had she been Constable Lynch, or been involved in his inquiries, Mr. Moss would have been number one on her list. For she had only that one glimpse of him at the Union Hall. He had had plenty of time to follow his former wife over here.

And what about that irate young man who had burst in the other day, roaring about his unsuccessful match? Daisy couldn't even remember what day that had been, or his name. But he had been so angry Captain Boyle had had to step in.

Clarissa Moss had been a matchmaker. Someone who built

happy endings for people. Why would anyone want to kill her?

Hot, stinging tears welled again in Daisy's eyes.

You owe her. As paltry as it is, go downstairs and give her the gift only you can give.

Oh, no. She was not becoming embroiled in another person's death. It had nearly cost her her life once before … and look what had happened in Santa Fe. Granted, no one but a villain had died, but still.

Stop lying to yourself. If not for the cancan and the loyalty of a young boy, you would be nothing but bones on the rocks at this moment, and so would Freddie. Put some steel in your spine, Daisy Linden. You are not going to be embroiled. You are simply being useful. To her.

Daisy's sketchbook lay on the nightstand. Her paintbox, with pencils and brushes in its narrow drawers, was in her valise.

Last time she had almost been too late to draw—stopping the gravediggers on the verge of their final duty.

You have time now. Do it. For her sake.

She hurried downstairs with sketchbook and pencils. There would likely not be time for color, but at least she could get the basic outlines down, in case they might be helpful later. She gritted her teeth and pushed open the kitchen door. Compassion alone—not courage, far from it—took her across the floor to the dreadful scene.

She breathed a few deep breaths, attempting to clear everything from her mind but the demands of her task. Cast-iron stove, woodbox, and table formed on the page in a few quick strokes. With a little water in a glass, she mixed her colors. Clarissa's body lay facedown, her arms above her head, the way babies often slept. Her head was turned to the left, her right cheek to the linoleum. Her eyes were still open. Gazing into eternity.

And her head—

Daisy put down her brush and allowed herself to really see what was under the tumble of golden hair. She could not bring herself to move aside even a single strand, but even so, the wound was visible.

And the blood.

With Clarissa's motionless form sketched in increasing detail—Detective Hayes would return at any moment, and she must get down everything she could—Daisy realized that she would have to add one detail more. She got out the rigger brush, found another water glass, and filled it.

The crimson pigment seemed to bloom on the paper not because the latter was so damp, but because there was so much of the former. Arcs of it, as though whatever weapon that had been used—the frying pan?—had come down upon the poor head again and again.

The lines of the walls ran off the edge of the paper, but at least she had the worst of the plume down, its shape and arc. She must record what she could before the drunken constable bumbled in here. An examination would be made, perhaps, though the thought of bearlike Constable Lynch touching this delicate form was abhorrent. Was there a doctor to perform that service? There would be a furious scrubbing of this kitchen by Mrs. Boswell, who was now without an employer. And at last, a funeral.

To whom would the house belong? Surely not Mr. Moss. Not if he was the guilty one. Oh, if she were a betting woman, she would place her money on him, she would indeed.

Where was Detective Hayes? It had been well over half an hour—long enough for her to add tiny details like the earring half visible behind one of the stove's curved feet. How strange that these houses did not have steam boilers to heat water for sink and bath. The stove appeared to use wood, of all things. What did they burn? Unused cabins? For there were no trees for miles.

What could be keeping him? He should have returned in ten minutes, not forty-five. Perhaps he had to sober the constable up. Perhaps he had given up on the latter and gone to find a doctor. Perhaps she had better go look for him.

But no. Someone must stay with Clarissa. There was nothing Daisy could do but exactly what she was doing. The water in the glass was by now wholly crimson. She poured it down the sink, filled the glass again at the sink pump, and began to mix the mossy green for Clarissa's dress.

Mrs. Lavallee, looking like a smug thundercloud, had apparently abandoned all hope of finding Mrs. Moss and mounted the box to announce the cake walk herself. Anxiously, Freddie searched the room even as she forced herself to take her place next to her cake, which appeared to be a lemon cream. Beside the coconut snowball cake on the table in front of her, Daisy's place was empty.

What on earth was going on?

Her worried gaze caught that of Peony Churchill, who was standing two cakes behind her. Peony, seeing the empty place, frowned and scanned the crowded ballroom for Daisy just as Freddie had.

In the space of an indrawn breath between the calling of the first young lady's name—Miss Selkirk—and that of her partner, Freddie realized that the sounds of shouts and yells had reached such proportions outside that heads had begun to turn.

"Alonso Gabriel!"

But Freddie had seen that gentleman escorted out under duress just a few minutes ago, so Elizabeth was safe from—

Goodness, there was Mrs. Moss!

She was coming toward Freddie in her green gown, completely ignoring Mrs. Lavallee, an expression of intense distress upon her lovely face. Had something happened to Daisy? Freddie's stomach plunged as Mrs. Moss extended a hand toward her, and her lips parted to say—

The sound of a gunshot made Freddie jump and the audience lost its interest in cakes and partners and whirled toward the exit as though they thought to see the gunman standing in the doorway, pistol raised. In that split second of inattention, Mrs. Moss disappeared, swallowed up by the crowd as surely as though she had never been there.

Mrs. Lavallee shouted, "Frederica Linden's cake goes to—"

Outside, a woman screamed, and then another, and then pandemonium broke loose as the double doors were slammed open by the crowd of dancers surging into the street.

"Mrs. Moss!" Freddie plunged into the melee. At least she would not have to dance with yet another importunate young man. The momentum of those pressed around her carried her out into the blessedly cool night air.

Another gunshot.

Where had Mrs. Moss gone? Why had Daisy and Detective Hayes not come back?

Her wrist was seized in a slender but strong gloved hand. "Freddie, where are you going? You could be killed!" Her train over one arm, Peony Churchill yanked Freddie to one side with the other.

"Daisy is looking for Mrs. Moss, but she's here, and oh, I'm so worried!" Freddie pulled her wrist from Peony's grasp. "What if she was shot?"

"She hasn't been shot."

"How do you know?" Freddie turned and plunged into the crowd, and from the string of impolite invective coming from behind her, Peony was hot on her heels. She burst out from between two ladies—goodness, Mrs. Chang and Mrs. Calvert! —to see a man lying on the ground.

Detective Hayes.

"Barnaby!" Freddie shrieked, and dropped to the ground beside him. "Are you dead? Please don't be dead!"

He groaned and opened his eyes. "Freddie?"

"Are you hurt?"

"Yes. Shot. Where's Lynch?"

"No idea. Where is Daisy?"

"At the house. With Mrs. Moss."

"No," Freddie said. "Mrs. Moss was just in the ballroom."

His eyes squeezed shut, and he gasped in pain. "Can't be. She's dead."

Freddie's skin went cold. No. It couldn't be true. He was delirious with pain, he had to be, and someone had just kicked her as they ran past, and *where was Daisy?*

A loud voice said in basso tones that expected to be obeyed, "You there! Bring that broken tailgate from that dray. Put this man on it. We must convey him to the doctor."

"Mister, the devil only knows where the doctor is, but he ain't here."

"Then convey this man to Casa Gallina and fetch him," Captain Boyle ordered.

"Who says?" the stranger demanded. Freddie was quite sure he had been one of her partners.

"Captain Alturas Boyle of the ship *Iris*, that's who," the captain roared. "Do as I say at once, or you—or—

"—and you shall have a kiss for your trouble," Peony Churchill finished with a winning smile, before the captain lost his temper and fisticuffs broke out.

The man took one look at her and leaped to his task, and thirty seconds later, he and Captain Boyle carried Detective Hayes between them, down the street and around the corner to Casa Gallina, a parade made up of Mrs. Boyle, Freddie and Peony, the two absent friends, and of all people, Elizabeth Selkirk, all following in their wake.

Poor Miss Selkirk. Things had reached a sorry pass when she preferred the company of a wounded man to the fifty or so partners who had been clamoring for her hand. But then, the wounded man was Detective Hayes. He stood in a class by himself. Or would, as soon as he was standing again.

At Casa Gallina, it was impossible to get the patient up the narrow staircase to his room without causing him more pain and likely aggravating his injuries. Captain Boyle said, "Is there a bedroom on the ground floor? We cannot very well put him on the dining room table, though I will if I have to."

"Through here." Mrs. Chang led the way into Mrs. Moss's bedroom. "I am sure that Clarissa will not mind."

"She—she—" Detective Hayes gasped as the gate was removed from beneath him. "Kitchen. Daisy."

Peony paid the young man with the promised kiss and pushed him out the front door. "Please locate the doctor and bring him back here," she said to him. "Quickly. For my sake." With a trembling smile that brought to mind a heroine waving her brave warrior farewell, she saw him up the walk and then slammed the door on him.

Even in her frantic state, Freddie could be awash in admiration for such a performance. It certainly got results.

"The doctor could be anywhere, blast him," Mrs. Calvert said with some heat as they hurried into Clarissa's room. "What are we to do?"

"By the time he comes, it could be too late. We must see to our patient ourselves." Mrs. Boyle pushed through the little crowd in the bedroom doorway and laid a gentle hand on Detective Hayes's forehead. Then she looked up at Mrs. Calvert. "Could you boil a large kettle? And I will need as many clean towels as you can find." Mrs. Calvert nodded and left the room. "Alturas, will you fetch my kit from the ship?"

"I will return in five minutes," he promised, and likewise departed.

"I will assist you," Mrs. Chang offered briskly. "Once, long ago, I trained as a doctor. I was unable to graduate, but I have not forgotten my anatomy lessons."

"Excellent." Mrs. Boyle beamed at her. "I have nurse's training, but it is nothing to my years of experience with burns, bullets, and broken bones in the Corps. That is where I met my husband. I set his arm."

"What shall we do?" Peony asked, taking Freddie's cold hand.

"Keep our patient company for the moment," Mrs. Boyle

told her. "This lady and I will catalogue our resources in the kitchen and return shortly."

"Daisy—" the injured man managed before his eyes rolled up in his head and his body went limp.

"Something has happened to my sister," Freddie ground out from between chattering teeth, fear flooding her veins like ice water.

The words were scarcely out of her mouth when they heard Mrs. Calvert scream.

CHAPTER 10

SUNDAY, SEPTEMBER 8, 1895

12:05 a.m.

*D*aisy sat at the kitchen worktable, her arms around Freddie, half comforting her sister, half reassuring herself that her sister, the person she loved most in the world, was all right. After being torn from the lifeless form of her friend, Mrs. Calvert had been taken home in hysterics by Elizabeth Selkirk, who presumably would assist her to bed.

Mrs. Chang and Mrs. Boyle were at work on Detective Hayes, if the occasional groan that floated down the hall was any indication, Peony hovering there, too, in case she was needed to find more towels or hot water.

Having delivered her medical kit to his wife, Captain Boyle now patrolled the street outside, watching for a sign of either the doctor or the constable, but Daisy did not have much hope of either.

"It was her *fetch* I saw," Freddie whispered against Daisy's shoulder. "In the ballroom. I should have known. She was trying to tell me something, but I did not understand. Who expects a fetch ... at a ball?"

Who indeed? There was nothing Daisy could do but rub her back with a trembling hand. "I am still horrified that the person who did this might still have been on the property as Detective Hayes and I came in. She could not have been ... gone ... for more than a few minutes, poor lady. Oh, if only we had come sooner!"

"You saw no one?"

"Not a soul. As you say, one does not expect murderers to be slinking about in the dark."

"In Bodie, apparently, one may." Freddie drew back a little to take out a handkerchief, and blew her nose.

Mrs. Chang appeared in the kitchen doorway. She had tied a towel over her burgundy silk evening dress, but it was not likely the dress would emerge unscathed for all that. "My dears, are you all right?"

My dears. Mrs. Moss had called them that. Daisy's throat closed, so that all she could do was nod.

Mrs. Chang observed the sketchbook lying open on the table. Her gaze went from the painting to its object, still lying on the floor awaiting attention immediately after the living were attended to. "You are very accurate," she said, and touched the paper as tenderly as she might have touched the body of her friend. "But it seems a gruesome subject for a young lady. Why have you done this?"

"It—" Daisy swallowed and tried again. "I have had a hard lesson in the difference between gruesome and helpful, ma'am. When we were in Georgetown, our friend met an untimely end. My sketch of her injuries helped to bring her killer to justice."

Mrs. Chang's dark eyes widened. "You make a habit of drawing your friends when they are killed?"

Daisy flinched, her face crumpling at such cruelty, and her throat swelled.

Mrs. Chang knelt to take Daisy's cold hands. "Forgive me, dear. That was horrid of me. I—I am as upset as you. More, for I have known Clarissa better than anyone these five years."

Daisy gripped her hands and nodded speechlessly.

"And now I must perform the service that only friends may. Will you help me to lift her up here on the table?"

"But the doctor—"

"If he comes before morning—or at all—he may examine her here. But I doubt they will find him at leisure any time soon. Two men lie dying in the street outside the Union Hall. Your Mr. Carnegey would have been a third, had he not been so fortunate to possess friends so close who could care for him so promptly."

It took Daisy a moment to remember who her Mr. Carnegey was supposed to be.

"How is Mr. Carnegey?" Freddie roused herself from her stupor long enough to say.

"He is doubly fortunate in that he was not struck by one of those terrible propelled bullets. This one went clean through him."

"So he will recover?" Life began to come back into Freddie's face.

Mrs. Chang paused. "I believe his chances are good. The bullet may have cracked his shoulder blade as it passed, however. That and infection are my two worries. But between us, Mrs. Boyle and I have cleaned and bound his wounds and will watch his progress."

"Thank goodness you are here, ma'am," Daisy said gratefully. "He is a good man, and his loss would hurt sorely."

"Many just as good are taken every day." Mrs. Chang's face quivered as she glanced again at Clarissa's motionless form. "Come. Let us do what we can for my dear friend, and hope that the doctor may turn up eventually."

He did, eventually, in the company of Constable Lynch, as dawn was turning the rim of the hills from black to purple on a clear Sunday morning. The doctor turned Clarissa's head none too gently, and glanced at her gown, now neatly arranged about her, though stained with blood.

"Head wound," he pronounced as though they had not seen any such thing, and jerked his chin toward the stove. "Looks like she slipped on the linoleum and struck her head on that corner. Was anyone home?"

"No," Daisy said. Struck her head on the stove? Was he mad? Did he not see the blood upon the wall? "Mr. Carnegey and I are boarding here. We wanted to speak with her, and believed she had slipped home on an errand before the cake walk at the ball. We happened upon her just after we arrived. The murderer may even have been going out as we came in."

"Murderer? Why would anyone want to murder Clarissa Moss?" Constable Lynch demanded. Though the smell of whiskey was strong on his breath, he appeared to still have his senses. "Why, the men in this town would have wanted to keep her alive to make their matches. Why would you say such an unladylike thing, missy?"

"I—well—the blood—"

"Looks like she went down hard." He waved a hand in the direction of the stove. "Arteries do that. Spray and whatnot. You listen to me. Don't go imagining things fresh out of your potboilers and scandal sheets." He shook his head in disgust. "A young lady ought to occupy her mind with higher objects, like poetry."

"I do *not* read—"

The doctor harrumphed to bring their attention back to him, and turned to Mrs. Chang. "That makes three tonight, same as last year, Selena. I swear I am going to retire before Christmas. This town is too much for me." He indicated the sad form upon the table. "I'll issue a death certificate. It's clearly an accident. Constable?"

Constable Lynch nodded in agreement. "Who are her heirs?"

Mrs. Chang shook her head. "We do not know. She never mentioned family, but there may be papers in the house."

"Right. Well, you may hold the funeral on Monday if you like. Was she a Methodist?"

"Episcopalian," Mrs. Chang said faintly, evidently nonplussed at this swerve in conversation.

The doctor evidently thought the same. "Normally I'd have her over at the morgue, but it is going to be full tonight. And since it's right next to the Miner's Union Hall with everyone milling about, our taking her over there would cause the kind of sensation that we don't want after tonight's events."

"I just left a crowd of hundreds in the street over there," Constable Lynch said, "half of them having a party and half a funeral."

The doctor shook his head in disgust. "You can wash and lay her out here, and I'll send the undertakers for her in an hour or two, before church."

Mrs. Chang managed to thank him before seeing him out.

When she returned with Mrs. Boyle to the kitchen, her face was as set and white as porcelain.

"Did you ask him to look at Mr. Carnegey?" Freddie asked. "What did he say?"

"I did not," Mrs. Chang said crisply. "I would sooner have Constable Lynch examine him, dead drunk. A coyote would make a better doctor than that one."

"Slipped," Daisy said, shaking her head in disbelief. "On the linoleum! When anyone with eyes can see she was struck from behind!"

"We have eyes," Mrs. Chang said grimly. "As do you. And we have ears where few people do. The unhappy fact of the matter is that if we wish to give our dear friend the justice she deserves, we are going to have to do it ourselves."

"I told you so," came a weak voice from the next room.

"You are supposed to be resting," came Peony's chiding but gentle tones from his bedside. "Far be it from me to threaten a gentleman, but I will ask Mrs. Boyle to dose you with laudanum if I must."

"Yes, ma'am," came the meek rejoinder.

Mrs. Chang's measuring gaze rested upon Daisy and Freddie. "It so happens that in yesterday afternoon's mail, I had a letter from Eileen Alvarez in Santa Fe. And she enclosed another from one of our absent friends in Georgetown. I would not have brought it up at this moment except that our extremity demands it."

Daisy's gaze locked with hers, and she felt a *frisson* of alarm.

"Apparently you young ladies have certain talents besides painting."

"Oh, no, we—"

"Apparently," Mrs. Chang went on relentlessly, "a murderer was brought to justice thanks to you, and a missing woman found."

"We were not alone," Daisy said. "We had help."

"Nevertheless, I would rather place justice in your hands than in the paws of Constable Lynch. In fact, it seems we must, for according to those two worthies, no crime has occurred here at all."

"But we are not Pinkertons," Freddie cried. "All we want is to find Papa!"

Peony left the invalid's bedside to come into the kitchen behind Mrs. Boyle. "I am no Pinkerton either, but if I can be of assistance, I hope you will employ me."

Of what use was Peony other than getting men to do her bidding? If she had been in the kitchen while the doctor was here, perhaps they might have had a different result.

"We cannot oblige you," Daisy said to Mrs. Chang, close to tears. "I am very sorry, but we cannot."

It was difficult to hold her head up when the gazes of all the occupants of the kitchen but one lay so heavily upon her.

"Very well," Mrs. Chang said at last. "We will leave it for now. Perhaps instead you might assist me in the last service I may perform for our friend? We must wash and dress her. Clarissa would hate to receive even undertakers in such disarray."

Daisy and Freddie had assisted in this service for their mother, undressing her, removing articles of clothing one at a time, washing pale skin, brushing out hair. It was a duty usually left to women, even if the deceased were a man.

As though Freddie had divined her thoughts, she said,

"Strange that it is the women who perform this last office. Not doctors or even husbands."

"Women brought us all into the world," Mrs. Chang said softly, gently rolling Clarissa's body over so that she might unhook her bodice and skirt. "Perhaps it is right that women should see us out of it."

After all the clothes had been removed and the silk gown taken outside to the burn pile, Peony went to check on Detective Hayes. She returned to the kitchen in less than a minute.

"Mr. Carnegey bids me tell you to wash the poor lady's wound carefully, and to preserve any—" She could not go on.

"Any matter in it," came the voice from the bedroom.

"Any matter?" Mrs. Chang repeated, her nose wrinkled in disgust. "Whatever do you mean, sir?"

"Daisy knows." His voice trailed away, as though he had been staving off unconsciousness only long enough to speak.

Again, Mrs. Chang's expression made Daisy quail. As steadily as she could, she said, "I believe he means that we must be careful. Sometimes the perpetrator may leave a hint of his or her identity behind."

"What sort of hint?" Even Mrs. Boyle was looking at Daisy as though she were a ghoul. Was this to be her fate each time she became even tangentially involved in such cases? People looking at her with such distaste? Though she was bound and determined not to become involved in this one after she left this room, she still must bear the burden now.

"I do not know," she confessed. "Anything. Or nothing. We must simply be careful, and observe."

"As you were doing, with your pencils and brushes?" Mrs. Chang indicated the sketchbook, which had been set aside on the counter when they had lifted Clarissa to the table. Could that be understanding growing in her face? For unlike Mrs. Calvert, who had screamed and fainted on top of the poor deceased's legs, Mrs. Chang had actually looked at the pages. "Your painting reminds me of the illustrations in my textbooks, long ago, in the old country."

Daisy had never seen a medical textbook, but she took this as encouragement. "Memory is faulty. But a sketch can tell the truth, even if we cannot see it at first." She took a deep breath. "If you will permit me to sketch while you carry out Mr. Carnegey's request?"

The two ladies exchanged a glance, one more pained than the other. Then Mrs. Boyle nodded, and Mrs. Chang said, "If such a distasteful task will help us find who did this, then I will not hinder you."

They left the washing of the wound for last. It was clear that no corner of a stove could have left such a deep depression in Clarissa's fragile skull. It was a jagged oval shape, as though she had been kicked by a horse. A small horse. From above and to the left, if the difference in depth from one side to the other was any indication. Daisy could not imagine what could have been used, for nothing but the frying pan had been out of place. Surely that would have left a different impression? More ... flat?

She set her questions aside, turned the now dry page of the sketchbook, and drew what she saw, pitiable and shattered as it was. It did not take long, and she did not use her colors.

Then, as the ladies gently bound up their friend's hair in a nightcap and dressed her in a clean nightgown trimmed in Irish lace, Daisy and Freddie gazed into the bowl in which the washing water had been wrung. Fragments lay in the bottom that were clearly bone. Golden hairs. A hairpin, bent double under sudden terrible stress. And a small, dark sliver that did not belong in the rinse from any woman's head.

Freddie fished it out and held it to the light. "What is this?"

Daisy squinted, as did Mrs. Boyle. "A shard of tortoise-shell?" the latter suggested. "Was she wearing a comb in her coiffure?"

Mrs. Chang shook her head. "She was not wearing a hair ornament of any kind, not even feathers. Her hair was so lovely put up in braids and curls that she often simply left it unadorned."

"Then I cannot imagine what it could be."

"Wrap it up in a clean handkerchief," Mrs. Chang suggested. "Alvira Manning uses a magnifying glass to do petit point. We might find it useful. I will ask her after church."

Daisy fetched a handkerchief from her room and wrapped the fragment in it. As she did so, Peony came back in from her vigil at Detective Hayes's bedside.

"He is asleep," she whispered. "And so am I, nearly." She followed Daisy into the kitchen and watched her tuck the handkerchief into the back of the sketchbook. "Mrs. Boyle, are you ready to return to the ship?"

"Yes, miss," Mrs. Boyle said. "For now, there is nothing more we can do."

"You have done all that you could, and more," Mrs. Chang said softly, gazing at the still form on the kitchen worktable. She had become rigid, but they had managed to cross Clarissa's hands over her breast, and she looked almost peaceful ... if you did not look at the mottling under the skin of her cheek, where she had lain on the floor. "And still it feels as though it is far from enough."

Her gaze rose to meet that of Daisy.

No, I cannot do any more. Do not ask it of me.

"Who will sit with her until the undertakers come?" Mrs. Chang asked as though this had been her only question.

"I will," Freddie said. "Daisy, you must get some rest."

"I cannot leave you here alone," Daisy protested. "And you have been awake all night, too."

"Please, dearest. Let me do this for her." Freddie laid a hand on hers, and belatedly, Daisy understood.

If there were any messages forthcoming from the deceased, Freddie would be the one to see or hear them.

"I—I suppose it is too much to hope that your plans to call upon us aboard *Iris* might still go forward?" Peony sounded uncharacteristically hesitant, as though aware she might be making a *faux pas*.

"Perhaps we might put it off until—until after the funeral," Daisy said. "I do want to, still."

"And perhaps Mr. Carnegey might have recovered enough to join you." Peony sounded hopeful.

"In two days, miss? I think not." Mrs. Boyle handed Peony her wrap. "Miss Linden, should he develop a fever, or show signs of restlessness or discomfort, you must send for Selena or me at once."

"Yes, ma'am."

"I will ask Alvira and Muriel to send word to our absent friends about this terrible event," Mrs. Chang said, pulling on her gloves though she only lived down the road. "They will not be able to come for the funeral, but they should know, all the same."

"And Mr. Moss," Daisy said. "He should know, too. I suppose he is staying at one of the hotels."

"I beg your pardon?" Mrs. Chang, normally so unruffled, looked astounded.

"Yes, did you not see him at the ball? Mrs. Moss's husband? He was wearing a black tailcoat and a man's waistcoat corset of the most bilious blue, like poorly mixed ink."

"Cyril Moss is in town? Are you certain?"

"Yes indeed," Daisy said. "He came in on the airship with us. He called here. He was dreadful, shouting and calling people names. Mr. Carnegey rendered him unconscious and dragged him from the house into the street."

Mrs. Chang said something in the Canton tongue that Daisy imagined had best not be translated. "Thank you for telling me," she said in English. "We must be on our guard."

"We ought to watch him closely," Daisy blurted. "For if ever a man were capable of doing this terrible thing, it would be he."

Mrs. Chang nodded, once. Decidedly. "I agree with you."

CHAPTER 11

1:20 p.m.

When Mrs. Boswell came in to make breakfast, it was to find her employer cold upon the worktable and everyone in the house sleeping the sleep of utter exhaustion. This Daisy learned some hours later, when she managed to dress and haul herself down the stairs to find the undertakers had come and gone, she had missed church, and Mrs. Boswell was wringing out the last of the cloths and sponges with which she had scrubbed the kitchen clean.

Exactly as Daisy had thought she might. No trace remained of the previous night's horrors save the painting in Daisy's sketchbook.

"It's a fright, miss," that worthy lady said, her eyes wet even as she set a cup of tea in front of Daisy in the dining room and sat across from her with one of her own. "I'm sure I can't think what monster could have done this. What shall we do?"

"Has your salary been paid, Mrs. Boswell?" If it had not, and the cook departed, Daisy was still prepared to feed herself and Freddie. But Mr. Pender would certainly have to leave, since a man could not sleep in a house with two young ladies unchaperoned. Detective Hayes, for the moment, did not pose a threat to their morals in the eyes of society, but when he was sufficiently healed, he too would have to depart.

"Yes, until the end of the month. So I may do for you boarders until then, at least. I hope Mr. Moss doesn't take it into his head that he ought to take over the business."

"She left the house to him?" Daisy could not keep the disbelief out of her tone.

"No indeed. It is left to the absent friends. Which I only know because I am one of them. That is what we do, you know, in the absence of children. We leave our properties to each other, that all may benefit."

The absent friends! What an enterprising group of ladies they were. "I must say that it a relief," Daisy confessed. "I was not looking forward to his tossing me from the house and announcing to everyone in the street that I was a desert flower."

"He's a piece of work, that man. You mark my words, he'll be at the funeral with a face as long as a wet evening, and then sniffing around here looking for a loophole in her will. But there isn't one. Clarissa Moss was no fool, and she had the best attorney in town looking after her business."

Monday, September 9, 1895 at 11:00 a.m.

Mrs. Boswell turned out to be a prophet of surprising accuracy. The Episcopal church was full to the windows for the funeral, and there in the first row was Mr. Moss, in black from head to foot, a black-bordered handkerchief in one hand. The pine casket was closed, naturally, but that did not prevent his throwing himself across it, making it rock on its cloth-covered sawhorses, sobbing and kissing the planks that separated him from the woman he had despised and abused.

Daisy glanced at Freddie in a moment of shared disgust. Freddie had told her earlier that there had been no communications from the dead in the interval before Mrs. Boswell had come in to work. But the dead were notoriously capricious when it came to passing on useful information, so Daisy had not been surprised. However, the day must be got through, though both she and her sister were still exhausted and emotionally wrung out.

Which may have been why Mrs. Manning and Mrs. Porter were able to trap Daisy so easily next to the coffee pot at the lunch in the Episcopal Church's public room following the burial. Mr. Moss had also come back, but Daisy predicted it would not be long before he adjourned to one of the saloons to drown his hypocrisy in whiskey.

"Selena tells us that you have declined to help us discover who ended Clarissa's life," Mrs. Manning said without preamble, disappointment in her eyes even as her ample form blocked Daisy's escape. "Muriel and I are here to beg you to reconsider."

Oh, dear. She was too tired to think, so words escaped her mouth, blunt and unconsidered. "We are here to find our father. Any moment spent on the passing of your dear friend is a moment taken away from our search."

"Not necessarily," Mrs. Porter said with a shake of her head. "Two searches may proceed simultaneously. We have already heard from three of the boarding-houses at the other end of town that Professor Linden was not seen there."

"You have? Why did you not tell me?"

"Because such a report leaves you no better off than before. Still, several more houses remain. We will make short work of them before we move on to the hotels."

Daisy blinked at her.

Mrs. Manning added, "You must give the newspaper men at Casa Gallina the facts, and put a missing persons article in the *Barker*. They publish them all the time."

Sadly, Detective Hayes was in no condition to be walking to the newspaper offices. Mr. Pender was busy as a jackrabbit following up on the two deaths outside the Union Hall on Saturday night. Might she ask Beth Selkirk for her help?

"So while the word goes out, you will have time to turn your mind to our sister," Mrs. Porter pointed out, two refusals evidently having no effect at all upon her. "Please, Miss Linden. We hear very favorable things of you."

"Very favorable," Mrs. Manning repeated, taking Daisy's cold hand and pressing it between her two warm ones. "If not to oblige us, then for Clarissa's sake."

Freddie, where are you? Come rescue me!

But deep in her heart, and in spite of her commitment to Papa, Daisy recognized a certain truth. She could not imagine staying in Bodie seeking news of him while a murderer roamed the streets free as air. She had too many questions, plaguing her like mosquitoes in the dark.

For one, why Clarissa? It could not have been that she had surprised the culprit in a burglary, for one did not burgle kitchens. Had she held secrets in her past? Was that why her husband had appeared without warning, spewing invective? Not that she expected Mr. Moss to confess on the spot. But if he were guilty, at least the facts could be turned over to Constable Lynch and an arrest made.

Her own curious mind had just confirmed the truth in her heart. Oh, dear. She really was going to do this.

Feeling rather as though she were stepping off the gangway of an airship in flight, Daisy nodded at last. "Very well. For as long as my sister and I are here in Bodie, we will do what we can to find out who killed your friend."

Mrs. Porter squeezed her hand and released it with a long breath. "Thank you."

"And do not worry about the roof over your head," Mrs. Manning added. "You may stay at Casa Gallina as long as you like, though you may need to launder your own unmentionables periodically."

"A roof is more important, and we are quite used to washing our own things," Daisy said. She had not even thought about leaving Casa Gallina, which told her that somewhere in the back of her brain, she had meant to see this through all along. "And you can assure me that Mr. Moss is powerless to take the house from the absent friends and throw my sister and I into the street?"

"Quite powerless," Mrs. Porter said firmly. "If he tries, we have ways and means by which to make him stop."

"You do not want to know," Mrs. Manning whispered behind her hand. "My sister keeps quite shocking company, but it is useful."

Daisy did not look at Mrs. Porter's reddened cheeks. Instead, she said, "Then there is no time like the present. I wish to know what Mr. Moss is doing here, and where he was during those few minutes last night. Excuse me, ladies."

A few minutes later, she materialized beside Peony

Churchill and Beth Selkirk. The latter was trying to convince her father to let her stay at the funeral lunch a few moments more.

"Peony, I need your help," she whispered as Beth lost the battle and left unwillingly with Mr. Selkirk.

"So does she." Peony tilted her head toward the departing pair. "Honestly, I am tempted to kidnap the poor girl and fly her anywhere she wants to go, just to get her out from under her papa's thumb."

"And then he would raise the Wild West against you, and that would clip your wings rather severely."

"You have not seen my wings," Peony said with a smile. "How may I be of service?"

"I want to question Mr. Moss, but I am not nearly as skilled as you are with the male sex," Daisy said in a low voice. "Our object is to find out where he was Saturday night, from just before the cake walk until Detective Hayes was shot."

"You are very precise in your estimations," Peony said in surprise.

"It is my nature, I am afraid," Daisy confessed. "I sometimes get so mired in the details that Freddie is forever pointing out to me the larger picture. Perhaps it is a result of painting, where the details *create* the larger picture."

"I like a clear, straightforward task." Peony touched her chignon, smoothing a strand into place and adjusting her black straw hat with its glossy blue and black feathers to a slightly more rakish angle. "Come. Let us beard the lion before he escapes to a den where we may not follow."

Peony floated across the room to where Mr. Moss was conversing with a pair of gentlemen. They fell back, their faces filling with admiration, as she extended her hand. Daisy was quite certain they did not even see her. Nor did Mr. Moss appear to. Then again, would he recognize the stranger in Casa Gallina's parlor as being the young woman before him in the navy walking dress? Daisy decided that if asked, she would pretend to be the famous Miss Churchill's rather mousy and fragile companion.

"Mr. Moss," Peony said in tones soft with sympathy. "I am so very sorry for your loss."

"Thank you." He took the slender gloved hand in his, completely engulfing it. "This is such a difficult time to be surrounded by strangers. Yet how wonderful to find such kindness as yours."

"I am certain we were introduced last night at the ball, sir, before these dreadful events occurred. I am Miss Churchill."

Still holding her hand, he made a half bow. "How could anyone forget a young lady of such beauty and presence?"

"You are too kind. But indeed, I could swear to it that yours was the name called for my cake, just before the cake walk. How is it that we did not dance?"

"The loss is all mine." He smiled down at her, and Daisy heard his corset creak. "But you are mistaken, for as an old married man, I should have been shot for attempting to claim a dance with you. No indeed, discretion was the better part of valor." His mouth opened as if to laugh, but with a quick glance about him at the assembled mourners, he seemed to remember this was no place for levity.

"So you were a wallflower for my sake?" Peony was finally able to withdraw her hand. "I suppose a man may find good conversation there as anywhere."

"Indeed. I spent a most interesting few minutes with a

Nubian aeronaut. It was his opinion that the sooner I invested in airships, the more success I should find."

"It seems likely such a man would know best," Peony agreed. "Did the fracas outside interrupt you?"

"Wasn't that a melée? I do hope you were not caught up in it."

"Certainly not." The feathers danced upon Peony's hat as she shook her head.

"I had barely secured a drink at the bar when in the rush for the door some oaf bumped my hand and spilled the entire glass."

"How tiresome." Peony pouted on his behalf.

"It was indeed, for in my distraction I missed the entertainment. Two men down, and there I was, wedged into the doorway with forty others! But as you may have observed, I am a man of some presence, and I soon freed myself. But by then it was too late, and the party was over anyway."

"Most disappointing for the Ladies' Aid." One could have spread the regret in her tone like butter. "The ball in pieces at the second interval! Had I been Mrs. Lavallee, I would have repaired to the nearest saloon to drown my sorrows."

"Exactly so, my dear Miss Churchill. We are of like mind, I see, for that is exactly the path I took. Selkirk invited me along, and so I went." The satisfied smile faded from his face with a little too much deliberation for sincerity. "It was not until the next morning that I heard the dreadful news of my dear wife."

"A terrible thing." Peony glanced at Daisy.

"What are your plans now, sir?" Daisy asked him in a whispery tone. Then, at his startled glance, as though he had only just noticed she stood there, she said, "Please forgive me, and accept my condolences, too. I am Miss Churchill's companion."

He gave her a nod with less than a tenth of the admiration he had bestowed upon Peony. Daisy had never been so pleased to know that a man found her so unremarkable that he did not remember her face ... or accusing her of being a whore a scant few days ago.

"My plans are not settled," he said. "But as I am sure you are aware, my wife has considerable property here. I expect that I will be called upon to decide its disposition. But all in good time." He reached for Peony's hand again, but was unable to capture it. "Miss Churchill, may I interest you in dinner at the American Hotel? I am staying there, and they serve an excellent pheasant, to say nothing of oysters."

"My goodness, sir, so soon?" Peony sounded more amused than scandalized. "Your dear wife is barely in her grave."

"But life goes on, does it not?" His voice became avuncular. "One must seize one's chances where one may."

"Indeed, sir. And I must seize mine. Come, Miss—er, I see Mrs. Boyle at the door. She will have a message for me from the telegraph office. Good day to you, sir—and again, our condolences."

In less than five seconds, Peony extricated them both from his company and from the room.

"My goodness," Daisy said, feeling rather as though she ought to be holding on to her hat. "You are awfully good."

"Why, thank you." Peony waved at Freddie, who had emerged from the door into the hot early afternoon sun in pursuit. "There are far too many boring men in the world, don't you agree? Thank heavens for people like Captain Boyle and your Mr. Carnegey. Neither of *them* would ask a woman to dinner on the day of their wife's funeral."

"Mr. Carnegey is not married," Freddie said breathlessly, joining them in time to hear this last. "Goodness, Daisy, I saw you speaking with Mr. Moss, but I could not believe my eyes. Whatever possessed you? I was on tenterhooks every minute, waiting for the explosion."

"Why should he explode?" Peony asked with interest. "Never mind, come back with me to *Iris* and tell me the story. I have had enough of being pleasant for one day and must loosen my corset a little."

"Oh, but we could not inconvenience you," Daisy protested. "Not after you have been so obliging."

"Nonsense. I must hear the story, and you must tell me if I was successful in my interrogation." They walked three abreast up the street, heading for Casa Gallina. "Besides, you promised to come when the funeral was over. And you're in luck—Mrs. Boyle has made a blackberry pie for tea. You must take a slice back to Mr. Carnegey with my compliments."

Behind Peony's shoulder, Freddie raised an eyebrow and exchanged a glance with Daisy.

Oh, no. Daisy determined on the spot that this beautiful young woman should not be the next to break poor Detective Hayes's heart. She would do everything she could to prevent it.

CHAPTER 12

3:05 p.m.

*W*hen they arrived at Casa Gallina so that Daisy and Freddie could change into something less formal, it was to find Mrs. Boyle there taking the matter of Detective Hayes into her own hands. He was on his feet, his left arm in a sling secured against his chest, and her son Timothy was coming down the stairs with his valise.

Mrs. Boyle faced her astonished employer in the foyer with a mulish expression in her brown eyes. "I can't leave this young man alone in this house. Who is to say that Mrs. Moss's assailant won't return? And him defenseless in bed."

"I say, Mrs. Boyle—" Mr. Carnegey began.

But Mrs. Boyle rode right over him. "He is hot to the touch, and must be watched. We have two spare cabins, miss. If I am to care for him I need him close to hand. Selena has her own household and boarders to look after as well as these young ladies and Mr. Pender. It is too much, and we must be sensible."

"Do you hear me arguing with you?" Peony inquired. She refused to allow herself to blush at the thought of Mr. Carnegey aboard her ship, in a highly interesting condition. "I think it a capital plan. See, Daisy? We need not bring the pie to Mr. Carnegey. He will bring himself to the pie."

"Or die trying," the gentleman in question managed, making his slow way to the door. "I am not in the least feverish. But since I appear to have no choice in the matter, I will do my best not to inconvenience you."

"Handsome men are never an inconvenience," Peony said with her best impression of airy unconcern. She was perfectly conscious that Daisy was gazing at her with a mixture of surprise and ... something else. Watchfulness? Dismay? But surely she had had no time to develop feelings for Mr. Carnegey, even of the protective, younger-sisterish kind.

Balderdash, snapped her conscience. She has had a day longer than you, and *protective* is not the word I would use for your feelings in any case.

I have no feelings where men are concerned. Not after having my heart broken by Sydney Meriwether-Astor.

But this seemed to offend her conscience so much that it did not deign to reply.

They made a slow parade up the hill to *Iris*—the injured man, white as a slack sail; herself and Mrs. Boyle, attempting to assist without wounding his pride; Timothy, carrying valise and the basket of bandages and other supplies; and in the rear the Linden sisters, Daisy with the reticule containing her sketchbook and goodness knew what else clutched to her chest.

Did she go nowhere without it? Possibly not.

What a puzzle of a young woman. How could anyone as

retiring and unremarkable as Daisy Linden find herself involved in the lives and violent deaths of the people around her? It could not be on purpose. Perhaps she attracted violence the way Claire Malvern attracted adventures. Daisy did not seem to be the adventurous kind at all.

Aboard *Iris* and in her own domain once again, Mrs. Boyle made Mr. Carnegey comfortable upon the sofa in the grand salon, with pillows behind his back and a knitted afghan over his knees. He gave a great sigh and gazed about him with interest.

"I say, this is a treat. This ship only becomes finer the closer one gets."

"Thank you," Peony said modestly, though pleased that his taste matched her own. "My friend Mr. Fremont in Philadelphia thought that a different, more streamlined model might be better for long-distance travel, but it was *Iris* for me and no other." She took off her hat and the black walking jacket she had worn to Mrs. Moss's funeral, and invited their guests to sit while Mrs. Boyle prepared tea.

"Mr. Fremont?" Mr. Carnegey said. "You are acquainted with Stanford Fremont? I believe he and Mrs. Fremont are in the Fifteen Colonies just now."

"Why, yes," Peony said in some surprise at his knowledge. "That seems to be a familiar name in these parts."

"That is quite the understatement," Freddie said. "We run into the Fremont name on a regular basis."

"How do you know Stanford?" Peony asked him. "And that they are in the east just now?"

"They departed in the summer," he said. "We had some dealings together during the Rose Rebellion. You may have heard of it."

Goodness! She knew the rough outlines, of course, but nothing of this man's involvement. Well! Their mutual acquaintance with the couple would have to wait until a less crowded hour. But there was one thing concerning this gentleman that she very much wanted to know now, and here was her opportunity.

"Speaking of names, Miss Freddie," Peony said pleasantly, "you must clear up a puzzle for me. I was standing just behind you when Mr. Carnegey was shot. You cried out, 'Barnaby!' as you ran to his side. But I could swear that he was introduced to me as David."

To Peony's surprise, the girl's face turned pale, and her fingers went to her lips as though to catch the words back, far too late. Her blue gaze found that of Mr. Carnegey, and filled with tears of contrition.

If the trifling matter was a puzzle before, it was a full-blown mystery now. Had Peony observed something significant? How delightful!

Mr. Carnegey sighed, his broad chest rising and falling and making him wince with pain. Daisy started forward in her seat, but he lifted his good hand.

"It is all right." Daisy subsided, but remained on the edge of her chair as Mrs. Boyle brought in the tea. "Mrs. Boyle, please seat yourself and join us. Freddie, do not worry yourself. If I am to be confined here, perhaps it is best that there should be truth among us." His smile was crooked. "After all, if one cannot trust the daughter of Isobel Churchill, who can one trust?"

"I should not make that assumption, sir." Why must she always be thought of in terms of her mother? It was highly annoying. "Are you telling me that David Carnegey is not your name?"

"Indeed, it is not. My name is Barnaby Hayes, and I am a Rocky Mountain Detective working *incognito* here in Bodie."

Mrs. Boyle, who was pouring, splashed a little tea into the saucer in her surprise. With an apologetic glance at Peony, she hastily wiped it up.

Peony closed her own sagging jaw with difficulty. Those were the last words she had expected to come out of his mouth. A Rocky Mountain Detective! She had no idea what that was, but wasn't he a mystery! "And Daisy and Freddie know this already?"

"Detective Hayes helped us trap the murderer of Miss Makepeace in Georgetown," Daisy said. "If not for him and the tools of his trade, it would not have been possible."

"And Daisy might well be dead," Freddie put in.

"Good heavens," was all Peony could manage. What depths this girl's ladylike exterior concealed! She was dying to know all the details, but tears still swam in Freddie's eyes. Nor did it seem decent to pump an injured man for information.

She would wait a suitable interval, and winkle the story out of him then.

"I will not ask you for details of your case, of course," she said with a nice mixture of virtue and sympathy. "Such a line of work would lend itself to aliases, I imagine."

"It does," he replied. "I ask you and your crew to continue to refer to me as David Carnegey. If my true identity were known, lives could be in danger."

Peony accepted her tea and a slice of the promised pie, swimming in cream. "I promise."

"I will see to it that the children understand the gravity of the case," Mrs. Boyle said.

"No need, Aunt Persis," Dinah said, coming in with the twins. "We heard. Is that pie?"

In the hubbub of seeing that her family had pie and tea, the discussion of aliases was set aside. But Peony had not finished with it yet, oh no indeed.

"You were going to tell me of Mr. Moss, Daisy, and why you deputized me to interrogate him," she said. "Had you had dealings with him?"

As Daisy told the story of the man's arrival in Bodie and his subsequent intrusion into and ejection from Casa Gallina, Peony set her fork down so that she might not miss a single detail. Fancy the patient upon her sofa knocking him unconscious and tossing him into the street!

"That brute," she exclaimed, taking a restorative sip of tea. "I am glad I knew nothing of this, otherwise, I should have been afraid to approach him. How strange that he did not seem to recognize you, Daisy."

"It is strange," she agreed equably. "But I am glad of it."

"The question is, what did you say to him, Miss Churchill?" Mr. Carneg—Detective—oh, bother. She would think of him as Mr. Carnegey. It was simpler, and she would be less likely to slip up and call him by his real name in moments of stress, like poor Freddie.

Rapidly, Peony filled him in on their conversation, aided by Daisy. His face pinched in disappointment.

"So we must strike him from our list of suspects? I was rather looking forward to turning him over to the law."

"I am afraid so." Captain Boyle took his tea from his wife with a smile of thanks. "I spent some time talking with him about investing in airships—the Meriwether-Astor Manufacturing Works in particular. We were engaged in conversation almost right up until the first gunshots. I did not go with him to the bar in the card room, but I certainly saw him there just beforehand, before the rush for the door."

"What a pity," Freddie murmured. "How bloodthirsty I am becoming, to want to see a man in gaol simply because he called me names."

"It sounds perfectly reasonable to me," Mrs. Boyle said crisply. "Though I doubt any magistrate in the country would agree with us."

"So we must look elsewhere for our culprit," Mr. Carnegey went on. "Who is next?"

"There is a young man," Daisy began hesitantly. "He burst into the house in much the same way, accusing Mrs. Moss of deceiving him about the match she had made for him. I do not remember his name, however."

"It was in the *Bodie Barker,* was it not?" Freddie asked. "He must have come straight from the paper after making a public complaint."

"This week's issues are in my room at the boarding-house," Mr. Carnegey said. "It will be easy enough to collect them. Who else?"

"That is the trouble," Daisy said. "With the doctor declaring poor Mrs. Moss's death an accident, and the constable consumed with the other shootings that night, there is to be no investigation. I have been dragooned into doing what I can to help by the society of absent friends."

"By whom?" Mr. Carnegey said. "I heard Selena say something about it, but I was not in my right mind at the time."

"All of them, it seems," Daisy said glumly. "In return, they have agreed to put out the word to all the boarding-house and hotel owners about Papa. Which reminds me, Detective. We must write a missing persons article for the *Barker* without delay."

"If Miss Churchill will supply us with paper and ink, you can write it. No need for my byline," Mr. Carnegey said. "Anyone may submit such an article."

"Unlike the articles Miss Selkirk writes under your name?" Peony asked in silky tones.

"Exactly," he said, and then turned his head to give her a sharp look. "Wait a moment. How did you know that?"

"Ladies talk," Peony said. "And that young lady has no one to talk to."

"She has me," he said, frowning. "It mystifies me still how I can be her only friend in this town when she has lived here for a decade. But getting back to our main subject, who might we put on our list besides the unhappy match? In this town, there must be many with a grudge and a temper."

After several moments of silence, Mrs. Boyle said, "Perhaps the grudge is in the past. Not her husband, but someone else."

"Perhaps." Mr. Carnegey nodded. "But it may be difficult to pursue them. What enemies did Mrs. Moss have here, if any?"

"I will ask the absent friends," Daisy said. "They know everything. Though it is odd that they did not immediately hazard any guesses."

"Perhaps they are used to keeping their mouths shut," Mr. Carnegey mused. "People who know much talk little, in my experience. It is the empty heads that cannot stop the endless flow of words, like a constant breeze between their ears."

Peony resolved to talk a little less and listen a little more herself, in case he should lump her into that despised company.

"I wish I could assist you, Daisy." Mr. Carnegey's brows drew together in pain once more, as he shifted on his pillows. "But I make a very good sounding board, should your inquiries lead you to form theories."

"I will depend upon your help," Daisy said. "And I hope there may yet be a mysterious device in your valise that could be useful."

"Not in my valise, but close by." His eyes twinkled. "One never knows when a Surreptitious Speech Transcriptor may come in handy. Now, speaking of that, if Miss Churchill will oblige us, you and Freddie might write that missing persons article while we are here at leisure."

Miss Churchill did oblige them. And following their excellent example, she slipped away into her own cabin and took out a piece of her crested stationery.

Mrs. Stanford Fremont
   Number 50 Washington Avenue
   Philadelphia, the Fifteen Colonies

Dearest Gloria,

How much I have to tell you since my last sent from Santa Fe! I have landed in Bodie, and within minutes made the acquaintance of the objects of my journey, the Miss Lindens. Was that not efficient of me?

I have not yet formed an opinion of either young lady. They seem rather unremarkable and retiring, yet have become embroiled in a murder while at the same time searching for their father. They are either astonishingly brave or utterly careless. I cannot decide which. In any case, I can see why Maggie formed a friendship with the younger one. There is a light in her eye that is very appealing.

They have made useful friends by some social alchemy, one of them being a young man called Barnaby Hayes. Apparently you and Stanford met him during the events of the Rose Rebellion? I must confess I am agog to learn the details of your friendship, if indeed you are friends. I expect he has an estate, a wife, and a brood of handsome children somewhere in the fens, but that does not signify. A woman may still have an interest for the sake of her friends, may not she?

It is very strange how well known you and your husband are in this pitiless country. I have begun to think that of your set at St. Cecilia's, you are quite the most celebrated of them all. Julia does not count. Notoriety is not the same thing as celebrity. And she would not last a minute out here anyway.

Back to the subject of Mr. Hayes. He is on some hush-hush mission about which he will say nothing, and is now under Mrs. Boyle's care here on Iris. He was shot two nights ago, at a ball. Well may your eyebrows rise at this. If there is a wife in the fens, say only that he is recovering—the bullet passed straight through his shoulder, though it nicked the shoulder blade on its exit. I will try my hand at nursing and hope my clumsy efforts do not hasten the poor man to an early grave.

As to that other matter, I no longer wish to sift it to the bottom. The little I did hear from Daisy Linden has settled my mind sufficiently. Claire was right, the maddening creature. He was not worthy of my love, and her intervention saved me from disgrace and ridicule. I suppose I must wait and see what the future holds in that regard. My heart glows at the thought of Claire's happiness, and yours. If only either of your lords of the manor had brothers!

I must close now, and waste a pigeon's time with this slapdash letter. I have never been so glad for friends like you, who supplied me with an airship, and Claire, who supplied me with a lightning pistol.

A bientôt, my dear. Kiss the baby for me, and share any of my scribbles with Claire if you write to her.

Your own

Peony

CHAPTER 13

5:30 p.m.

*I*t feels wrong somehow, to leave Detect—er, Mr. Carnegey among people we hardly know. Oh, Daisy, what a fool I felt. I did not even know I had blurted out his name."

Daisy patted Freddie's hand and tucked it into the crook of her own elbow. "I do not believe there is any harm done, dearest. Miss Churchill moves among people of our—well, your acquaintance. I am quite certain she and her crew can be trusted—for Mr. Carnegey did not hesitate to reveal himself to them."

"That is true. Well, what's done is done, and we must turn our minds to the task we have been given."

"I have begun a list in the back of my sketchbook, and with regret will strike Mr. Moss's name," Daisy said. "Let us take this article about Papa to the newspaper offices, and then after supper, approach the absent friends to see what other possibilities we might gather."

The first errand took only ten minutes and a twenty-five cent piece, and they left having garnered polite condolences and, more important, assurances that it would run in the morning edition.

After an excellent supper provided by Mrs. Boswell, their next call was to Mrs. Alvira Manning, whom they found sitting with Mrs. Muriel Porter in the parlor after dinner. The parlor had an excellent view of the street, and all the comings and goings along it. After the initial pleasantries, Daisy posed the question that might produce more names for the list.

"Now, my sister will never tell you this," Mrs. Porter said in a confidential tone, as if the former could not hear her. "She tends to care too much for what people think. But this is too important. I don't care whose name gets dragged through the mud, if we have justice for Clarissa."

"Whose name do you mean, ma'am?" Daisy had a difficult time not dropping her voice to match.

"I can think of two—and believe me, I have been thinking of nothing else since the funeral this morning."

Daisy waited, pencil poised.

"Vincent Selkirk," Mrs. Porter whispered, "and Judge Bonnell."

Daisy had the names written down in her careful script before the sense of them penetrated her brain.

"Wait—"

"Mrs. Porter, what?" Freddie said at the same time.

"You may well look surprised." The two ladies nodded wisely at each other. "But when I tell you that they both proposed to her and were both refused, well then … it stands to reason, doesn't it?"

Elizabeth's father? And a judge? One of whom proposed to

Mrs. Moss and then murdered her? It didn't stand to reason in the least. But perhaps that was love for you. It made people do unreasonable things. Like yearn for someone you hardly knew and would probably never see again.

Freddie recovered her powers of speech while Daisy was woolgathering. "How long ago was this?"

Mrs. Manning considered. "The judge was at least two years ago. He retired last autumn, and it was a year before that, I'm sure. He was the circuit judge for this side of the mountains."

He had had two years to work out the legalities of murdering a woman who had refused his suit? That made no sense.

"And Mr. Selkirk?" Daisy asked.

"His offer was more recent," Mrs. Porter confided. "In June, when he thought Elizabeth was going to accept the offer from that boy from Edmonton. He would have covered her in diamonds. And yet, she refused him, silly girl."

Daisy made a mental note to have tea with Beth Selkirk at the first opportunity. "It seems to me that it would have been more logical for the judge to have killed Mr. Selkirk," she suggested. "Out of jealousy."

"Vincent Selkirk would be notoriously difficult to kill," Mrs. Manning said. "He is never alone, for one thing, forever at the mine offices. And when he is at home, he has guards about the house. He fears being murdered. The mine, you know."

"But not by a judge, surely," Freddie said, brushing away such speculations. "What proof do you have, ma'am, outside of their proposals to Mrs. Moss?"

"Why, none. We merely suggest a motive. It is up to you girls to find the proof." Mrs. Porter and her sister sat back and beamed, as though they had bestowed upon them a gift.

As if this thought had reminded her, Mrs. Porter added, "Before you go, girls, I have something for you." She hurried out of the parlor, and returned a moment later with two leather gunbelts, a holstered revolver dangling from each one. "I dug these out of the shed yesterday after church while I was getting a quart of rhubarb sauce, since I had promised them to you."

A gun for each of them? Since the events of Saturday night, Daisy's opinions concerning firearms had undergone a radical change. She accepted a belt and holstered revolver, turning it this way and that.

"It is fastened like this." Mrs. Porter draped it around Daisy's hips and fastened the buckle. The gun dragged at her right side, dangling practically down to her knee while on the other side the belt rode up her waist.

Freddie, following along with the other belt, looked so comical that Daisy had to smile. "We look like children playing dress-up."

Mrs. Manning considered them both. "If you were a man, the pistol would be tied around your thigh with those leather strings. Hmm. Muriel, what can we do?"

"Put it in my reticule?" Daisy suggested, twisting this way and that to make the equipage sit properly.

"Some of us do," Mrs. Manning allowed. "Hm. You know, Mrs. Boswell's daughter-in-law is a harness maker. Hasn't she been experimenting with a lady's rig?"

"You might ask Mrs. Boswell," Mrs. Porter said to Daisy.

Daisy and Freddie thanked the two ladies, and departed with every intention of doing no such thing. The sun had already slid behind the rim of the hills, leaving a dim twilight that in these parts was deceptively short.

"I do not wish to be out in the dark," Daisy said, quickening her step, though Casa Gallina was within sight, being only across the road and down half a block.

Freddie said, "It is not likely I will be wearing a gun, Daisy, no matter how dangerous it is here, dark or daylight. Why, the weight alone makes me list to one side."

"I agree. We shall simply have to make bigger reticules."

"When are we going to call upon Mr. Selkirk and the judge?" Freddie asked as they went through the wrought-iron gate and up the walk.

"It hardly seems likely that either would have harmed Mrs. Moss, but it is an excellent reason to call upon Beth," Daisy said. "We'll go tomorrow."

They found Mr. Pender in the parlor reading a newspaper that was not the *Bodie Barker*. Prominently featured on the front page was a headline announcing a new installment on page four of *Tales of a Medicine Man* by An Educated Gentleman. Oh, good! Daisy had come to enjoy the Educated Gentleman's stories, as lurid and astounding as they sometimes were. She felt an affinity with the man—with him, and with all fish out of water in the Wild West. Perhaps that was why he was so popular.

Mr. Pender put down the paper to regard them both in astonishment. "Is this a hold-up? For I assure you, I have nothing to my name but a five-dollar gold piece, and I must save that for a train ticket."

"That is more than we have, sir," Daisy said with a smile, and hefted the belt with its iron burden. "These are a gift from Mrs. Porter down the street. Apparently their previous owners no longer have any use for them."

His face betrayed his shock. "Not the two dead men from Saturday night?"

"No, an earlier mishap," Freddie said. "I confess I have no idea what to do with a gun. I do not even know how to put the bullets in it. And if I did, like as not I would shoot myself rather than some miscreant threatening me."

"Let us hope not," Mr. Pender said. Daisy was quite certain he was trying not to smile at their odd predicament. "There is nothing more useless than a gun if one does not know how to use it. Here is an idea. May I escort you up to the baseball field tomorrow morning for some target practice?"

"First," Daisy said, "I do not know what a baseball is, and second, I am quite certain I could not hit one."

He laughed. "It is a sport that used to be quite popular here, a bit like cricket. They are talking about turning the field into a race track—the better to gamble on, I suppose. At the moment it is unused, and there are hillocks as tall as I am where we could set up a few bottles and coffee cans as targets."

Daisy looked at Freddie, who shrugged as though leaving the choice up to her. "We must pay a call tomorrow, but I suppose we could put it off until the afternoon."

"We will set out before it gets too hot, then," he said, settling back into his chair with the paper. "Say nine o'clock?"

They agreed, and lugged their awkward burdens upstairs to their room. Daisy set hers carefully on the planks of the floor under the bed, wary in case the thing should go off. Mrs. Porter had assured them the chambers were empty, and had pointed out the pouch of bullets on the belt, but since Daisy did not know how to open the gun to confirm it one way or the other, it was best to be safe.

Then she sat on the bed with her sketchbook, and turned to the last page. Under Mr. Moss's crossed-out name, she wrote:

Badly matched man.
Vincent Selkirk.
Judge Bonnell.
Someone from the past?

~

FROM THE BODIE BARKER, morning edition
Tuesday, September 10, 1895

RESPECTED PROFESSOR MISSING

Professor Rudolf Linden, lately professor of engineering at the University of Edinburgh, Scotland, has been missing since the spring of this year. He was believed to have been in Bodie at the end of August, and may in fact still be in our fair town. However, due to a blow to the head during the events leading up to the Rose Rebellion, he may not be in possession of all his faculties.

Professor Linden is about six feet tall, solid of build, with dark hair graying at the temples, giving him a distinguished appearance. He speaks with a faint Prussian accent. According to family members, he remembers the distant past but has difficulty recalling the events of the last year. He has only recently remembered his own name. He was last seen wearing a Prussian blue greatcoat of military provenance, and may be attempting to reach Victoria, in the Canadas.

If you have seen a man answering this description, or know of his present whereabouts, please reply care of this publication at your earliest convenience.

9:00 a.m.

At the appointed hour Daisy and Freddie found an aged but serviceable two-seater buggy waiting at the gate, with Mr. Pender up on the driver's seat. Daisy was not surprised that he had hired it; she had seen very few steam landaus in Bodie, perhaps because the only way in was by train and the only way to get about once here was on appalling dirt roads full of rocks and potholes. Mr. Selkirk had a two-piston landau, and she had seen one or two others, but most people either walked the mile from one end of town to the other, or used a horse and buggy. The roads, after all, were less a convenience than an insult to a fine landau.

The abandoned ball field lay up the hill past the cemetery, where they saw that Mrs. Moss's grave had been filled and smoothed over. Soberly, Mr. Pender saluted her by a touch of his whip to the brim of his hat, and they passed on.

Daisy had been a little worried about their shooting lesson, knowing little more than that a gun must be held at one end while a bullet came out of the other. But Mr. Pender turned out to be a good teacher, patient with their ineptitude and encouraging when at length they began to wing the coffee cans he had set up on a knoll.

"But really, it is not fair," Daisy complained, laughing. "Your pistol is as neat and comfortable in the hand as a hairbrush, while this … Colt, did you call it? … is as long as my forearm and twice as heavy."

"You will be sore tomorrow," he admitted. "But here is a proposition for you. If you will trade that thirty-eight to me, I will give you my dress pistol."

How Mrs. Moss would have enjoyed such an offer, for she had admired it so!

"Mr. Pender, are you certain?" Daisy said. He had told them that his was a Thaxton single shot, made in the Louisiana Territory. It really was a pretty piece, with its engraved brass, its ivory grips, its golden barrel with a tiny flare at the end. "You must have chosen it because you liked it, and I would by no means deprive you of it."

He smiled, the brim of his bowler shading his eyes against the merciless sun. "I picked it up in Reno because I thought I ought to have something, not because I had any idea of what I was getting into in Bodie. To be honest, I am tired of being a laughingstock in the saloons. That Colt of yours will restore my reputation in short order. It appears to be a popular choice among many of the other men."

Daisy promptly handed it over, in two hands as he had taught her, and unbuckled the leather belt about her hips. "Done. I am ever so grateful to you."

Once it was in her possession, Daisy promptly aimed the little Thaxton at the coffee can, sighting down the short barrel and through the notch. She squeezed the trigger, whose action was so smooth there was no one more surprised than she when the can went spinning off the back of the knoll into the sagebrush.

"Oh, well done!" Freddie cried.

"They will be calling you Deadeye Daisy at this rate," Mr. Pender said with approval. "Miss Freddie, your turn."

Freddie hit the can on the second attempt with the Thaxton, and Daisy applauded.

"I still say I got the best of the deal." Mr. Pender took aim at the third can and knocked it neatly top over bottom into the brush. "This Colt is a fine peacemaker. Well cared for. I am indebted to you."

"You are indebted to Mrs. Porter," Daisy corrected him, "but you must not thank her. I should not like her to know I traded away her gift at the first opportunity. She meant it kindly."

"My lips are sealed," he promised.

He made them fire Freddie's Colt revolver until they were at least able to hit the cans, even if they did not knock them off the knoll, and when they returned to Casa Gallina he showed them how to clean both types of gun and oil the leather belt so it would not crack.

"You will find cleaning supplies anywhere in the Wild West," he said, when Freddie wondered aloud how heavy her valise was going to become. "Just remember to take care of your guns, and they will take care of you should you fall into a tight spot."

They thanked him, washed the oil and powder from their hands, and consumed the sandwiches Mrs. Boswell had left upon the sideboard. Then they took the time to re-pin their windblown hair in preparation for their call upon Beth Selkirk.

Daisy made a point of slipping the cleaned and reloaded Thaxton into her reticule with her sketchbook, where it barely made a bump. "We are walking unescorted through Bodie," she said in reply to Freddie's raised eyebrows. "Now I am prepared."

CHAPTER 14

1:05 p.m.

*B*odie could not really be said to have neighborhoods. There were the saloons, hotels, and gambling establishments that lined the two main streets, thick as a crowd on Coronation Day. There was Maiden Lane and the narrow streets of the Canton community on the north, below the sluice ponds from the mine. And there were the houses and churches that sprawled up the hillsides behind the streets, much like a matron might pick up her skirts so that they might not be sullied by what lay at her feet.

Daisy and Freddie were directed to the Selkirk house, which was large and as imposing as a foursquare clapboard structure could be without gables, turrets, or any other architectural feature. What it did have in abundance were many-paned windows.

"Imagine how much those cost," Freddie whispered as they went up the walk. "And the difficulty of transporting them here."

Daisy imagined instead how the Selkirks might see nearly the entire town from any prospect. On the other hand, the entire town could see them. The family must have incurred another fortune in employing seamstresses to make the drapes.

Elizabeth was delighted to see them when the maid showed them into the front parlor overlooking the street. She slipped the paper on which she'd been writing under the blotter and greeted them with a smile. "I hope you have come with news of Mr. Carnegey."

"He is as well as can be expected," Daisy said, "and under Mrs. Boyle's care aboard *Iris*."

Beth's expectant expression became fixed. "*Iris?* Miss Churchill's ship?"

Since there were no other ships of any kind in Bodie, Daisy passed over the obvious. "Mrs. Boyle was convinced that he would make a sitting target should the murderer return."

"And were you convinced?" Beth's gaze searched Daisy's face, her fine brows crinkled in concern.

"A person who wanted to harm Mrs. Moss might not have the same reasons for harming one of her boarders," Daisy said carefully. "And Mr. Carnegey was not even home at the time to be a witness. The perpetrator has nothing to fear from him."

"Then Miss Churchill has put Mrs. Boyle up to it," Beth said with flat certainty. "What cheek!"

"There is some merit to the plan," Freddie said. "It saves Mrs. Boyle running up and down the hill, and he is far from out of danger. She fears infection and fever."

"He ought to be under the doctor's care, and not that of a

stranger." Beth got up to ring for tea. "But neither you nor I have any say in the matter, I suppose, being merely his friends."

"You know you have found a friend in Miss Churchill," Daisy said, watching her closely. "And should you ever decide to leave Bodie, I hear there is a spare cabin aboard *Iris*."

In the act of turning from the bell pull, Beth froze, her gaze on something—or nothing—outside. "What makes you think I have any interest at all in leaving Bodie or my father?"

Oh dear. Daisy wished she had kept her mouth shut. When would she ever learn? But how interesting that she seemed to have changed her mind about her independence. Perhaps it was telling that the girl had introduced her father into the conversation when they had not.

"No reason," Daisy said at last. "Speaking of your father, we have heard recently that he once had feelings for the late Mrs. Moss. I hope her death has not affected him adversely?"

Now Beth dragged her gaze from the window, draped in gold brocade, to stare at her openly. "Where on earth did you hear that?"

Was she was about to be ejected from the house? "From some of the ladies of the town. At—at the funeral lunch, I think."

"Nosy old cats." Beth dropped into a corner of the sofa. "It was probably Mrs. Lavallee. Clarissa Moss and my father had no such relationship. While he may have called upon her in the course of business, nothing else was going on."

"Are you certain?" Freddie asked. "For it would not be unusual for a man not to confide in his unmarried daughter about such things."

"Father does not confide in me at all, thank heaven," was

the curt rejoinder. "The less we speak, the more I am able to bear my life. But you knew that already."

Daisy scrambled for a suitable reply to this unexpected confidence. "Not—not in so many words."

Beth sighed and rubbed her forehead with her fingers, one elbow on the arm of the sofa, which was covered in a yellow and cream striped silk that turned her skin nearly the same shade. Really, this was a most unflattering room for her to receive callers in. "I am so unhappy," she whispered.

Which of the several moods she had displayed in the last five minutes was her real feeling? But even as Daisy was asking herself the question, Freddie had moved to sit beside the girl on the sofa.

"You are quite right that we are all Mr. Carnegey's friends," she said softly. "But Daisy, Peony, and I are your friends, too."

"On what basis?" Beth flapped a hand. "One ball and my inability to keep my feelings to myself in feminine company?"

"Longer friendships have been based on less, I am sure," Freddie said with a smile. "But we trust Mr. Carnegey. And he has a great regard for you."

"So great that he has permitted Miss Churchill to remove him and keep him all to herself?"

"I do not think that was her motive," Daisy said. "And she had nothing to do with it in any case. When Mrs. Boyle gives orders, even she and Mr. Carnegey must obey."

Beth bit her lip. "Forgive me. I cannot keep my temper today. Everything seems to hurt."

The tea arrived, and in the orderly ceremony of preparing cups for her guests, she seemed to find her composure. As she handed Daisy her tea, she said, "But tell me, why do the ladies think Father was courting Mrs. Moss? For there must be more to it than appearances."

"They think he proposed and was refused, if you want the truth," Daisy said. "Do you think it could have been so?"

Beth took a sip and gazed at her over the rim of the fragile cup. "I honestly do not know his feelings toward her, other than what he showed me, which was admiration at a distance for a lovely woman. My mother had passed away by then, of course."

"Of course. Apparently there was a Judge Bonnell, too, who paid court to her," Freddie said. "To your knowledge, is there any truth in that?"

The cup remained suspended below Elizabeth's lips for a moment before she sipped again. "People's memories are very long when it comes to courtship, aren't they? I had forgotten all about him."

"So it was true," Freddie pressed.

"Oh, yes. The judge was madly in love with her. Bodie never saw so many cases come before the bench as it did when he was courting her. We were almost civilized for the span of six months. Once we even went without a shooting for an entire week."

"Might he have been in love enough to harm her after he was spurned?" Daisy asked.

Now Beth put down her cup. "Why are you asking me these things? Do you think the judge had something to do with her death?"

"We have no idea," Freddie said. "We are simply trying to blunder our way to the truth."

"But why should the truth mean anything to you?" Beth

looked honestly confused. "She was merely your landlady, was she not, and a stranger?"

Oh goodness. In for a penny, in for a pound. "The boarding-house keepers have asked us to look into her death," Daisy explained, "despite the fact that the doctor believes it to have been an accident."

"Look into her death?" The color drained from Beth's cheeks. "What does that mean? Like the Pinkertons?"

It was on the tip of Daisy's tongue to say, *No, like the Rocky Mountain Detectives,* but she clamped her lips upon the urge. It was not her place to reveal Detective Hayes's identity. If he had not confided in Elizabeth Selkirk, then she must not do so.

"Not like the Pinkertons," she said. It was terribly awkward to be caught between truths. "More like friends who wish to see justice done."

"It is nonsense to believe that Clarissa Moss slipped and struck her head on the stove, as the doctor said," Freddie added. "Someone hit her from behind, and that someone is at this moment walking around Bodie thinking he has gotten away with it. Daisy and I object to his doing so, that is all."

"Goodness." A new respect seemed to be dawning in Beth's face, and what little color she possessed seemed to be returning. "So you are now wondering if my father or the judge could be that man."

"It has occurred to certain of the ladies of the town to wonder," Daisy said carefully. "We are simply making preliminary inquiries on their behalf."

"Well, you have done the right thing in calling upon me first," their hostess said. "Father would toss you out on your ears for saying such things, and have Constable Lynch clap you in gaol for slander."

This confirmed her worst fears with a vengeance. "I fully expect you to do the former." Daisy looked about her for her reticule. "I apologize if we have caused you distress."

"Oh, you haven't." Beth patted the air, and after a moment, Daisy settled back into her chair. "I suppose the first thing one does in such cases is look into anyone who might have had a bone to pick with the deceased." She laughed, a single huff of air. "Fancy starting with Father."

Daisy felt she ought to apologize to the girl for this lapse in taste and respect. "And the judge."

"I think you may leave out the judge." Beth rose and left the room, to return in a moment with the same paper Mr. Pender had been reading that morning. "He is making head-lines, it seems."

"Hanging" Judge Bonnell to Resume Career
by O. Nordgaard

RENO— Once the most feared and respected member of the circuit courts in the Texican Territories, Judge Wilson Bonnell retired at the age of 50, looking forward to passing sentence on miscreants no more serious than garden pests and carpenters. His ambition was to build a home in Reno that would be a showpiece of Texican architecture, and indeed, until this week he could be seen on the property, directing builders and entertaining garden designers from as far away as Italy.

The calls for his return to the bench have long gone unheeded, but none have been more desperate than those from Port Townsend, which surely rivals Bodie for its lawlessness, crime, smuggling, and piracy. The judge on Saturday called a press conference upon the steps of the Reno courthouse to announce that he has been convinced to accept the post.

Port Townsend, as many know, has the worst reputation in the Canadas, a slap in the face impudently situated directly across the strait from Victoria, a gracious and flower-bedecked city named for Her Majesty and known as the Pearl of the Pacific. Citizens of the Texican Territories wish the judge well as he brings his particular kind of justice to the maritime post. Pirates and opium smugglers may well wish to find another center from whence to ply their trade.

Judge Bonnell, along with his two son, and his daughter, plan to move before the snow flies. They will keep their residence in Reno until he retires for the second time.

"He called the press conference on Saturday," Daisy said after a moment, handing back the paper. "It took us two days to reach Bodie from Reno on the train."

"Precisely." Beth dropped the newspaper under the sofa. "So unless he has an airship that would bring him here Saturday night and take him home again—which he does not, to my knowledge—that eliminates one of your jilted suitors. But I am afraid I have no such proof of my father's where-abouts, except that he escorted me to the ball in full view of everyone."

"Yes, well, Mrs. Moss was in full view of everyone, too, but that didn't prevent her being killed," Freddie pointed out with what Daisy felt was admirable logic.

"She could not have been in full view all of the time," Beth said. "What possessed her to return home before she was to announce the cake walk?"

Daisy gazed at her, chagrined that she had not thought to ask this very question even as she and Detective Hayes had gone in search of her. "We do not know. It seems out of character, does it not? She took her duties at the ball every bit as seriously as Mrs. Lavallee does."

"And that lady would have to be dragged out the door by main force before she gave up the speaker's box," Beth said. Daisy wondered how many times the president of the Ladies' Aid had clashed with the foremost young lady of Bodie society in order to produce these uncharitable remarks.

"Was your father in view all evening, Miss Selkirk?" Freddie asked.

"I cannot say," she admitted. "I was dancing, and fending off proposals, and lost track of everything but—" She stopped, and colored.

Daisy took pity on her. If she had been waiting to be rescued by Detective Hayes, Daisy wasn't about to speculate aloud. "Does it happen at every social event?" she asked instead. "These endless offers of marriage? I fielded six at least."

Imagine if she confided *that* to Aunt Jane in a letter! That worthy lady would be on *Persephone* in a moment, coming at speed to make Daisy accept one of them.

"Oh, yes." Beth made a face. "But everyone knows that to succeed with a young lady, a man must first be vetted by Mrs. Moss. Only think what our lives are going to be like now. It will be like the Gold Rush of fifty years ago. Every man for himself, and the devil take the hindmost."

Freddie swallowed. "We shall all be taking refuge on *Iris* at that rate, with the mooring lines played out to their furthest extent as we hover over the shouting crowd."

Daisy caught Beth's eye, and the image made her burst into giggles. Beth began to laugh … and laugh … until she was finally forced to set down her tea before she spilled it. Wiping tears from her eyes, the girl said, "That confirms it. We are meant to be friends. I am sorry I was so cross. I will include Miss Churchill in that number, for she has been nothing but kind. We shall all four be leaning out of the viewing ports, waving our handkerchiefs at the crowd below as we—"

"As we depart Bodie for calmer shores?" Daisy finished when Beth cut herself off.

"Do not breathe a word." The girl sobered as abruptly as if a candle had been blown out, and glanced at the empty parlor doorway. "Do not even think it within these walls."

After a moment, Freddie said, "Very well. So you cannot account for Mr. Selkirk's whereabouts the entire time we were at the ball. Can you think of anyone else who might have believed they had a reason to harm Mrs. Moss?"

"Besides Mrs. Lavallee?" Beth quipped, clearly attempting to regain her former humor.

"We are going to speak with a man who came to the house to shout at her about his poor match," Daisy said. "He made his displeasure publicly known in the *Barker*, too."

"Oh, you mean John Parsons? Dear me, yes. What a horrible man. Emily is well rid of him. If you are not escorted by a large man when you speak with him, go armed. He has a temper."

"We know," Freddie said, her face losing a little of its color all the same. "Where does he live?"

"On California Street, a tiny little house with front steps painted blue."

"Were you friendly with Mrs. Parsons?" Daisy asked, for these details were too accurate for any lesser acquaintance.

"I was, before she was married," Beth replied. "She is in Bridgeport now, so I do not suppose we will see one another above once or twice a year."

Daisy gathered up her reticule. "I suppose there is no time like the present to speak with the man."

"We have been learning to shoot," Freddie supplied helpfully, at Beth's alarmed eyes. "Mr. Pender took us out to the baseball field this morning and taught us. Daisy has his pearl-handled Thaxton in her reticule."

Its weight was a comfort, under these circumstances, though six months ago Daisy would never have dreamed such a thing could be possible.

Then again, six months ago she had been a different woman, in a different place.

"How ... practical of him," Beth said. "He is the newspaper man, isn't he?"

"Yes, and we are very glad he is boarding at Casa Gallina," Freddie said. "Though I suppose he will need to make other arrangements if a chaperone cannot be found while we are there. Mrs. Boswell goes home at night."

"Perhaps *you* ought to take that cabin on *Iris*," Beth suggested with a smile. "I would ask you to stay here, but ..."

Daisy had not the least desire to stay where the master of the house made his daughter so miserable, to say nothing of possibly being a murderer. Nor did she believe that Peony deserved to have *every* visitor to Bodie staying aboard her ship. "The boarding-house keepers will see to the situation," she said. "Thank you for tea, Beth. And for your knowledge of society here."

"You do not seriously suspect Father, do you?" the young woman whispered. "We have our differences, but he could not have wished Mrs. Moss harm. He has never struck me in my life, though goodness knows I—I have provoked him to rage often enough ... and he finds ... other ways to see that discipline is meted out."

Daisy could not imagine what such a confession might have cost her, and what dreadful memories the brief sentences might conceal. "Are you in a position to ask him about his movements during the ball, dear?"

"Goodness, no. That would mean initiating conversation, and I prefer not to do so."

"That would mean possibly clearing his name, too."

"His name is in no danger," the other girl said bluntly. "He simply has too much to lose to take the risk of killing anyone. Bodie Consolidated is in enough trouble without that."

"Is that the mine?" Freddie asked. "We have not yet gone up the hill to see it."

"Believe me, you do not want to," Elizabeth said. "I would not go if I were not forced to, for cutting ribbons on new tunnels and other horrid things."

"They have ribbon-cutting ceremonies on mine tunnels?" Daisy tried to imagine it, and failed. "That seems ... unusual."

"It is superstition. You will never find a more superstitious lot than miners. Particularly the Cornish ones. Apparently when the mine was first opened there was a terrible accident in a tunnel that had not been blessed by a woman, so ever since I arrived, it has been my unhappy lot to do the honors."

"So it is not like steamships, then, where women are considered bad luck?" Freddie asked.

"Not at all. I do not believe in bad luck at mines, either. The things that happen there are usually the result of poor training or carelessness. But that does not stop the miners from demanding my presence every time they are ready to send the men down a new bore. I am to go tomorrow, heaven help me. Thank goodness I was not necessary when they brought in the second automaton at the stamp mill. I could not imagine how I was to christen it—break a bottle of absinthe over its knee? The things are twenty feet tall."

It all sounded appalling, but all the same, if they went along they might have a chance to speak to Mr. Selkirk. "Would you object to some feminine company?" Daisy asked.

Beth drew in a breath, hope breaking over her wan features like sunlight. "Do you mean it?"

"I do," Daisy said firmly. "I have never seen a mine, or a stamp mill, though I have seen one or two Cornishmen."

"Then you are in luck." Beth's smile now rivaled her laughter of a few minutes before. "I would count it the greatest of favors, and will owe you a good turn."

"There are no such debts among friends," Daisy assured her, and stood to make their farewells.

"I will collect you at Casa Gallina in the landau at two o'clock tomorrow afternoon," Beth said, taking her hand and clasping it warmly.

"You pilot a landau?" Freddie said in surprise as her hand was shaken with equal warmth.

"You recollect the part about provoking my father to rage?" But this time her face retained only humor, not distress. "Ninety percent of it was over my insistence on learning to pilot his landau. And taking it out without permission." She tilted her chin proudly, as if this were a great accomplishment.

"Good for you," Freddie said with admiration, and on that happy note, they took their leave of the luxurious house that simultaneously revealed all that did not matter, and concealed everything that did.

CHAPTER 15

2:55 p.m.

Mr. Parsons answered the door of the house with the blue steps himself, blinking at them owlishly. His face was unshaven, his shirt hastily tucked into his pants, his hair standing on end. Daisy very much feared they had awakened him from a dead sleep.

"Two young ladies," he said blankly when they had introduced themselves. "To see me?"

"Yes, on a matter of some importance," Daisy said. "May we speak with you for a moment?"

He stood aside and ushered them into a sitting room so neat it was clear a female hand had been at work. "Excuse me while I make myself presentable. I work the night shift at the mine, you see, and sleep during the day."

Oh, dear. "We do apologize," Daisy said in real distress over their unwitting intrusion. "Ought we to come back another time?"

"No, you are here now, and I have just cleaned the house. That's something, at least. I will only be a few minutes."

His was the tidy hand? Daisy was guilty of it again—making assumptions about people. That would not stand her in good stead in finding a murderer. She must wait for people to reveal themselves and not paint a mask upon their faces before they even opened their mouths.

They had only a few minutes, as promised, to evaluate his surroundings, examine the spines of his books, and rifle through the papers on his desk before he returned to find them sitting politely upon the divan.

Sadly, there had been nothing at all in their rummaging that might have pointed to his being the man who had killed Mrs. Moss, but what guilty party would have such evidence lying about in the sitting room? Still, it had to be done.

His offer of refreshment being declined, he hitched up the knees of his trousers and seated himself opposite. "Now, how may I help you?"

Daisy said, "As we said, we are the Miss Lindens, formerly of Bath, and lately of Santa Fe. We are staying at Casa Gallina while we search for our father, who is missing."

"Your father is the missing professor?" He sat back. "I read the article in the *Barker* over my supper this morning. My sympathies. I do hope you find him."

For a moment, Daisy wondered if they had the right house. How could this pleasant young man be the raging intruder from the other day? But no, it was definitely the same man. Perhaps he was the Dr. Jekyll half, and only needed a little provocation to turn him into Mr. Hyde.

"Thank you, sir," Freddie said softly. "We are doing everything we can to that end."

"You say you are lately of Santa Fe? Perhaps we have acquaintances in common. Do you know Cora and Eliza Comstock? Their late father built the railroad that runs in here from Reno." He paused, as if a thought had struck him. "I suppose they own it now."

Daisy gave him her most winning smile. "Indeed we do know them, sir. In fact, we were guests in the Comstock home recently. That is … until the unfortunate events that led to Mr. Comstock's death."

Freddie was doing her best to look politely vacant, and betray nothing of her involvement in said events.

"Wasn't that something?" he said, shaking his head. "Did you hear what happened to Mrs. Comstock?"

"No indeed. Is she facing trial?"

With a snort, he said, "Of course not. The clever baggage has fled the Territories, taking her daughters with her. The Texican Rangers in Santa Fe never had the sense to lock her up. House arrest!" He laughed. "Maybe I should try it. A shot in full view of the public, house arrest, then give them the slip and off home to Virginia." His gaze fixed upon the hearth, he seemed to be miles away, in a world where such schemes were possible. "I miss it. Virginia. All the green. The trees. If it weren't for the money here, I'd be off like a jackrabbit."

"Having disposed of your marital entanglements," Daisy said softly.

"Yes. Er, no. What?" He came back to himself with a start. "I'm sorry. Homesick. But you did not come to listen to me ramble, and it's not likely you have a message for me from the lovely Cora Comstock. Do you?" Hope lit his eyes, the irises a shade halfway between blue and green.

"I am sorry, but no," Daisy said. "In any case, you are a

married man, so it would hardly be becoming in us to bring you such a thing, would it?"

At this he got restlessly to his feet. "I would hardly call myself married. Not now that Emily has returned to her father in Bridgeport, for all the good that will do her."

"You do not seriously mean to employ the means that Mrs. Comstock did to secure your freedom, do you, sir?" Freddie asked anxiously. "I should hate to see it go awry and you find yourself in gaol—or worse, facing the hangman's noose."

His expression smoothed out and he regarded Freddie with something approaching affection. "Do not fear. I have more sense than that. Emily may have provoked me to the point of murder, but certainly not past it."

"I am glad to hear it." Freddie laid a hand upon her heart. "For you called on Mrs. Moss the other day in such a fury that I feared for her life."

Goodness. If Daisy had not already seen Freddie upon the stage, she would have believed her to be sincere. Freddie could fool even those closest to her if they weren't paying attention.

Mr. Parsons actually colored. "Were you girls there, behind that closed door? Not my finest moment, I admit."

"You agreed to meet Mrs. Moss, then, the night of the ball? To apologize?" Freddie's eyes could have melted the hardest heart. Had this been Mr. Gabriel, he would already have been down on one knee, proposing.

"The night of the ball? No indeed. Why would you think that?" His brows pulled together in confusion.

"It seems what a gentleman like yourself would do," Freddie said, giving the impression that she considered him a gentleman of the highest order.

Mr. Parsons gave a nod of understanding. "Perhaps, but even if I wanted to, that opportunity has passed, now, hasn't it?"

"Yes," Freddie said sadly. Were those tears beginning to swim in her eyes? "She was such a kind lady."

"I am sure that the females in town thought so," he allowed, "but I make no secret of the fact that I believed her methods were flawed. No—" He held up a hand as though Freddie were about to argue. "I would not have apologized for the truth of my case. Only for my loss of temper. I could not have done so the night of the ball, anyway. I was at the mine and did not even attend."

Daisy thought it safe to ask her own question. "Did they not give the gentlemen the night off for such an important occasion? I understand the Autumn Ball to be one of the highlights of the year."

With a single huff of breath, he displayed his disdain for such shallow amusements. "You ladies might have a different definition of *important* than the men who devote their careers to the mine. With Bodie Consolidated losing value hand over fist, we in the offices are working night and day."

This was the second time they had heard of something going wrong at the mine, which was so enormous it was difficult to believe it could lose money.

"What does that mean, sir, to lose its value?" Daisy tried to look interested but not very intelligent. "Do you believe someone is stealing gold from the mine?"

He shook his head. "If only it were that simple—and easy to remedy. No, we cannot seem to pin it down. We are processing the same amount of ore, but are being offered less and less for it. Heaven help us when the newspapers get ahold of the story. If it gets out that—" He stopped. "By Jove, did you say you were staying at Casa Gallina?"

"Yes." Daisy felt her stomach drop at the sudden intensity in his gaze, as though a hawk had just noticed a mouse in the grass and was wheeling about for another look.

"There are newspaper men staying there."

"Only one," Freddie said, and that awful gaze moved to her. "Mr. Pender."

"You'd better know how to keep your mouths shut, you two."

"Sir!" Daisy protested. She laid her hand upon her reticule, which lay between herself and Freddie, and after a moment, pulled it slowly into her lap.

Equally as slowly, though infinitely more threatening, he rose, laid a hand on the arm of the divan, and leaned over Daisy, holding her alarmed gaze. "If I hear you've been blabbing to the papers about this, you'll be sorry."

"Mr. Parsons, please step away from my sister," Freddie said, sitting up very straight and extending a trembling hand.

While he was distracted by her distress, Daisy slipped her own hand into the gathered velvet neck of her reticule and closed her fingers around the pearl grips of the Thaxton.

"I won't," he said, returning his venomous eyes to Daisy, "until she gives me her word."

She suddenly understood with the clarity of empathy exactly why Emily Parsons had left her husband. Even if he had not struck her, it was absolutely clear that if she moved, he would.

"One word to Pender, missy, and I'll know who to punish. I'll know who to send the miners after for ruining their livelihood. Do you want to know what happens to desert flowers after they've been with a gang of angry miners?" He leaned in even farther, so that his breath puffed in Daisy's face. "They die."

She drew out the Thaxton and thrust its barrel none too gently under his belligerent chin. "Step away from me, sir. Immediately."

He drew a long breath as he straightened slowly, his eyes nearly crossed as he tried to see what kind of gun she held. Both hands went up in an attitude of surrender. "Do you—" He choked as she rose with him and pushed the gun a little more firmly into the soft spot under his chin. "—know how to use that?"

"I do. I have been shooting targets all morning," she informed him pleasantly.

"Don't—" He took a step back and Daisy braced herself in case he tried to take the little gun from her. Freddie was on her feet, clearly anticipating the same thing.

But instead, the chair on which he'd been sitting caught him behind the knees. Daisy needed only to exert a little more pressure under his chin for him to overbalance and crash to the floor. He roared in pain and surprise. Daisy stepped over the fallen chair and both she and Freddie gained the door.

"Good afternoon, Mr. Parsons," she said. An inarticulate gurgle came from the floor. "I trust you will not be threatening us again."

She got herself and Freddie out the door and down the steps to the street, sure every moment they were about to be leapt upon from behind. But they were not. They walked as fast as they could, losing themselves in the crowds of Main Street and heading in the general direction of Casa Gallina.

"Aren't you a cool one," Freddie said breathlessly, her arm

tightly linked with that of her sister. "I honestly thought you were going to shoot him."

"I do not think I am capable of shooting anyone," Daisy managed through trembling lips.

"You are shaking, Daisy. Come, let us get home as quickly as possible. I believe there is still some sherry on the sideboard in the dining room."

"I am perfectly well." But she did not slow her pace. "What a horrible man. Emily Parsons is well rid of him."

"I should say so. But do you suppose he was telling the truth about being at the mine during the ball?"

Daisy turned in at their own gate with a prickle of relief. "It is an easy thing to check. If they are working three shifts in the offices, his absence would be marked, and it would take more than a few minutes to run from up there to Casa Gallina, kill Mrs. Moss, and run back. It would be all of three miles."

"You are quite right. Nonetheless, we should inquire while we are there with Miss Selkirk tomorrow. I wonder what is going on at the mine?"

"It is none of our business." Inside, Daisy went straight to the sideboard, where Mrs. Boswell, bless her, had not forgotten Mrs. Moss's tradition of leaving a decanter and glasses for the boarders. She laid her reticule down and poured the two of them a tot each. "Our business is first to locate anyone who might have news of Papa, and then to do our best to carry out our commission from the absent friends. But I would like to leave the latter for tomorrow."

"That makes two of us." Freddie sipped the sherry, the tension in her shoulders slowly relaxing.

Daisy's breath began to come somewhat normally. "There

is nothing like being threatened with my life to bring out the urge to paint. Perhaps I will try to capture the reflections in this crystal decanter ... after we both have had another."

6:40 p.m.

After dinner, Daisy heard a knock at the front door and found young Lucas Boyle on the step. "Pardon me, miss," he said to Daisy, who had answered it in the absence of anyone else, "but Mr. Carnegey asks could you wait upon him at your earliest convenience."

Daisy stomach dipped in fear. "Is he all right? Has there been a change to his condition?"

"No, miss." The boy smiled, and her heart slowed to its normal pace. "I believe he is tired of us already, and wants someone new to talk to."

She laughed, and she and Freddie collected their hats and shawls, for the evening had turned cool after the heat of the day.

They were welcomed aboard *Iris* with tea and pie—peach, this time—and found Detective Hayes once more ensconced on the sofa among his pillows.

"Are you quite certain there has been no change for the worse?" she asked Mrs. Boyle, sure to find the truth in that quarter.

"Rest assured, Miss Linden, that he is mending as well as can be expected. He is sore, and tetchy, and in need of distraction. I hope you may provide it."

If Peony, who perched on a chair opposite, could not provide sufficient distraction, then Daisy was nearly certain she could not.

"Tell me what you have been doing today," the detective begged. "I must hear news of others, if I cannot relate anything but moans and groans myself."

"You will be proud of us," Freddie said. "We accompanied Mr. Pender up to the baseball field this morning, and learned to shoot the pistols Mrs. Porter gave us."

"Topping!" young Lucas exclaimed to his twin.

"And then Daisy traded her Colt for Mr. Pender's little Thaxton, which was providential, for not three hours later she had to use it."

"Did you shoot someone?" Lucas's brown eyes were as round as saucers.

"I did not," Daisy said, laughing. "I merely warded him off, the way the man in the traveling circus wards off the tiger with a whip and a chair."

Of course the whole tale had to come out, then, as well as news of their visit to Elizabeth Selkirk and the subsequent invitation to accompany her the next day to the ceremony at the mine.

"But here is something I find very curious," Daisy said when their stories were told. "Both Elizabeth and Mr. Parsons mentioned something about trouble at the mine. It is being devalued, apparently, a process about which I know nothing, but which is causing a great deal of concern in the management offices."

"And now that Daisy has told you that, I must also tell you that Mr. Parsons threatened to kill her if she said any such thing to a newspaper man." Freddie glared at her, as though she absolutely believed Mr. Parsons would carry out his threat, and if he did, it would be Daisy's own fault.

"What a lucky thing that I am not, in fact, a newspaper

man," Detective Hayes said mildly. "But I say, Daisy, it would set my mind at ease if you didn't call on him again."

"I have no intention of doing so," she said crisply, and pulled the little Thaxton out of her reticule. "Miss Selkirk advised us to go armed, and she was quite right. He had much more respect for this than he did for me." She slid it back into its velvety concealment.

"I am glad you took her advice seriously," Peony put in. "Imagine such advice being given between ladies in London!"

Ladies in London, Daisy suspected, had other ways to protect themselves from powerful men. Which brought her back to the matter that had made her curious.

"What would it mean for the mine, Detective Hayes, if it is devalued?"

He took a moment to consider. "Let us set aside the possibility that it is happening naturally because the gold is playing out, and go with the supposition that it is being triggered artificially. There are only two reasons for this. The first is espionage, because someone wants the mine closed for reasons of their own. Someone whose father or son was caught under the stamping automatons, for instance. Or whose family was killed in a tunnel collapse."

"Would such a person or family have the resources to cause a mine as large as Bodie Consolidated to fail?" Peony asked.

"An excellent question," he said with a smile.

Unaccountably, she blushed.

Daisy looked away, as though the girl had shown her corset in public, like the cancan dancers in Santa Fe. Peony Churchill, a woman who had traveled the world, who called famous people friends, blushing! Perhaps it was not Detective

Hayes who was in danger of having his heart broken. Perhaps it was she.

"It is doubtful that espionage of that kind would be effective," he said in reply to Peony. "Too small a scale. It would take something on the order of a few tons of dynamite to make a dent in the processing works, and crates of that kind of thing coming in on the afternoon train without the Consolidated guards present would certainly be noticed."

"And the second reason?" Daisy prompted.

"In the more likely case," he said, "There is someone out there who wants to buy the mine."

Captain Boyle nodded slowly, swallowing his bite of pie. "And to get it as cheaply as possible, that someone finds ways to decrease its value."

Detective Hayes nodded. "No loss of life, hardly any effort, and presto, the mine can be had for a pittance."

"If that is what is happening here, I am sorry for it," Daisy said. "But it is not likely to have anything to do with Mrs. Moss's death."

"And it certainly has nothing to do with our locating Papa," Freddie agreed. "We must stay true to our purpose, and mind our own business."

"I quite agree," Peony said, and poured them both another cup of tea. "It is bad enough you are putting yourselves in danger for Mrs. Moss's sake. It is quite out of the question for you to do so for the sake of something as soulless as a gold mine."

Detective Hayes twinkled at Daisy. "Are you going to tell all that you have told us to Mr. Pender, and risk your life a second time? He is a good sort, and it would not hurt to put him on his guard in case Mr. Parsons regrets his loose lips and comes to the house to renew his threats."

Daisy had not thought to do so, but really, if Mr. Parsons had been so foolish as to blab his employer's concerns to strangers, then she owed him nothing. "Perhaps I shall. The more friends we have around us who are fully in the picture, the better I will feel."

"And if nothing else, Mr. Pender is not much of a talker," Freddie added. "Our confidences are likely safe with him."

CHAPTER 16

WEDNESDAY, SEPTEMBER 11, 1895

10:20 a.m.

The next morning, Peony stepped off the gangway of *Iris* with Dinah Boyle, who had said she wanted to see the town but was not willing to go alone. Since the young woman was at least as tall as she, and very fit from wrestling steam boilers and levers and ropes for a living, Peony thought privately that if anyone could look after herself, it was she. It was not until they had reached the bottom of the hill that it occurred to Peony that she had been bamboozled. It was herself, not Dinah, who was in need of escort.

She took the young woman's arm. "Has your father assigned you to me this morning to keep me out of trouble?"

"Yes." Dinah patted her hand. "I hope you are not offended. He has the measure of this town, and was consequently unwilling to let you go alone."

"I am merely calling upon the Miss Lindens," Peony protested. How novel to have someone concerned about one's comings and goings. How touching, in a way. And how completely unnecessary. "In any case, I have a lightning pistol in my reticule. The likelihood of my being set upon or hurt is very low."

"I would not gamble on those odds, around here." Dinah thrust a hand into the pocket of her canvas skirt and drew out the grip of her own small revolver briefly, then slid it back into concealment. "But with the two of us armed, perhaps they are better."

They found the Miss Lindens on the point of going out themselves. "Mr. Pender has just come in with this," Daisy said with some excitement, holding out a slip of paper bearing the masthead of the *Bodie Barker*.

June Chu, maid at Palace Hotel, knows something about missing professor.

"We must go at once." Daisy did not exactly chivvy them down the walk like so many chickens, but she looked as though she wanted to.

"Let us accompany you," Peony suggested. "You know how good I am at getting information out of people."

"This is a female," Daisy pointed out dryly, "and it seems she has already expressed willingness to give us information. But we will be glad of your company all the same. Will the two of you return with us for lunch?"

"Will Mr. Pender be joining us?" That gentleman had followed them out of the house and down the walk, and Peony included him in the conversation as a matter of course.

He smiled at her, the curls under his bowler falling on his forehead in a most appealing fashion. "I appreciate the thought, but I am at this moment due at an interview. One of the men who was shot has regained consciousness, and if he recalls the gunman, I may collect a reward." He lifted his hat to them all and passed out of the gate, his long stride soon carrying him out of sight.

"Such an appealing gentleman," Peony remarked. "Did you disobey instructions and tell him about the troubles at the mine?"

"While we will not be dictated to by brutes, I was cautious about doing so at first," Daisy confessed. "But somehow the story came out."

Peony laughed. "He is a newspaper man, after all. I expect he is as good as I am at making people speak … incautiously."

"At least I was able to couch it in a way that made it seem as though we were merely putting him on his guard, not betraying state secrets." Daisy sounded a little defensive.

"I do not imagine any gentleman wishes his life to be threatened, particularly by the Mr. Parsons of the world," Freddie said, as though her sister needed reassurance. "It was the least we could do."

It did not take long for the little party of four to make their way over to the Palace Hotel. While the Savoy it was not, it was a large, clean establishment, and in the street in front a twelve-mule passenger wagon and two carriages were jostling for space to allow their passengers to board or alight. Peony pushed through the doors without hesitation, for the dust billowed up from the street in clouds.

The interior of the hotel was cool, but just as busy as the street outside, minus the vehicles. Porters ran hither and yon with baggage, well-dressed people stood conversing in the polished lobby, and from a dining room came the sound of cutlery on china, though it was the middle of the morning.

A husky man wearing a morning coat, his skin a shade darker than Dinah's, approached them. "Good morning, ladies. I am William O'Hara, the proprietor of this establishment. How may I help you?"

Daisy curtseyed. "We are not in need of rooms, sir, but of information."

His brows rose. "Indeed. Well, I am not the *Bodie Barker*, but I will do my best."

Daisy held out the scrap of paper. "My name is Daisy Linden, and my sister and I are searching for our father—the missing professor. Perhaps you read of him in the *Barker*?"

"I did indeed." The man's dark, liquid eyes filled with sympathy. "I hope you find him, Miss Linden." He read the bit of paper at a glance. "Ah. June Chu, one of our chambermaids. If you will step into my private sitting room, ladies, I will send for her."

"That is very kind of you, sir," Dinah said.

His gaze rested upon her like a blessing. "Being a happy family man myself, I have strong feelings about the separation of families, and do not hesitate to assist on those rare occasions when I may."

He showed them into a small, neat sitting room, its shelves covered in leather-bound books. Peony prowled the spines restlessly, not really reading them, while Daisy and Freddie showed their anticipation in their posture, hitched forward to the edges of their seats. Only Dinah seemed relaxed, walking from one painting to another as though battlefields and horses actually interested her.

Perhaps they did. She was a student of history and geography, Peony had discovered. When she wasn't tending the fine Daimler engines in *Iris* and making them purr, she was curled up in some chair or other, reading.

After a few minutes, the door opened and a pale young woman of Canton descent sidestepped into the room. She was painfully slender, her tiny uncorseted waist accentuated by the sash of the ruffled white apron over her black cotton dress. Her hair was tucked into a mob cap, and under its lace trim, her eyes were huge.

"Do not be afraid," Mr. O'Hara said to her gently. "These ladies are the Miss Lindens. They are looking for their father, and they have come to ask you about him."

He smiled at them in turn, bowed, and left, closing the door behind him.

Daisy rose to guide the frightened girl over to a chair, but she would not sit. Instead, she wrung her hands, gazing up anxiously. Daisy sat, so that she was looking up into Miss Chu's face in a beseeching pose, and showed her the note. "Do you know something of our father? This note says that you do. We should very much like to know anything you could tell us."

Peony read it again over her shoulder, but on second reading, it sounded peculiar. "Daisy, I do not think she left this message. It almost reads as though someone is carrying tales. No wonder she seems to think she is in trouble."

The poor girl was shaking, and as they both looked up from the paper, she began to speak in the Canton tongue, her voice high, as though she were begging.

Dinah abandoned the paintings and joined them, and Miss Chu flinched as she reached for her hand. Dinah said a few syllables in a low, calming tone, and the girl gasped.

One could have knocked Peony over with a feather, too.

It was clear that Dinah's Canton was not smooth, or colloquial, or even very fluent, but the girl heaved a sigh of gratitude nonetheless. She said something in reply, but Dinah shook her head. Too fast. The girl repeated it, more slowly, and now Dinah looked up.

"She wishes to know which of us is going to beat her for not ironing the sheets. She says she cannot do the job without a steam boiler. The little flatirons are good only for throwing at men."

"Oh, dear." Freddie's face crumpled, as though she did not know whether to laugh or cry. "The poor thing. She sounds very much like a young friend of ours. Please help her to understand our true purpose."

Slowly, with several repetitions, Dinah did so. The girl looked from Daisy to Freddie to Peony, confused. Dinah said a few sentences more, and indicated the note.

Miss Chu's face cleared, and she spoke again.

In German.

"You have not come about the sheets, but about the professor? I must say, I am very happy about that. I was not looking forward to being beaten."

After a moment of stunned silence, Daisy said in fluent German, *"Fraulein* Chu, how is it that you come to speak this language?"

Peony's German was as fluent as her French, thanks to her tutors, but Daisy's was better—the kind spoken in the home as easily as English. What a surprising lot they all were!

"I know four languages," came the astonishing rejoinder. "I have a degree in engineering from the university in my country, but no one in this devil's land will employ me. I am

175

reduced to housework, and laundry, and saving every penny in order to pay passage home." She switched to English halfway through this astonishing speech, and Dinah laughed.

"You gave my Canton quite a working-over," she said.

"It is better sometimes to reveal little," Miss Chu told her. "But I see in your eyes that there is no deceit in you."

"Nor is there in my friends here," Dinah told her solemnly. "You may speak freely to them without fear."

Switching back to German, Miss Chu said to Daisy, "The professor is your father?"

"*Ja*, he is. Have you seen him?"

"He was staying at this hotel, but he did not have enough money, and Herr O'Hara was sad to be obliged to ask him to leave." Distress pleated her brow. "*Der Professor* was to have taken me with him, but when I came to his room, he was gone."

"Wait—" Freddie pressed a hand to her heart, as though to still its rapid beating. "Papa was here, in this hotel? How long ago?"

Miss Chu thought for a moment. "A week?"

Peony's heart squeezed at the sight of Daisy and Freddie doing their best not to weep with disappointment.

"He may have left the hotel, but ... is he still here in Bodie, do you think?" Peony asked the girl, still in German, to give the sisters a moment to recover.

"I think not. I do not wish to think badly of him, but he might have told me he was going. I gave up my position at my old hotel, and when I came to his room to make plans, I had to pretend to be a maid, or be taken for a desert flower. Then it was I learned he had gone. Luckily a maid had just left to marry a miner, so there was a place for me."

"If he has left Bodie, I do not think I can bear it," Daisy whispered, sinking back in her chair. Only her corset saved her from curling into a bow of distress. "Are we to forever be one step behind him, never catching up?"

There was no answer to this question, so Peony asked the next of several on her mind. "Miss Chu, you said the professor was to have taken you with him? What did you mean? And take you where?"

"Why, back to Old Gold Mountain, of course," the girl said. When Peony's face must have expressed her confusion, for she did not understand what that meant in either German or English, Miss Chu explained, "San Francisco."

Dinah said what Peony assumed were the words in the Canton tongue, and Miss Chu nodded. "It is what we call it, because of its seven hills, and because the hills across the bay are gold in summer. I should never have left it. But they promised gold here, so I came." Her gaze lowered and her mouth set. "It turns out that only men may get gold for themselves. I did not last a day."

"You came as a miner?" Dinah said. "You are brave."

"Foolish, perhaps." Miss Chu sighed. "But mines must be engineered as well as airships. I believed I could find work in my field, and if not, at least I could use a pick. I was wrong on both counts. So when the professor said he would go to the Barbary Coast and work his passage on a ship, I jumped at the chance to go under a man's protection. I knew he would not demand payment from my body, like some."

Freddie made a muffled noise, and pressed a hand to her mouth.

"The Barbary Coast?" Daisy whispered.

"Yes. That is what they call the docklands at Buena Vista Cove."

"Miss Linden, do not even think it," Dinah warned, seeing as Peony did the direction of Daisy's thoughts. "I have heard tales of its depravity and danger. Of cargoes of opium and black powder. Even the Viceroy's power and justice are limited there. You would certainly be killed."

"A ship going where?" Daisy asked as though Dinah had not spoken. She hardly appeared to be breathing. Peony braced herself to spring up and catch her should she tumble off the chair in a faint.

"I do not know."

"How could you not know?" Freddie wailed. "Did he not say where he was bound?"

"We did not have time for further talk, nor did we make our plans, as I just said," Miss Chu said tartly, in English, clearly taking exception to her tone. "One moment it was as though he had remembered an important errand, and the next he was being asked to leave the hotel. And then, when I came to his room with my bag, he was gone. As though he had forgotten me." She scowled.

"Professor Linden has an injury of the brain that has rendered his memory unreliable," Peony said when it was clear the Linden sisters were beyond speech, and in fact doing their best not to weep ... or scream. "It may be that he did indeed forget you, but he cannot be blamed for that."

"It is too late for blame," she was informed, with dignity.

"I do not want to go to San Francisco." Freddie began to cry. "I want to go home."

Daisy said nothing, only gripped her sister's hand as tears slid down her own cheeks. Peony, who would cheerfully have identified herself as the least likely to weep under most provocations, felt a clutch in her own throat. She slid a comforting arm around Daisy, half expecting the reserved, awkward girl to pull away, but she did not. Instead, she laid her forehead on Peony's shoulder and let herself go altogether.

The storm passed after an interval that seemed very long to Peony, but surely could not have been more than a minute or two. At length, Daisy straightened and pulled a handkerchief out of her sleeve. Peony allowed her arm to fall away, but in the meanwhile, perhaps there was more comfort to be gained from words than actions in a case like this.

"What do we know of the Barbary Coast?" she said to Dinah. "The steamships there—where are they bound?"

Dinah considered. "Mostly, they ply the waters of the west coast. Sailing and steam ships do not go across the Pacific to the eastern kingdoms any longer when the airships out of Victoria are so much more efficient. Nor would they go to the southern reaches of the Texican Territories or the kingdoms of the southern continent. Airships based in Santa Fe have taken over those routes in this modern age."

Peony wished she had a map in front of her, but short of rifling kind Mr. O'Hara's sitting room for one, imagination would have to do. "So may we safely say that if the professor were indeed planning to take passage, it would be to somewhere on the coast of the Royal Kingdom, or the Oregon Territories, or the Canadas?"

"Since we are merely guessing, that will do for a start," Dinah said with a smile. "We aeronauts do not pay much attention to seagoing ships."

"But ports are ports, are they not?" Peony persisted.

Dinah shook her head. "A sea port may have a harbor, but if it has no airfield, the captain my uncle would not regard it. Look at Bodie—it has a train depot, but no airfield. One cannot assume that a port will have both. San Francisco, with its steep hills and deep bay, was never settled with air travel in mind. The laws against it have been in place since the Kingdom was established."

A spasm of what might have been disgust passed briefly over the face of June Chu. "The Californios put their faith in trains and railroads and ships," she said. "Until very recently, they believed that airships were the work of the devil, because they flew in the face of God. There is no engineering work of that kind to be had there at all. At least, not when I came there."

"Dear me," Peony said faintly. An entire country managing without airships until the new Viceroy had come to power, and with Gloria's help, had seen the light of progress. Would *Iris* have the skies to herself if she should venture over the mountains? What a strange thought.

"Even now there is no airfield in San Francisco," Dinah said. "Captain Boyle says if an airship were to go there, it would have to be moored above a pier in the harbor, or else find a field outside the city and have a landau aboard to travel back and forth."

"Which we do not have," Peony said with some regret. Neither her pocketbook nor her will o' the wisp life had allowed for the purchase of a steam landau, and it did not look as though one lay in her future, either. But really, if one had *Iris*, what more could one ask for? Landaus could always be borrowed from friends. "So to the main point, if the professor were leaving San Francisco on a seagoing vessel, he could be anywhere along the coast. Well, I suppose that narrows it down a little."

What was she saying? Did she mean the search would be narrowed for Daisy and Freddie, or for herself and her crew, with the Lindens as their guests?

Oh, dear me, no. She had what she needed from Daisy. She ought to be asking Timothy to set a course for the Fifteen Colonies and thence to London, not indulging in idle speculations about missing fathers.

"You said he behaved as though he had remembered something," Daisy said hoarsely to Miss Chu. "Do you know what it was?"

When the girl shook her head, Peony had to admit she felt as deflated as Daisy looked.

"I must return to my work," Miss Chu said. "I have been too long already."

"Thank you for your help." Daisy took the girl's hand as she rose. "We appreciate it very much."

June Chu met her gaze. "You have come from Santa Fe, have you not?"

"We have."

"If you decide against San Francisco, and return instead to Santa Fe, will you take me with you? For I have heard that engineers are respected there, even female ones." Color suddenly suffused her face. "And I know of someone whose home is there, and who may return by and by."

Peony smelled a romance, and could not help but wish her well. Someone ought to be lucky in love, despite the steep odds in present company.

"If we go," Daisy said steadily, "which I cannot promise we will, I will come and tell you, so that you may choose."

The girl nodded, and slipped out the door.

"I suppose it was too much to hope for," Freddie said, once she was in command of herself. "That Papa would have mentioned his destination to her, I mean, the way he did to Mrs. Holt in Santa Fe."

"Shall we continue to hope he is in Bodie?" Daisy asked rather pathetically.

"The missing persons article may yet bear fruit," Peony said in her most bracing tones. "Do not give up."

Daisy nodded. "You are right. In the meantime, I suppose we must keep our engagement this afternoon, at the mine."

"Your engagement?" Peony said, surprised. "Whatever could take you up there?"

"Beth Selkirk is cutting a ribbon for a new tunnel, or some such. She has invited us to go along."

Here was an opportunity for something new and amusing that did not involve flying into the dens of opium smugglers. Peony had never imagined herself having any interest in a mine at all, but the chance was not likely to come again. Unless she married a man who owned one, of course. "Would you object if Dinah and I joined you?"

Daisy actually smiled, poor girl, doing her best to rise above the wreck of her earlier hopes. "I think that five young ladies turning up all at once might cause a riot. But as far as we are concerned, you and Dinah would be very welcome."

CHAPTER 17

2:30 p.m.

S tanding before the entrance to the new tunnel, Elizabeth Selkirk wore a very smart walking costume the color of charcoal mixed with cocoa, and trimmed with pale viridian ribbon—a fashion choice so daring that it made even Peony Churchill sit up and take notice.

"Doesn't she look smart in that ensemble," she murmured to Daisy. "Like a different woman. Has no one told her that she must never wear yellow or pink?"

Indeed, with more viridian ribbons trimming her hat, bringing to mind the color of the sea in warmer climates, Beth hardly resembled the wan, sallow young woman in the sitting room that morning. Daisy really must do a study on how warm or cool pigments might or might not flatter a woman's complexion. She was quite sure such knowledge would be in instant demand.

But at the moment, there were other things in demand,

here in the sun at the top of the hill to the north of the Bodie Consolidated offices. Such as themselves.

She had not been entirely in jest when she had told Peony that the arrival of five young ladies—one of them being the lovely Miss Churchill—would incite a riot. It very nearly had. It was only when Mr. Selkirk had shouted for rifles to be fired over the heads of the crowd that the miners, prospectors, men off the streets, desert flowers, laundresses, and anyone else who had heard about the ribbon-cutting ceremony had fallen back and given them a little breathing room.

How long the peace would last, Daisy did not know. Not long, if they had any luck. For Freddie looked dreadful—so white it looked as though she might faint.

"What is it, dearest?" she whispered under cover of Beth's rehearsed remarks to the crowd. "Have you been too long in the sun?"

"I will tell you later," Freddie said with an effort, "when we are away from here."

Had she taken suddenly ill? But she had been perfectly well on the ride up in the landau, even laughing and cheering Beth's skill with levers and wheels.

Beth made short work of the ribbon, snipping it in two with her sewing scissors, declaring the tunnel officially open. The miners put on their leather helmets with moon-globes in sockets on the front, hefted their dinner pails, and marched into the tunnel two and two, bowing as they passed the managing director's daughter. One man attempted to clasp her hand in fervent admiration, but he was quickly swept along by his companions before Mr. Selkirk caught him.

"Come along, Elizabeth," that worthy said once the men

had gone to work. "Your friends, too. We will have tea in the offices."

"Father, should I not help the townspeople to the traditional toast?"

For they were already lining up behind a wagon loaded with a multi-armed apparatus attached to a brass barrel filled with of some kind of liquor, pulled up here by mules far stronger and more patient than any Daisy had ever seen. A dozen or more tin cups waved up and down on the jointed copper arms. A spigot squirted, and the arm presented the cup to the waiting recipient, who took a swig and stepped aside for the person pressing in behind. When the cup was empty, the arm retracted to the spigot for a refill.

Ingenious. Only in Bodie would such a device be devoted to the serving of liquor. What, Daisy wondered, must the saloons be like?

"Now, girl," Mr. Selkirk blustered. "Hang your traditions. The townsfolk can look after themselves."

"Is it quieter in the offices?" Daisy said to Beth as they made their way through the crowd, the men with the rifles acting as escort. "The stamping of the automatons is deafening."

"The reason I keep my remarks brief," she said. "Yes, it is quieter, though not by much. I am afraid you are the fortunate one, living at the farthest end of town."

"I can barely hear myself thi—" Something caught Daisy's eye in the crowd, something small and bright and very much out of place. "Wait—what is that?"

There it was again, on the white collar of a girl who was clearly a laundress. Her raven hair was bound up in a white scarf, and with those cheekbones and eyes that seemed to see into a great distance, she could be a daughter of Alaia, the shaman of the Navapai cliff village above Santa Fe.

"I will follow you shortly," she said to her companions. "I must speak to someone."

Freddie looked helplessly over her shoulder as the riflemen closed around her, but Dinah evaded them the way smoke slips through green branches laid on a fire.

"You can't be out here alone," she said briefly as she joined Daisy.

"I have my Thaxton."

"And I my Browning." Dinah smiled. "Two is always better than one. Now, what did you see?"

"Something out of place." She pushed through the crowd to the cup line, where the laundress, in company with several others, had just finished and stepped aside for a desert flower behind her.

"Excuse me—miss?"

The girl looked startled, and ready to flee. "Who are you calling miss?"

"You, if you will forgive me. May I ask you something?"

She looked at Daisy, her eyes now filled with suspicion. "It'll cost you."

Daisy dug in her reticule and unearthed a five-penny silver coin. The girl snatched it from her fingers with the swiftness of a chicken striking a lizard, then pocketed it and walked away, heading down the slope toward the ponds that lay between the mine and the rowdy end of town.

"Miss, what about my question?"

"You already asked it, lady."

"I did not!"

"You asked can you ask me something. If you want another question, it'll cost you another silver piece."

Daisy and Dinah hurried to catch up, Dinah's long stride making it look effortless.

"I'll do no such thing," Daisy said when they were within hearing. Then she threw some bait, though the odds this fish would bite were nearly nonexistent. "Alaia would be ashamed of you."

The girl stopped dead in the middle of the slope, her shoulders rigid, and Daisy felt a spurt of satisfaction that her baseless assumption had managed to hit its mark.

"How do you know that name?" The girl turned, and if her eyes had held suspicion before, it was nothing to what they held now, narrowed and glinting.

Daisy resisted the instinctive urge to step back, and clutched her reticule closer instead.

"We are acquainted."

"You." The dark gaze swept her from head to foot with contempt. "*You* know the greatest shaman in the Wild West."

"As it happens, I do. She was very kind to me when I was in Santa Fe recently. Tell me, are you a relative? For I can see her in your cheekbones and in the way your hair parts with a whorl, just here." Daisy touched her own hairline to indicate the spot.

To her astonishment, the suspicion and dislike melted, and the girl's lip trembled. "Tell me—is she well? And Tobin and Maria and the children?"

"They are all very well." Daisy could hardly recover quickly enough from her surprise at this change. "Tobin saved my life just a few weeks ago, in fact."

A wavery smile broke upon the girl's face. "He is a man

most capable of that. He is my cousin. My mother is—was—the youngest sister of the shaman."

"I am sorry you have lost your mother," Daisy said softly. "I lost mine, too, last year. The wound has not grown over yet, and I suspect it never will." She extended her hand. "I am Daisy Linden, and this is Dinah Boyle, first engineer aboard the airship *Iris*."

The girl flicked a glance over her shoulder at the airship, moored on the far side of the valley but no less obvious for the distance, then gazed down at Daisy's hand as though not quite certain what to do with it. Then she shook it, and Dinah's with more confidence. "At this time on my name trail, I am called Atsa."

"Your name trail?" Dinah asked. "What is that, if you don't mind me asking? Because I haven't got a five-penny piece."

Atsa smiled, her eyes now glinting with mischief. She did not offer to give Daisy's coin back, either, now that they had been introduced. "We Navapai may be called different things at different times in our lives. Now I am Atsa." The glint faded. "If I ever go home again, to take up my aunt's work as she wishes me to, perhaps it will be different. When I am different." She lifted her chin, as proud as ever Alaia could be in her white skirt and blouse. "What question did you have for me, Daisy Linden?"

"I only wished to know where you got that pin you wear upon your collar."

Atsa's hand touched the red enamel zinnia. "It was a gift."

"From the society of absent friends?" Daisy asked eagerly, touching the pin at her own throat.

The girl's face clouded with confusion as she gazed at it. "I do not understand. What is that?"

How odd that she did not know. "It is an unofficial society, formed of absent friends—of boarding-house keepers in the Wild West," she said. "This pin indicates that you are either one of them, or a trusted friend."

"I know of no society, and I do not live in a boarding-house." Her jaw firmed, and the tension returned to her shoulders. "I live in a house of desert flowers, and wash their clothes."

Daisy nodded, this being not unusual in her experience here. "I have a friend who did the same. One cannot be fussy about where one finds employment in this country. There is no shame in being a laundress. I imagine one knows many secrets in such a trade."

Atsa looked as though she had expected to be struck, or spat upon, and the loosening of tension was almost comical. "It is unusual for a fine lady to hold such views."

Daisy snorted. "I am no fine lady. I am simply a woman, like you, making my way as best I can. But please, if you did not have the pin from an absent friend, where did you get it?"

"From a man." Atsa lifted her chin. "Not a customer. I take in laundry for others. What the madam does not know will not hurt her."

This was even stranger. Could the man have been an absent friend?

Daisy fumbled her sketchbook out of her reticule, and turned to the painting of Clarissa Moss.

Atsa gasped and stumbled back. "That is a terrible picture! It is death!"

"It is. I am sorry to have distressed you. But—ah." Here it was. The sketch of the awful wound. A study of Clarissa's face, in profile as she lay in state upon the kitchen table. The neckline of her green silk gown, bare of the tiny red enamel zinnia that Daisy was positive had been nestled in its trim during the ball.

All of the absent friends had worn them, a sign of sister-hood, even at a social event. The other ladies wore the pins in a rainbow of colors—yellow, orange like her own, pink, purple. Clarissa's was the only red one Daisy had seen. But there must be many of them scattered through the Wild West. The zinnia flower had a limited palette, after all.

"He gave you the pin as payment for the washing?" Dinah was saying, and Daisy came out of her thoughts and back to the windy, dry hillside. She closed her sketchbook and slipped it into her reticule.

"N-no," Atsa said. "It was in a bundle with his shirts, and those of others. In a pocket. I took it out so it would not go through the mangle."

"Do you know the man's name?" Daisy was not interested in whether the girl had rifled the man's pockets and stolen the trinket. She was deeply interested in how it had arrived in said pocket, however.

"The shirts come from certain customers at the board-ing-houses. But his name is Alonso," the girl said. "He is a friend, and promises to take me with him when he is married—back to Santa Fe, where I will be able to see my family again."

"Alonso—not Alonso Gabriel?" Dinah said in surprise.

"Yes, that is he." Atsa's eyes held curiosity, not suspicion. "Do you know him?"

"Yes, we met at the ball Saturday night." Dinah's gaze caught that of Daisy, her wry expression conveying that she had also been one of the young ladies fielding his proposals.

What was the wretch doing, proposing to all and sundry while promising to take this proud, penniless girl with him?

"Did he say where he got it?" Daisy asked. "Perhaps there is a peddler? Or he bought it at a shop?" Both possibilities were unlikely, but Daisy would ask one of the absent friends where the pins came from as soon as she returned home.

"I do not know," Atsa said. "I found it when I washed the shirts. He had gone by then."

Daisy did not much look forward to asking these questions of Mr. Gabriel, who would likely think that her seeking him out meant she was madly in love with him.

"Thank you, Atsa." She offered her hand once more, and this time the girl took it in a manner that, if it did not mean friendship, exactly, meant acceptance. "I appreciate your speaking to us."

"I will tell Alonso I found the pin in the laundry," she said, sounding both defensive and nettled. "I am no thief."

"I never believed you were," Daisy said with a smile.

Dinah shook her hand, too, and then the two of them made their way back to the road, where they found a white-faced Freddie waiting for them in the company of a severe-looking individual carrying a rifle.

"Thank you, sir," she said to him, "but my sister and our friend will see me home."

"Very good, miss," he said, turned smartly, and headed up the hill to the mine buildings at a great pace, as though to distance himself from his duties as nurserymaid.

"Please take me home," Freddie begged, clasping Daisy's arm tightly.

"You *are* ill." Dinah took her other arm, as though she was afraid Freddie might collapse in the street. Together, they walked down the hill between the miners' cabins as rapidly as they could. "Do you not take tea with them all? I'd have thought Miss Selkirk might have driven you home."

"I did not want tea, nor to be driven home in state and be asked a thousand questions," Freddie said. "Besides, Peony is with her. Miss Selkirk will have enough to do getting away from her awful father and piloting the landau through town with Peony in it."

There could yet be riots today.

"I had better fetch Captain Boyle, in that case," Dinah said grimly. Perhaps the same thought had occurred to her. "Daisy, will you be all right walking your sister home?"

"Indeed, yes," Daisy said. "I think you may be right about Peony. Does this kind of thing happen everywhere she goes?"

"Certainly not. It is Bodie that drives men to such lengths. Peony only came here seeking information about one man from you. She cannot help it that all these others are mad." And with that Dinah left them, loping down the street at a ground-eating pace that soon took her out of sight.

"You must tell me what is the matter at once, dearest." Freddie clung to Daisy's arm now with both hands. "You are frightening me."

"Not half as frightened as I was at that tunnel." Freddie choked. "Oh, Daisy, the dead!"

In the time it took to blink, the entire excursion took on a completely different cast. Daisy could have slapped herself for being so blind. "My dear," she breathed. "I am so sorry. It never occurred to me that you were not ill, but being ... visited."

"There are hundreds, Daisy. Perhaps even thousands. That mine is housing the population of a small town in ghosts.

How do they keep it running? Do people not protest the number of men who have died there?"

"I do not know." Mrs. Moss would have known. But now the dead of Bodie included her in their number, and she would be forever silent. "This is a deadly place, if two and three men—and women, for that matter—die every day."

"And yet still people come," Freddie said in wondering tones. "For the gold. Dinah is right—they are mad. How soon can we leave?"

"Freddie, even without our inquiries into Papa's stay here, we must do the best we can for Mrs. Moss and the ladies. We cannot leave yet."

Freddie shook her head, the ribbons on her second-best hat moving restlessly. "I do not want to stay here any longer. I shall be beset on every side by ghosts, and that is infinitely worse than fending off proposals from the living."

A chill ran over Daisy's arms, as though a shade had touched her in passing. Or in warning.

"Shall I inquire as to whether Mrs. Chang or Mrs. Manning might have a room for us? At least you would never be alone, and susceptible." For in the past, the … visits … to Freddie had been when she was likely to be alone or separated from her company. How overwhelming it must have been today, with the dead so numerous they could not help but show themselves.

They were nearly at the corner of Green Street. "Yes," Freddie said. "Yes, that is a good idea. Or we might beg that last cabin from Miss Churchill."

"I like that idea. At least there you would be close to Detective Hayes, and I would feel infinitely better about leaving during the day while I make my inquiries."

"Let us visit the detective soon, then," Freddie said, her voice sounding stronger already. "If I look sufficiently ill, Mrs. Boyle may do all my work for me, and I will not need to ask."

"If ghosts can attach themselves to *Iris*, you may not find yourself pretending." What an appalling thought. "They can't, can they?"

Freddie squeezed her arm in reassurance as Casa Gallina came into view at last. "I do not think so. They seem to be tied to the place that meant the most to them in life. Which is not likely to be that bare hill where the ship is moored."

"What a pity you have seen hundreds of others, but not Mrs. Moss since her fetch appeared to you in the ballroom," Daisy said. "I have a question or two for her."

"Do not say things like that, Daisy," Freddie whispered urgently as they went up the walk. "Not even in jest."

CHAPTER 18

8:45 a.m.

*D*aisy opened the front door the next morning to find Mrs. Manning on the step holding what appeared to be the latest edition of the *Bodie Barker*. "Miss Linden, have you read the morning edition?"

"Why, no. We have only just finished breakfast. Do come in."

Now that she thought of it, there hadn't been a paper yesterday, either. In fact, there had been none delivered since the funeral on Monday. Mr. Pender must have got the Bridgeport paper from one of the hotels. Did the *Barker* automatically stop delivery to people whose deaths it reported?

Mr. Pender had already gone out, but Mrs. Boswell appeared in the kitchen doorway at the sound of her friend's voice. "Good morning, Alvira. May I offer you some coffee?"

"Thank you, Dora, that is very kind. Have you seen the paper this morning?"

"No. Don't start without me. I'll be back in two shakes."

When all four of them were seated, Mrs. Manning shook out the paper, slid it in front of Daisy, and planted a quivering finger on the front-page article. "There. Read it aloud."

MINE OFFICER MEETS TRAGIC END
by D. Carnegey

It is with deep sorrow that Mr. Vincent Selkirk, Managing Director of the Bodie Consolidated Mine, announces the untimely death of the mine's director of accounts. The body of Mr. John Parsons of California Street was found last night by a neighbor.

"He was just lying there across the back steps," said Mrs. Jessie White, who has lived in Bodie since the Occidental Hotel burned down. "My husband and me, we never seen the like in all our born days. We think he was shot."

Constable Lynch is following up on a number of leads. "He wasn't an opium eater, nor a frequenter of the saloons, though he did more of that since his wife left him. He was a good man. A little tempery now and again, but with his domestic situation, who could blame him?" The lawman is convinced that robbery is the motive, since he is convinced Mr. Parsons was a friend to everyone, and had no known enemies. "He was very highly regarded up at the mine," the constable stated. "A man more familiar with a pencil than a pistol." Then he shook his head.

"Ah, little town, thy streets for evermore
  Will silent be; and not a soul to tell
  Why thou art desolate, can e'er return."

Mrs. White, being no admirer of Keats, further states, "There were two young ladies called on him the morning he died. Emissaries from his wife? You tell me," she says darkly. "Maybe they poisoned him."

This reporter doubts that a young lady would be responsible for the kind of lead poisoning that led to Mr. Parsons' death, but at the time of the interview, Mrs. White was determined to bring her theories to Constable Lynch's attention. Should anyone else have witnessed the visit of the two young ladies, they are requested to vouchsafe their information to the representative of the law, and no one else.

Funeral services will be held Saturday at eleven o'clock in the morning at the Miners' Union Hall. The crowd is expected to be large, due to the general regard in which the deceased was held. One hour's leave will be given to all Bodie Consolidated employees should they wish to attend. A lunch prepared by the Ladies' Aid will follow.

Daisy lifted a troubled gaze to meet the expectant face of Mrs. Manning. "What are we to make of that?" the lady demanded. "Clarissa told us all about his bursting in on her that day. Next thing we know, she is dead. And now so is he."

So he was, apparently, indeed ... and the byline had to be Miss Selkirk writing under Detective Hayes's *nom de plume*, for he was not yet allowed out of Mrs. Boyle's sight. Daisy's breakfast had begun to churn in her stomach by the end of the second paragraph, and by the last line, she felt positively ill. "Mrs. Manning, Mrs. Boswell—" She could not go on.

Freddie's face had lost its color. "Daisy, we called upon him yesterday. Surely they do not think—that we could have had anything to do with—"

"You called upon him?" Mrs. Boswell repeated. "Whatever for?"

"I should think it was obvious, Dora." Mrs. Manning leaned toward her. "The young ladies have been speaking to anyone who had a reason to be angry with Clarissa. Mr. Moss, that pompous wretch. Mr. Parsons. Who else?" She turned to Daisy.

"Why—why, I hardly know." She must pull herself together and speak coherently. "Judge Bonnell. Mr. Selkirk."

"You spoke to Mr. Selkirk?" Mrs. Boswell said on a gasp. "You told him you suspected him of *murder?*"

"No, of course not. We spoke to his daughter, to feel out the lie of the land, as it were." Daisy pushed her coffee away. It was making her mouth dry. "We managed to eliminate Judge Bonnell and Mr. Moss by virtue of their being nowhere near Mrs. Moss when she was attacked."

"Mr. Parsons, too," Freddie said. "When we called upon him, he said he was at the mine offices, working, the night of the ball," Freddie said.

"So he told you, at least," Mrs. Manning said in a tone that cast doubt on every word out of his mouth.

"We have not had time to corroborate it," Freddie admitted. "We would have yesterday, except that I became ill, and we came home instead of taking up Mr. Selkirk's invitation to tea at the offices."

"That you can tie to," Mrs. Boswell told Mrs. Manning. "I took her some soup myself."

Which reminded Daisy of the enamel pin on Atsa's collar. "Mrs. Manning, perhaps you can tell me something. We met a young lady yesterday who wore a red zinnia, yet she said she had no connection to any of the absent friends."

"She must have," Mrs. Manning said, folding her arms over her comfortable bosom.

"She is a laundress, and said she found it in a shirt belonging to Mr. Alonso Gabriel. Does he have a connection?" Daisy asked.

"I have never heard of him," Mrs. Manning said.

"He was at the ball, Alvira, proposing to anything in skirts." Mrs. Boswell shook her head at such behavior. "He is the one with the longish hair. You remember, I remarked upon how he needed a visit to the barber."

"He did not propose to *me*."

"Or me, but that does not signify. *We* are not single young ladies."

"Thank you for that reminder, Dora."

"The point is," Daisy said, feeling as though this conversation would run away with her if she did not rein it in, "are there any other red zinnias among you? Because I realized yesterday that Mrs. Moss's pin was missing when we found her."

Two sets of eyes stared at her. "Missing?" Mrs. Boswell finally said. "I never thought to look. And why should I? My poor dear friend." Her eyes filled with tears.

"I wore mine that night," said Mrs. Manning. "We all did."

"I confess I did not," Daisy said, "but then, it has more significance to you ladies. Can you tell me if there is more than one red zinnia among the boarding-house keepers in town?"

"I cannot positively say," Mrs. Manning said. She pushed away her cup. "Selena can tell us. She has them made. Let me ask her."

Ten minutes later, Mrs. Manning was back. "Selena says

there are five red pins among the absent friends in Bodie, including Clarissa's … and her own. Which was on her collar, right where it ought to be."

Daisy leaned both elbows on the table and rubbed her temples. "So … Mrs. Moss leaves the ball just before the cake walk is announced. She hurries home for reasons we do not understand, takes off her pin and gives it to Mr. Gabriel, who puts it in his pocket and returns to the ball to propose to any number of other young ladies."

"But before he does that, he kills her." Mrs. Boswell's cheeks had begun to fly red flags of anger. "The beast."

"He could not have," Freddie said, putting down her cup. "For Mrs. Moss's injuries were such that the perpetrator's clothes would have been spattered with her blood."

"Yes, but did anyone see him afterward?" Daisy asked. "I was his partner for the first dance, but I managed to avoid him after that."

"I cannot remember, either," Freddie frowned into her cup. "But there could be any number of reasons for a pin to be slipped into a pocket. It may not even be Mrs. Moss's pin. It could belong to Mr. Gabriel's landlady. He might have offered to have it repaired, and forgot it was in his pocket."

Except that the pin on Atsa's collar was not damaged.

"It is easy enough to check," Mrs. Manning said. "We are having a quilting bee Friday morning, and two of the other three absent friends possessing red zinnias will be there. It will simply be a matter of glancing at a collar to see if one is missing."

"If all are present, that still does not clear Mr. Gabriel," Daisy pointed out.

"But it does eliminate a possibility," Freddie said. "I should not like to go about accusing young gentlemen of murder with nothing more substantial to go on than the presence or absence of an enamel pin."

"Quite right," Mrs. Boswell said, rising and commencing to clear the table.

Mrs. Manning got up, too, waving a hand at the newspaper. "Keep it," she said. "All my gentlemen saw it earlier." Then she turned back. "Miss Freddie, have you been to see Mrs. Boswell's daughter-in-law about having a rig made for that revolver?"

"I—why, no," Freddie said. "I am afraid that we have been much occupied. I did learn to shoot the Colt on Tuesday, though. Mr. Pender took us out in a buggy and gave us lessons."

"Did he?" Mrs. Manning beamed, and Daisy felt a sinking feeling in her stomach. In the next moment, her trepidation was justified. "And how did you find the Colt, Miss Linden? Did it serve you well?"

"I—I must confess I found it very heavy," Daisy stammered. It was the truth, as far as that went. "I am no expert, but I may need to find something easier to hold. I had no idea that revolvers could weigh so much."

Mrs. Boswell laughed at such naïveté. "That is why Lorraine, my son Carter's wife, expanded her repertoire from horse and mule harness to leatherwork for ladies and gentlemen. Truly, you must visit her and see what she can rig up for you. The blacksmith's and livery is in the red barn, across the road from the Methodists and next to the stables."

"Thank you," Freddie said with a glance at Daisy's guilty face. "We will be sure to visit, after such a recommendation."

When Mrs. Manning had seen herself out and Mrs.

Boswell had returned to her kitchen, Daisy and Freddie collected their hats and reticules and made their escape.

"That was close," Daisy said, turning naturally toward the hill above which *Iris* bobbed gently on her ropes, and not toward the blacksmith's. "I knew I should be caught out."

"You wriggled out of the trap very well," Freddie told her. "Likely it will not come up again. Besides, it is reasonable that you should trade for a different gun. Why shouldn't you?"

"I do not want to hurt her feelings." Daisy picked up her skirts to climb the slope. "She is a kind woman, and so helpful."

"Is there a reason we are calling upon Miss Churchill?" Freddie said presently, as they reached the top and walked toward the ship.

"We are calling upon Detective Hayes," Daisy corrected her. "But I shall be glad to see Miss Churchill, too. I want to know what happened at the tea yesterday."

"And I would like to ask her about that last cabin. She can only say no."

They found Peony and her crew at breakfast—even Detective Hayes was seated at the table in the dining saloon, spooning up whipped eggs with one hand. Chairs were pulled up for them, and with far too much fuss Daisy and Freddie found themselves once more in front of a cup of tea, with the welcome addition of scones bearing generous dollops of clotted cream and jam.

"Mrs. Boyle, you make a wonderful breakfast," Freddie sighed, licking cream off her upper lip. "Even Mrs. Boswell is not so good a cook. I cannot believe I have eaten two breakfasts this morning."

Daisy could. The only mystery was how she remained so slender.

Mrs. Boyle looked pleased. "Thank you, Miss Freddie. It's a shame our niece takes more to steam boilers than to cookery, but I hold out hope for Lucas." She smiled fondly at her younger son. "It was he who made the scones. Not every boy of ten can make scones light as air and shoot a target at fifty feet besides."

Captain Boyle tousled his son's hair with approval. "What brings you to us so early, Miss Linden? Have you found Mrs. Moss's killer?"

"Have you not read the paper, then?" From the curiosity in the circle of faces, Daisy gathered they had not. "Mr. John Parsons—you remember him, Captain—"

"I do indeed," he said imperturbably. "I believe I threatened to throw him from the porch of your boarding-house, and like a man of sense, he went on his own."

"Has something happened to him, Daisy?" Peony spread jam upon a scone.

"He is dead." Into the silence, she gave the details of the article. "Mr. Carnegey, yours was the byline. I assume Miss Selkirk had the details from her father."

Half frowning, he said, "Clever girl. I wish she would reveal herself, and take the credit due her. I must say I am concerned about the two mystery women who were seen. They were yourselves?"

"Yes," Daisy admitted unhappily. "We were not to know a murderer would be his next caller, however."

"One never does," Peony remarked, as though she had had some experience along that line.

For all Daisy knew, she had.

"Are you in any danger?" Mrs. Boyle's brown eyes held concern. "What if this Constable Lynch decides the two young ladies already connected to Mrs. Moss's murder are responsible for this one, too?"

"He does not strike me as the sharpest of tacks," Daisy said. "He swallowed without a qualm the doctor's verdict that Mrs. Moss had slipped and struck her head upon the corner of the stove. Even after I showed him my sketch, he would not change his mind."

Mrs. Boyle snorted. "He does sound like a buffoon, but even buffoons may get the answers right from time to time." She rose from the table. "Miss Churchill, might I have a word?"

Peony dabbed at her lips with a napkin and followed her from the salon, while Daisy's attention returned to Detective Hayes. "How do you feel, Detective Hayes? I take it as a good sign that you are up and about."

"I am healing," he said, "but it will be some time before I can lift my arm. I am under strict orders from Mrs. Boyle not to make the attempt."

"I am glad you are under her care," Freddie said in her kind way. "Imagine being laid up at the boarding-house, with no one to look after you but us."

"I am sure that I would survive it very well," he said with a smile. "Mrs. Chang has been put to the inconvenience of walking up here with potions for me, though, instead of merely strolling down the street." His smile faded. "I am a little concerned on your behalf, Daisy. Mrs. Chang said that despite Mrs. Boswell's presence in the house during the day, there will soon be talk about your staying there alone at night, even with Mr. Pender sleeping on a separate floor. I know you are in no danger from him—on the contrary, he would be the first to leap to your defense—but there is the appearance of impropriety."

"Yes, in fact, we had meant to ask one of the ladies if a room might be available in another house," Freddie said, "but it seems Mrs. Manning only takes gentlemen, and we have not yet spoken to—"

"Mrs. Boyle has come up with a solution to the difficulty." Peony came in with a rustle of silk twill skirts and seated herself once more at the table. "I am ashamed that I did not think of it myself, with that empty cabin staring me in the face every time I walk down the corridor. Daisy and Freddie, would you like to bring your things aboard *Iris*, and stay with us?"

The correct thing to do, of course, was to decline with thanks, to refuse to put them to such an inconvenience, to trudge down the hill in search of a room elsewhere. But sometimes a sensible woman had to choose between *correct* and *right*.

"Oh, yes," Daisy said fervently, as Freddie took her hand and squeezed it. "We did not know how to ask. Thank you so very much. I promise we will be no trouble to you. You will hardly know we are here."

"That would be unfortunate," Detective Hayes remarked with a smile.

"It is more than propriety," Mrs. Boyle said, bringing in a fresh pot of tea. "If this Constable Lynch is determined to pin a murder on two young ladies, he will have a hard time apprehending you if you are twenty feet in the air."

"An excellent point, Mrs. Boyle." Detective Hayes turned his smile on Peony. "Miss Churchill, for my part, I thank you for your generosity to my friends. It does you great credit, particularly with me already underfoot."

"You are far from underfoot, sir. You have been a most welcome addition to our number."

And to Daisy's chagrin, she blushed. It seemed her speculations on the condition of Peony's heart might be all too accurate.

CHAPTER 19

THURSDAY, SEPTEMBER 12, 1895

Miss Peony Churchill
*   CAS Iris*
*   Via air*

Dearest Peony,

You are in Bodie! Stanford says it is one of the wildest places in all the Territories, and you must lift at once before you are killed— or worse. How on earth did the Miss Lindens find themselves there? Surely their father—whom Stanford persists in referring to as Dutch since their time together in gaol—cannot have lost himself in such a place. He would have been better off staying in the Royal Kingdom of Spain and the Californias.

And Barnaby Hayes is there too! I am simply bereft of speech. He was in gaol with Stanford, too, for weeks and weeks, but we lost track of him after the Rose Rebellion. But I knew him even before that. He kidnapped me, you know, in Venice, that time I went to view the exhibition. I told you of my father's political machinations; well, Mr. Hayes—Captain Hayes, at the time—was in his employ, steaming about the Aegean in an undersea dirigible helping him foment a war. To be fair, it is not likely Barnaby knew what my father was up to.

Once in his hands it did not take me long to decide I was going to make my imprisonment far more unpleasant for him than for me. Claire helped me to escape, and I made my way back to the Fifteen Colonies, only to get into enough scrapes to fill a book. At least said scrapes led me to Stanford and my darling Honor Isabella Claire, so they were worth it in the end.

And while I make no claims to celebrity, you goose, it is certainly true that I made wonderful friends during my adventures. One of them is there still—Mr. Evan Douglas, who is cousin to Maggie and Lizzie. Their grandmothers are sisters, or some such. In any case, he is now a privy councilor to His Royal Highness the Viceroy, and engaged to be married to a grandee's lovely daughter, so it is plain he means to stay and make his life there. Perhaps you ought to call! Heaven knows the intrigues of court are nothing compared to the dangers of Bodie.

Now, back to the fascinating Barnaby Hayes. Contrary to expectations, he does not have a wife and family tucked away in the fens. He does, however, have a pretty estate only ten miles from that of Captain and Lady Hollys, in Somerset. He is the baseborn son of Julia Mount-Batting's husband's grandfather. The old duke sired him in his old age, settled one of the lesser estates on him, and expired. Can you credit it? She, of course, does not know he exists, and would cut him dead if she did.

Claire let slip one evening that he is well regarded in political circles, and in fact is spying for the Crown, but I have absolutely no proof of any of it. Lady Dunsmuir would likely know. I would not have the courage to ask her, but you know her better than I.

Barnaby can be very charming, and is certainly handsome, but beware your heart, my dear. He is one of those exasperating men who possess a Higher Purpose, and it is my belief that no mere woman can hold him. A man like him would rather be conducting secret missions in faraway lands than concerning himself with crop rotations and dining with the neighbors. I have no doubt you have met such men before, considering that your esteemed mama probably dines with them six days out of seven.

I must finish this letter, or no matter the speed of its propellers, the pigeon will go down from sheer weight. Please take care of yourself, and give our best regards to Captain and Mrs. Boyle. I swear if you allow any harm to come to them before you get them out of Bodie, Stanford, Honor, and I will take ship ourselves and chase you down.

Je t'embrace, cherie.

Your own

Gloria

P.S. My dear, I have this moment received a letter from my cousin Hugh, and will pass on its news immediately. It seems that Sydney has made one conquest too many—a married Englishwoman living in Cairo. Her husband challenged him to a duel and proved the superior marksman. Hugh reports that his brother has already been interred there, in the Christian cemetery. The heat, you know. I am sorry that I cannot give you this news in person. I hope you are with those who will understand a woman's feelings for an old love, be he ever so faithless.

My feelings are certainly mixed. Sydney was the amusing companion of my childhood, the knight to my princess. But as a man ... So much potential for good, wasted in discontent and disloyalty.

—G.

2:15 p.m.

*C*urled up in the window seat of the arched viewing port in her cabin, Peony laid Gloria's closely written pages in her lap with a sigh. Sydney dead! And under circumstances that seemed to be a fitting end to his spiraling career of increasingly disastrous choices.

Imagine if you had been in Egypt with him, and caught up in it. Imagine if you had married him, loving him despite what you knew of him.

She would still be disgraced, and he would still be dead. As was Emma Makepeace. And his innocent child with her. All dead.

And Peony's love? Poor, frustrated, anxious emotion that it had been? Also dead, buried in the reality that she had not loved him at all. For she had not known him. She had been in love with a creation of her own making—someone who was good, and exciting, and worldly. Well, she had been right about the last two, anyway. What a good thing that creation had died first, when Claire had made the scales fall from her eyes, or she would be in quite a state now. As it was ...

Peony gazed out of the viewing port, which, being on the port side of the ship, furnished a view of golden hills and the vivid blue sky of autumn. From here, there were no cabins jostling for space, no people, nothing to stop the eye from rising into the endless blue, or the heart and mind from rising into freedom.

She was free.

Free of her own mistakes, her own petty self-delusions. Oh, it was more than likely she had a number still to make, but at least these ones could be shed like an old skin and left behind. They would plague her dreams no longer, tying her to a past she no longer wanted.

Free.

A tap came upon the door. "Come in," she called.

Mr. Carnegey—Detective Hayes—oh bother, *Barnaby*—slipped in, leaving the door open as propriety and Mrs. Boyle dictated.

"The Lindens will be here soon, with their bags." He took in her relaxed pose on the window seat, with its colorful cushions, her half-boots on the floor, the letter in her lap. "Am I interrupting your reverie?"

"No indeed." She waved at the easy chair, and he crossed the cabin toward it.

"News from home?" Then he colored. "I'm sorry. Your correspondence is none of my business."

She folded Gloria's letter. "As it happens, this is from Gloria. Is it true that you are a spy for the Crown?"

In the act of seating himself, his knees seemed to give out, and he landed in the chair with a grunt of pain as the upholstered arm bumped the elbow in the sling. He stared at her owlishly. "What is that girl up to?"

"If by *that girl* you mean Mrs. Stanford Fremont, she was just passing along a rumor, as we *girls* do. Such excitement during the Rose Rebellion. I am agog to know all your stories."

"That was in the past, and has no bearing on the present." He squirmed in the chair, then gave it up as a bad job and went round to lean on the back of it instead.

"If the Lindens go to San Francisco, and you happen to be personally acquainted with a privy councilor to the Viceroy, it could have a significant bearing on them."

"My, my, Gloria did brief you well."

"Which is a lucky thing, since you seem reluctant to do so."

He did not even look abashed. "I do not speak of my work. Secrets, you may have learned as a child, are meant to be kept."

"People who are in the care of other people should not patronize them, sir."

He glared at her. "I was dragooned here, if you remember. I can go back to my boarding-house at any time, if my company irks you."

She raised an amused eyebrow at him, ignoring the falling sensation in her middle at the thought of his actually going. "It is not your company that irks me. It is your lack of honesty."

His jaw set, but to give him credit, he did not cross the few feet of carpet to loom and intimidate. "My honesty could put you and yours in danger, Miss Churchill. I shall not risk it."

"Very well." Her acquiescence left him flat-footed, and she felt a spurt of satisfaction. "Perhaps you might tell me instead how you came to kidnap Gloria in an undersea dirigible."

"What!"

Now she did laugh. "Oh, come, Detective Hayes. You forget to whom you are speaking. My mother does confide in me, you know. It is quite likely that I possess as many secrets as you. And Gloria and I have become friends in a way we never could have been in our schoolgirl days. She has told me of your estate in Somerset, and that Claire helped her escape your evil clutches, you villain."

"I am not evil. Or a villain."

"Do not sulk. It is most unbecoming in a man."

"Pert insults are equally unbecoming in a woman."

"Did you fall in love with her?" She asked a ridiculous question, hoping to disconcert him again as she circled around to a real one, but to her surprise, he looked as though she had slapped him.

"She told you that?"

Good heavens. Had she hit upon one of his secrets?

"No indeed." She thought quickly. "But she is a very pretty woman, and rich, and was your captive. Only a man made of iron would not fall in love with her."

To her complete surprise, he laughed, though she had not meant to be funny. "A man made of iron *did* fall in love with her, and she turned him down, too," he said, his face alight with humor and memory. "Evan Douglas, the aforesaid privy councilor. He is the only man to my knowledge—besides Captain Fremont and myself—who can operate a forty-foot-tall battle behemoth." He chuckled again. "A man of iron, indeed. Isabela is a fortunate woman."

By which she realized that he had been cleverly leading her away from all discussion of his current activities. And she had not missed the "too." *She turned him down, too.* So her shot in the dark had found its mark—he had cared for Gloria, and been rejected.

At least they were on equal footing in the lost love department.

"Are you really a Rocky Mountain Detective?" she asked.

He nodded, clearly happy to discuss anything but his connections with the Queen's government. "They are a secret group of investigators who operate with or without the sanction of the Texican Rangers, on behalf of those who are too poor or too cautious to obtain justice through normal channels."

"There is a word I have heard in the streets here," she said. *"Vigilantes.* Are the Detectives like that?"

"No indeed." He frowned. "We come when we are needed, one at a time, not as a posse. We receive requests through channels known to only a few. Daisy, for instance, needed my help in Georgetown, and I happened to be close enough on my way out of Denver that word of her case came to me."

"And someone like Daisy needed your help here?" She did not look at him, instead smoothing the crumples in Gloria's letter.

"N—" he began before he stopped himself. "Very clever. But I shall not be trapped into giving you facts."

"Hmm?" She lifted her lashes, the picture of innocence. He had been about to say no. So he was not here as a detective, but as ... what?

An agent of the Crown.

But why? What could possibly interest Her Majesty in a town like Bodie?

There is no other town like Bodie. Bodie is unique. Because of the gold. Hundreds of thousands of Texican dollars in gold.

Her Majesty, it must be said, was deeply interested in gold.

Trouble at the mine, Daisy's voice repeated in her memory. *It is being devalued, apparently ... causing a great deal of concern in the management offices.*

"Are you somehow causing a drop in the value of the mine, Detective Hayes, so that representatives of the Crown may buy up its shares in Her Majesty's name?"

He pushed his weight off the back of the chair so suddenly that it rocked on its carved feet.

"Where in heaven's name did you hear that?" he snapped. Now he did loom, standing over her, his knees brushing her silk skirts as they draped to the floor, his eyes wide. "Peony, answer me."

He was not angry, she saw at once. He was afraid.

For her.

"I—I did not hear it," she stammered. "I merely guessed. The way I did about your falling in love with Gloria."

He stared down at her, confounded. "I should like to take a voyage through the labyrinth of your mind," he said at last. "As it happens, you are wrong. But you are close enough to being right to truly frighten me. Peony, I am in earnest. You must never say those words aloud. It could mean your life. Or the lives of others. Promise me."

Mr. Parsons had said similar words aloud, and it had certainly meant his life. "I—I— Not even to Daisy?"

"No. This has nothing to do with the death of a boarding-house keeper, or with her search for Dutch."

"You mean Professor Linden."

"Yes. Dutch is what the Californios called him when he could not remember his name. I think it comes from *Deutsch*."

German. But why were they talking about Daisy's father?

Because they both needed to calm down. To step away from the Canton fireworks that their conversation had become.

To back slowly away from the knowledge that she now shared something with him … and he was deeply afraid because of it.

THE LINDENS ARRIVED, bag and baggage, some thirty minutes later. It was all Peony could do to welcome them and escort them to their cabin without her face betraying how unsettled she felt.

"I hope you will be very comfortable," she said as Daisy set their valises down, and Freddie rolled in a very nice traveling closet with the initials *EMM* stamped upon the front clasp.

"I do not think we can help it." Daisy straightened to look at the sleeping cupboards, the window seat in the viewing port (smaller than Peony's own, but still, not a common feature), the pipes through which one could have both hot and cold water. "This is the nicest cabin I have ever occupied … and that includes *Persephone* and *Swan*."

Peony smiled. "*Persephone* is a commercial long-distance ship and *Swan* is a military vessel. Compared to them, *Iris* is a well-dressed flirt in company with wise old ladies in bombazine."

Much like herself, if it came to that. She and her ship were well suited.

"Like many flirts, I imagine she has secrets that would surprise us all," Daisy said with a smile.

"You may be right. I trust Captain Boyle to draw the best from her, and for the rest, I am happy that she has room to make my friends comfortable." Peony walked to the door. "When you have settled in, come to the main saloon and we will have tea."

When they had all assembled except for Timothy, Scooter, and Dinah, who had taken the twins off on some adventure of their own, both she and Detective Hayes managed not to look at one another as they filled their cups and settled on comfortable chairs and sofas.

Daisy did not waste time on pleasantries. "Peony, please

allow us to offer our thanks, again, for your generous hospitality."

"It is nothing, truly. Your circumstances are far better here than in the boarding-house."

"Indeed they are. Freddie and I both feel much safer. But I have one more request for you."

"Certainly." Had the twins put towels in the room? Did Daisy have some peculiar eating habit that must be satisfied?

"What happened at the tea yesterday, when Freddie and I had to come away after the ribbon-cutting at the mine?"

Oh. Well, curiosity was easier to satisfy than peculiar eating habits. "Were you expecting something to happen?" Peony asked with interest. The entire affair had seemed rather dull … or perhaps it was Beth Selkirk who had been dull despite how well she looked. Despite the chance for a ride in her landau, Peony would have been better off reading to Detective Hayes or doing some other useful thing than going to the tea.

"No, not exactly," Daisy confessed. "Unless you caused a riot?"

Peony had to smile. "No. However, one can only take so many men pressing compliments and whispered proposals of marriage upon one. I could barely get sips of tea in between refusals."

"We hoped only for a single fact—whether Mr. Parsons was indeed at the offices Saturday night," Freddie said. "Though I suppose the point is moot now. If he killed Mrs. Moss, then he has received his just desserts."

"As it happens, he did not," Peony said. "I happened to overhear Beth Selkirk asking the night manager if anyone there had gone to the ball, and the answer was no. Parsons and the other financial men were at work from ten o'clock until well after four in the morning."

Daisy sat back, as though her spine had wilted. "So we may remove him from our list ... and Emily Parsons may wear black knowing that whatever else he was, at least her estranged husband was not a murderer."

"I doubt she will know that, dearest, since she does not know he was ever on our list," Freddie said.

"Daisy, may I see your list?" Awkwardly, Detective Hayes put his cup and saucer on the tea table. Daisy handed him her sketchbook, after locating a page at the back for him, where Peony could see a number of lists and scribbles and notes in pencil, along with what looked like the outline of a teacup. He gazed at the page for a moment, then looked up. "You seem to have eliminated all your suspects save one—Mr. Selkirk."

Peony shook her head. "I cannot believe that that pompous, controlling stick of a man could be a suspect."

"Mrs. Manning says that he once harbored a *tendre* for Mrs. Moss, and actually courted her," Daisy said. "He was refused, from all accounts, which could be a motive for harming her. But my goodness, he is the next thing to the lord of the manor here, and would certainly have been missed had he left the ball."

"Does Beth think her father capable of such a thing?" Detective Hayes asked in some surprise. "For I certainly do not."

"I have learned not to assume what anyone may be capable of," Daisy said after a moment. "She does not even believe he courted Mrs. Moss. His admiration, according to her, was bestowed from afar."

"I am long overdue for a call upon Beth. I must get out for

some exercise. I shall ask Selkirk myself, if he is at home." Detective Hayes handed back the sketchbook. "In the meantime, we must enlarge our list."

"How?" Daisy bit into a teacake as though it offended her. "The people with any reason at all to wish Clarissa Moss harm have been crossed off. What other reasons might there be?"

"If one eliminates revenge, there are still love … fear … even greed," Peony pointed out.

"We covered love, did we not, with Mr. Selkirk and Judge Bonnell?" Freddie took a teacake, and passed the plate.

Captain Boyle took one. "What did anyone have to fear from Mrs. Moss? She seemed a very pleasant lady."

"We must still go through her personal papers at the house," Daisy said thoughtfully. "There may be something in there."

"Blackmail letters?" Peony was only half joking. "What could anyone fear from a matchmaker other than a bad match?" Though no one said it, Peony was quite certain they were all thinking that the matchmaker had had more to fear from the bad match than the match did from her.

"It is still worth looking into," Detective Hayes said. "What about greed?"

"It is a shame Mr. Moss has been eliminated," Daisy said. "He believes he is entitled to the boarding-house. He was there while we were collecting our things, shouting at poor Mrs. Boswell and making a great to-do."

"That is why we were late. You should have seen Mrs. Chang and Mrs. Porter," Freddie said with admiration. "They came sailing down the road like a pair of Valkyries, and when he threatened them with harm, Mrs. Porter whipped out her revolver and stuck it under his chin, just like Daisy did with Mr. Parsons."

"I *beg* your pardon?" Detective Hayes exclaimed. If he had still been cradling his teacup in his working hand, he would have spilled it. "Parsons threatened you? You did not tell me that."

"It didn't last long," Daisy said. "He fell over a chair trying to get away from my little Thaxton." She pulled it out of her reticule and waggled it with some satisfaction.

"Is that Pender's Thaxton?" the detective demanded.

"Yes. I traded the Colt for it. Isn't it pretty?"

"I'd rather it was useful. But not for physically threatening men who are bigger than you are."

"In such cases, one has no choice," she informed him.

Peony smothered a smile. My, my. The mouse knew how to roar. Daisy and Freddie Linden were turning out to be much more interesting than they looked.

"But back to Mr. Moss," Daisy said. "He left in a temper, heading for the attorney's office. I do not know what he can do. The ladies assure me that the wording they use in their wills is ironclad. The society of absent friends inherits the property of any friend who passes without heirs. And since Mr. and Mrs. Moss were no longer married, he is not her heir."

"For such mercies we may be thankful," Peony murmured. "Can anyone else be suspected of greed?"

It was a poser, and no one aboard had any other answers.

"Very well, then," Detective Hayes said, rising from the sofa, careful of his posture, and keeping his arm in its sling tight against his chest. "I shall call upon Selkirk under the pretext of visiting Beth, and Daisy, you and Freddie must comb through the papers left at Casa Gallina in search of evidence of deadly sins. Mrs. Boyle, what time do you wish us back for dinner?"

"Seven," she said. "Fancy searching for evidence of deadly sins. I am afraid to wish you luck."

CHAPTER 20

4:35 p.m.

*D*aisy had known they would have to go through Mrs. Moss's papers at some point, but she had not been looking forward to it. Even though Mrs. Chang had assured them that all the ladies stood by to help, and they were free to do whatever they must in bringing the murderer of their friend to justice, it seemed a ghoulish task, raking through a woman's life in search of the reason a person unknown might have had to end it.

She and Freddie went to the back of the house to the large bedroom belonging to Mrs. Moss, most recently occupied by the injured Detective Hayes.

Mrs. Boswell poked her head out of the kitchen. "Oh, it's you. I had hoped that corseted devil had not come back with Constable Lynch." Seeing them in the doorway of Mrs. Moss's room, she said, "I've changed the sheets and made up the bed. Selena tells me I'm to stay on, and the other ladies will run the boarding-house as usual. I hope they can get the rooms filled. It's dreadful quiet now that you're gone and I have only Mr. Pender to look after."

"I am glad he is still here," Daisy said impulsively. "It is better that a man be on the premises when you go home, with all that has happened."

"Indeed it is." Mrs. Boswell nodded firmly.

"We are here to look through Mrs. Moss's papers," Freddie said. "We have eliminated most of those who might have had a reason to harm her. Now we must expand our search."

"And you wonder if there might be a reason in there." Mrs. Boswell indicated the room behind them with her chin. "You are welcome to look. She kept everything recent in the roll-top desk. You will find the key behind the daguerreotype of her mother."

"She did not have a separate office?" Daisy asked.

"No indeed. A boarding-house has no rooms to spare for such luxuries. If a bed will fit, a bed goes in."

"You said *everything recent*. What about records from the past?" Freddie asked. "Are they kept in the attic?"

Mrs. Boswell thought for a moment. "I keep the attic tidy in case we need to house people there. I do not recollect any such records offhand, but they must be there." She smoothed her apron. "I will go look."

"Thank you, Mrs. Boswell."

The good lady hustled up the staircase, and Daisy and Freddie turned their attention to the roll-top desk. The key was where it was supposed to be, tucked into the back of the frame of a severe-looking but attractive lady bearing a faint resemblance to Mrs. Moss.

"I wonder if anyone has written to notify her family," Freddie said.

"Married or not, it is Mr. Moss's duty." Daisy rolled up the top. "I will start up here, if you will take the drawers."

They were poring through lodging receipts, records of grocery deliveries, and letters from prospective boarders ("Look, Freddie, Miss Harding and Miss Levesque are not figments of our imagination—here is a letter of introduction from the former") when Mrs. Boswell returned carrying a rectangular leather box.

"Here are the old registers. She liked to keep them to remember returning boarders—and those whom she would not allow to return."

"Why would she not allow some to return?" Daisy tapped the letters together and returned them to their cubbyhole.

"Nonpayment of their bill, usually," Mrs. Boswell said. "But sometimes rowdy or immoral behavior. She marked them with a red *X* in the margin. The returning boarders are in green ink, everyone else in blue or black."

"Thank you for fetching the box," Freddie said. "We will not keep you from your duties."

"They are few enough now that you have gone," Mrs. Boswell said sadly, returning to the kitchen. "Mr. Pender is not a demanding gentleman."

Daisy swallowed the guilty urge to ask if they might stay for supper, just to give the lady some feminine company. She turned instead to Freddie. "Any luck in the drawers?"

"No. Just the household accounts, stationery, pens, and ink. And some cards from friends. You?"

"No." She gazed thoughtfully at the bed, the dresser, the little bookshelf with its china vase, now empty of the flowers she remembered seeing there Saturday night. "If I wanted to hide something important to me, though, where would I put it?"

"In the flickers, people hide things under the mattress. But Mrs. Boswell has changed the bedding. She would have found whatever there was to be found, and told us of it, would she not?"

Daisy ran her hands under the mattress anyway. "Best be thorough ... no, there is nothing."

"The books? Remember *Passion in the Rockies*? There was a false one in the villain's library that turned out to be a trea-sure-box."

But the books yielded nothing but two bookmarks made of ribbon, a letter from Clarissa's mother dated five years back, and a squashed insect at which Daisy did not look too closely. While she was doing that, Freddie pulled the drawers out of the roll-top, this time running her hands along their undersides, then reaching in to feel if something had been taped to the back.

"Nothing. How disappointing," her sister said.

"I feel like a very poor detective, and a worse burglar," Daisy confessed. "Living in Mr. Hansen's house in George-town did not feel quite this intrusive."

"We are trying to help, not to steal," Freddie said in reas-suring tones. "Where else? Shall we turn up the corners of the carpet?"

Nothing, except more proof that Mrs. Boswell was an exceptional housekeeper.

"Bother," Daisy said, gazing at the walls. "The backs of the pictures?"

Luckily, there were only two besides the portrait that

concealed the key. One, a gloomy oil of a bouquet of moss roses that did not seem to Mrs. Moss's taste at all, hid nothing but—

"Freddie."

Her sister looked up from the leather box in her lap, from which she had just removed the lid. "Did you find something?"

"Two things. In the language of flowers, moss roses stand for voluptuous love—and past love. Second, it is odd, is it not, that their frame has a hinge?" She lifted the painting down and laid it on the bed. It was about eighteen inches by twelve, and the frame was slightly thicker than picture frames tended to be. On one edge was a hinge so small and innocuous it could hardly be seen. On the other, where one might expect a hasp to be, was ... nothing. Daisy ran a fingernail around the seam, but could not lift the back.

"What is the purpose of a hinge with no hasp?" she said aloud.

Freddie shook her head. "Treat it like a Canton box. You remember the one Uncle Edward was so proud of because only he could open it?"

"I never did open it," Daisy said with some irritation. Oh, to be so close and yet so far! "Do you suppose anyone would mind if I simply broke the wretched thing over my knee? These roses are an offense to good taste."

She took it in both hands, just long enough for Freddie to look alarmed, and glared at the frame.

Which had a tiny hole in it.

Oh dear. Were there termites in the house? Surely not.

Besides, termites would eat more than one hole in something. "Freddie, take out your hat pin and insert it, just here." When she did, they both heard a tiny click and the back of the frame popped up. Daisy smiled with satisfaction. "Well done. That makes up for the Canton box. In spades."

While Freddie reinserted the long pin in her hat, Daisy opened the back of the frame to find letters. Notes. Billets-doux. Closely written in a masculine hand and obviously well read. All were addressed to Clarissa using increasing terms of affection.

"V," Daisy said. "That is the sender of this note. Oh, look, this one on top is signed. From Vincent. They must be the same man."

"Vincent Selkirk?" Freddie sighed. "All this effort to hide letters from him when his interest in her was known?"

"Not by his daughter." She held it out.

Darling Clarissa,

I long to see you. Dolores cannot last much longer—every day she fades a little more. Consumption is a terrible disease, made worse by the fact that this climate was supposed to help her. The only light on my horizon is you, my dearest. Once my period of mourning is ended and Elizabeth can accept another woman in my life, we may court openly, and then be married. The days cannot pass fast enough for me.

Your own Vincent

Daisy folded up the letter, feeling like the worst kind of voyeur. "His interest in her *while he was married* was certainly not known. But he never did marry her. They must have quarreled."

"With promises like that, I am surprised she did not kill *him*," Freddie said. "How long ago was this?"

Daisy peeped into the letter, and the next, and the next, all written in the same vein. "Three years ago. Two years after she came to Bodie."

"Hmph. And before she began to see Judge Bonnell. Do we still think Mr. Selkirk might have been responsible for her death?"

"How can one say? She didn't marry the judge, either. She and Mr. Selkirk seemed to meet in public without signs of heartbreak—at the ball, at least. But I am no expert in these matters."

Nor would she be, if William did not follow them as she had thought he might, choosing instead to plot the course of his life in a different direction. Something in her middle clenched in dismay.

"So we are left with dull and boring ledgers." Freddie pulled the box toward herself once more. "Best put those back where you found them."

"Should I burn them in the stove?" Daisy dragged her thoughts from the hopeless to the immediate. "I cannot imagine she would want anyone to see them. Think if Elizabeth were to find them, reading what her father wrote of her mother ..."

"Perhaps when all this is over, we may give the painting to Mr. Selkirk." Freddie's smile held mischief. "They are *moss* roses, after all. Perhaps he will discover their secrets himself. Perhaps not. In either case, we need say nothing about it."

Daisy returned the letters to their hiding place, and hung the moss roses up again.

She had just turned and removed a ledger from the box

when Mrs. Boswell popped her head in. "Still here? Mr. Pender will be home soon. Will you stay for dinner?"

The poor lady looked so hopeful that Daisy hated to disappoint her. "You are very kind, but we are engaged to dine aboard *Iris*, with Miss Churchill."

Mrs. Boswell nodded. "I thought you might be, but this stew turned out to be more than I expected. Did you find anything to help?"

Daisy shook her head. "Only that Mrs. Moss was a very orderly businesswoman. We have only the ledgers to go through now. Will it be all right if we return tomorrow?"

The cook waved her hand at the box. "Take them with you. They start with last year and go back as far as Clarissa had the house—five years now, I suppose. Oh, that reminds me. Selena and the others would like you to take a memento from the house. To remember us by."

"Why, how kind," Freddie said.

"If you are successful in your inquiries, I feel quite certain they will find a way to pay you, but in the meanwhile, take anything you like, excepting the things in my kitchen."

"Dear Mrs. Boswell, we do not need to be paid," Daisy protested. "We are having no success at all."

"Never mind. You may yet. Go on. Choose something."

"I should like this picture of the roses," Freddie said promptly, nodding at the excrescence on the wall.

"Go right ahead." Mrs. Boswell turned to Daisy. "And you, miss?"

Daisy gave up. "The petit point of the yellow zinnias in the sitting room is very pretty." It was also very small, and might be tucked into luggage or posted to Bath without too much inconvenience. And the zinnias would be a nice remembrance of these ladies who had been so kind.

"A good choice." Mrs. Boswell smiled sadly. "Clarissa loved her petit point. She worked that one last winter, when the snow was up to the eaves and Mr. Pender had to dig us out of the second-floor landing window."

"Good heavens," Freddie exclaimed. "So deep as that?"

"Oh, yes. Winter is fierce here. You won't want to stay much past the end of October … unless you accept a proposal of marriage and have a home of your own to winter in, with horses to get about on. Carriages, you know, are quite useless in the drifts."

"Quite so," Daisy said faintly. Snow to the eaves? What an appalling prospect.

"Speaking of horses, have you been to visit my daughter-in-law yet, as Alvira suggested?"

"No, not yet." Whether or not their inquiries were successful, Daisy had a feeling they were not going to be allowed to leave town without first seeing about a holster rig for Freddie.

"We will go in the morning, Mrs. Boswell," Freddie promised, taking the moss roses from the wall and slipping them under her arm. "I am quite looking forward to meeting your family."

Daisy slid the strings of her reticule over her wrist and picked up the leather box. "Thank you for letting us examine Mrs. Moss's papers. We had better be getting on."

"I hope you find something interesting in the ledgers, though I can't imagine what. Bring them back whenever it's convenient." Mrs. Boswell hurried into the sitting room, took down the cheery yellow zinnias, and laid them on top of the box. "There you are. Thoughts of absent friends."

Her eyes filled with tears, and when Daisy reached the gate and looked back, she was dabbing at her cheeks with the corner of her white apron. Mrs. Boswell had clearly held her employer in great affection. So had many others.

Why, then, could they find no evidence of the person who had been driven to end her life?

CHAPTER 21

9:30 a.m.

The next morning, after breakfast aboard *Iris*, Daisy, Freddie, Peony, Detective Hayes, and Timothy each took a ledger. "What are we looking for?" the young man asked, pushing his spectacles up on his nose. "A confession?"

"Don't we wish," Freddie said ruefully. "We are looking for anything odd or out of place. Repeated patterns. Possible reasons for someone to have had a quarrel with Mrs. Moss."

The ledgers were of the kind Daisy had seen open on hotel reception counters—long, leather-bound, with lined pages. But they were not thick, and it was not long before they reached the final pages and stopped to compare notes.

"She has made crosses with notes next to five names in this one—let's see, 1890," Detective Hayes said. "Drunkenness, breaking a lamp and starting a small fire, a lewd proposition, and a refusal to pay a week's board because he did not like the food." He flipped toward the back. "And Pender is in here. He managed to travel in December, brave man."

"He is in mine, too, in green ink," Daisy said. "Twice in 1892. And three men and a lady were not allowed to return." They were not the same three as in his ledger, though that was to be expected.

"Mr. Pender does not appear in 1891 at all," Freddie said. "He seems to have skipped a year."

"Perhaps nothing newsworthy happened in Bodie in 1891," Detective Hayes said with a smile. "Miss Churchill?"

"He stayed here no less than five times last year, but no more than a few days each time."

"He has been here since before we came to Bodie," Daisy said. "And it seems he stayed a long time during the winter. I must remember to check the current ledger, at Casa Gallina."

Timothy lifted his ledger. "Mine must have been a very quiet year, too—1893 has no crosses at all, and only one visit from Mr. Pender. I don't see what his being here or not has to do with anything."

"It doesn't, really," Daisy told him. "It is just interesting, that's all. Mr. Pender is a newspaper man. He would have come in search of a story. I suppose we may be glad we were not in Bodie during those years. Imagine what horrors are considered newsworthy here, if death and mayhem are not."

"You're in Bodie now, and so is he," Timothy pointed out, as maddeningly logical as Freddie.

"Then let us hope we are not involved in something newsworthy." Daisy clapped the ledger closed. "We have done our duty and found nothing. I will return these to Mrs. Boswell."

"What a pity," Peony remarked. "I had quite hoped to see a few names with deadly sins marked next to them. Or notes about someone smuggling gold into the Royal Kingdom. That would have been exciting … or at the very least, useful."

The trouble with making inquiries of this nature was that they were rarely exciting. "Do you find yourself doing things like this during an investigation, Detective?" she asked Barnaby Hayes. "Reading ledgers and other dull things, and finding nothing?"

"Constantly," he assured her. "But the devil is in the details. Something small can turn up and make all the difference, as you know."

That was the truth. Skirt ruffles, for instance. They had reason to know such insignificant things could mean the difference between life and death.

Daisy and Freddie pinned on their hats, and put on their walking costumes with warm jackets. "We will return these, and then we must visit the harness maker or Mrs. Boswell and Mrs. Manning will begin to be offended." They took their leave, promising to be back for tea.

They reached the bottom of the hill to see Mrs. Chang coming toward them at a brisk walk. "Good morning," she said when they reached her. "Just the people I wanted. Now I do not have to climb that hill."

"Do you wish to see us?" Freddie asked.

"I do, in the matter of red zinnias."

For a moment, Daisy was all at sea, and then she remembered. Atsa, and an enamel pin in the washing. "Yes?"

"Including myself and Clarissa, five of us remain in town with red zinnias. Two were at our quilting bee this morning, sporting them upon their collars as usual. The third was not, but I saw her wearing hers when I took tea with her yesterday."

Daisy nodded, thinking. "So it was definitely Mrs. Moss's pin that Atsa was wearing. Mrs. Chang, I am speaking of a laundress at one of the flower houses. She says she takes in laundry from the boarding-houses. Is that the usual custom here?"

"Yes, certainly," Mrs. Chang said. "For you see, the flower houses have steam boilers on the ground floors. For baths for the miners. A miner's cabin has only the most rudimentary of necessities—certainly not a bathroom. They are shacks, lucky to have doors that close properly, and the beds are used by men rotating in from their shifts. So the miners bathe at the flower houses, and have their laundry done there, too."

"I see. Can you hazard a guess as to how Mrs. Moss's pin might have gone from Casa Gallina to Atsa's flower house?"

"I expect a gentleman would bundle up his washing and take it there, dear. Hardly any of the boarding houses have boilers, and even gentlemen who are not miners enjoy a bath. Perhaps one or two other benefits as well."

Hot color flooded Daisy's cheeks. "Thank you, Mrs. Chang," she managed to say past her embarrassment. "This has been … illuminating."

She and Freddie curtsied and took their leave, walking down Green Street toward the big red barn they could see beyond the Methodist Church.

"It still does not make sense, Daisy," Freddie said. "Has Detective Hayes had his washing done since the ball? Or Mr. Pender? I know we have not, but that is because we wash our own things. But even if they did, how did Mrs. Moss's pin get into their laundry?"

"I cannot tell you," Daisy said helplessly. "We will ask Detective Hayes when we return to the ship. For now, you must resign yourself to talking about gun harnesses for fifteen minutes."

"I do not want a gun harness. What woman wants a big heavy Colt constantly banging on her leg?"

"We have promised to go, so we must. We are not obliged to order anything. Just look interested."

Freddie muttered something under her breath that Daisy chose not to hear. They reached the red barn that housed the smithy and livery stable, and through the open sliding doors, large enough to admit an entire carriage, could smell the familiar scents of horses, hot metal, and oil. The heat inside was welcome, for the day, though bright, was cool even at noon.

A man approximately the size of an ox, his face flushed with exertion, and wearing a leather apron, looked up from the hearth. "Help you ladies?"

"Are you Mr. Carter Boswell?" Daisy called.

"I am. Are you the Miss Lindens?" He handed over control of the levers of the bellows to a young man and came toward them, pulling off his leather gloves, his ham-sized hand outstretched.

"We are, sir." His grip was surprisingly gentle, though Daisy suspected his wife might make him rehearse it when in the company of ladies. "Your mother has been very kind, and has directed us here to see Mrs. Lorraine Boswell about a ladies' harness. For a Colt revolver."

"Well, well, come through here. My wife will be happy to meet you. Mother has had only good things to say about you young ladies."

"We are happy to hear it." What a good thing they had come. The question was, did the blacksmith know that she and Freddie were also investigating Mrs. Moss's death? For he must have known his mother's employer. Perhaps she had even made his match.

"You said you had a Colt, Miss Linden?" he asked over his shoulder.

"Not I, but my sister."

Freddie pulled the Colt from her reticule and handed it to him.

"This is a nice piece." He turned it over in his hands, where it looked much smaller. "A little large for a lady, but it will bring down a man with one shot."

"I hope it will not come to that," Freddie said faintly.

"Around here, you never know." He handed it back. "You're still at Casa Gallina?"

"At the moment we are visiting elsewhere, sir," Daisy said.

"Ah, never mind." He picked up the largest pistol Daisy had ever seen, and sighted down its cannon-like barrel. "I was going to ask you to send Pender by if you saw him. The grips on this hogleg of his are in poor shape. I cleaned all the dirt out of them, but there's no saving them. Full of cracks and chips. If I'm going to replace them, I'll need to know what wood he wants me to use."

"His … hogleg, sir?" This was not the Colt Daisy had traded for the Thaxton. The piece in Mr. Boswell's hands could fell a bear. "Are you certain that is Mr. Pender's? I believe he has a Colt similar to Freddie's."

"A man can have more than one gun, little lady," he said with genial cheer. "This is a Colt Army Model 1860. Cap and ball, trusty as a good horse. I don't know what happened to it, though. Looks like it's been through a war. Here. Give it a heft."

Daisy did not want to touch the thing, but a cold feeling

was settling in her stomach. Hesitantly, she took the gun. It must have weighed nearly three pounds—more than her arms could bear. Even with two hands on the grips, she couldn't hold it level—it wobbled and tilted until she lowered it.

As she did, she got a good look at the butt of the grip.

"What kind of wood is this, sir?" she said.

"Walnut, I think. Needs to be hard. The good thing about this gun is, once you bring down your animal, if it's not dead you can save a bullet and knock it on the head." The smith laughed, then sobered. "Sorry, miss. My wife would smack me a good one if she heard me talking that way to ladies. I forgot myself."

"Think nothing of it. The, er, material in the grips that you cleaned out … that might have come from being used just as you said, mightn't it? To dispatch an animal?"

For there was no arguing with the fact that the gun would make a fine club. Leaving a singular depression.

Not a triangular one, such as the corner of a stove might have made.

Not a flattened area, such as a frying pan might have made.

An oval one, like the butt of this gun might have made.

The chill in Daisy's stomach became outright nausea as she adjusted her hands on the gun, holding it gingerly like a club, as though illustrating her own words.

"Probably did," Mr. Boswell agreed. "It had hairs in it, and dried blood. You wouldn't really want to use a gun for that, though. That's what I'm saying. The walnut has to be replaced now. See? Like this."

Next to his pointing finger, Daisy could see that a small piece of the walnut grip had been sheared off. A small piece about the size of the one tucked in the back of her sketchbook at this moment.

She laid the gun on his workbench with a smile as convincing as she could make it, but was probably a rictus of falsity. "We will stop by Casa Gallina and pass on your message," she said. "Now we had better meet your wife."

Freddie gazed from the gun on the workbench to Daisy's rigid face, puzzled and concerned. As they followed Mr. Boswell into the livery, she whispered, "Daisy, are you all right?"

"I will tell you when we leave," she whispered back.

She hardly heard the introductions. Mrs. Lorraine Boswell was a hearty individual of the rangy, tweedy type. If she had lived in England, she likely would have been as comfortable with boilers and steam as she would with horses and hounds. Her smile was luminous, though, and when she looked at her husband, it was with pride and happiness.

Freddie was drawn into her enthusiasm for the ladies' harness in spite of herself, leaving Daisy for the moment unnoticed. She slipped back into the smithy, to the work-bench, and removed the sketchbook from her reticule. After unwrapping the bit of what she now knew was walnut, she laid it in the grip of Mr. Pender's hogleg.

It fit perfectly, making the shape of the grip whole again.

A long sigh left her lungs.

"Back again, Miss Linden?" The blacksmith had come up behind her and she hadn't heard a sound. With the racket in the smithy—the pounding of hammers on iron, the roar of the fire, the whoosh of steam—that wasn't surprising. But it could have been Mr. Pender, walking up behind her the way he had come upon Mrs. Moss, his hogleg inverted like a club in his hand.

"I found the missing bit of this grip," she said as though there had been no break in their conversation. She held it out to show him.

"Right you are." His eyebrows rose. "How did you come by that? Not that I can do anything with it, mind."

"Cleaning," she said simply. "Tell me, Mr. Boswell, am I right in assuming that gun would have a report commensurate to its size?"

He laughed. "If by that you mean does it have a bark as big as its bite, the answer is yes, little lady. You could hear it halfway across town. Which is good, I suppose. The only reason you'd want to use this gun is to stop an attacking bear or catamount or some such. You'd want people around you to know about the danger."

"So you would." She rewrapped the bit of walnut in the handkerchief, and replaced everything as it had been in her reticule. Then she looked up at him, and smiled. "Thank you. I've had quite an education today."

"Glad to help. You won't forget to tell Mr. Pender I need to speak with him?"

"No," Daisy said as steadily as she could manage. "I won't forget." Then, "How long have you had his gun for repairs?"

"A couple of days. No." His wide brow furrowed. "No, it must have been Monday. I remember, because he brought it in when my wife was all of a flutter to get to Clarissa Moss's funeral. Usually I write up an order then and there, but I didn't that day, or I would have made us late."

"And he is clearly in no hurry for it."

"Doesn't seem to be. Which is good. If I have to order in

pearl grips or some such, they'll take a week or two to get here on the train. Nothing I hate more than being nagged to finish a job."

"Pearl grips on a gun of this size?" she asked in some surprise. It seemed a feminine detail for such a large and deadly weapon.

He laughed. "No, probably not. He's had an awful time with men chaffing him about his silly little Thaxton. Nonsense waistcoat pistol, it is, that no self-respecting man would carry. If I were to put pearl grips on that hogleg, he'd never hear the end of it. He'd have to leave town."

"I wonder he did not carry this, then, instead of the waist-coat pistol. To stop the men from laughing."

But the blacksmith only shrugged. "No telling, miss. It's a heavy piece, awkward to wear. He mentioned it was his father's. Likely he just kept it for protection—and sentiment. Well, I must get back to work. Good day to you." And he did so, whistling something that might have been "After the Ball."

"During the Ball" might have been more apropos. For during the ball, Mr. Pender had slipped away and bludgeoned Mrs. Moss with his heavy gun. To shoot her would have made too much noise, and alerted all of Green Street. He could have hidden it somewhere, then when all the excitement had died down and Constable Lynch and the wretched doctor had effectively declared he'd gotten away with his crime, brought it to the smithy to be repaired.

Daisy's stomach heaved. If not for Peony's invitation, she and Freddie would still be sleeping in the house with a murderer just upstairs. He had taken them out in the buggy, so cool and friendly—talking about wind direction and helping them with their aim as though he had not snuffed out his landlady's life with a gun as long as Daisy's forearm.

Breathe deeply. You must not be ill. You must think.

She now knew who had committed the dreadful crime.

What she did not know was why.

But did she need to know? The absent friends had their man. Did they need his motive, too?

And now another thought struck Daisy, as she walked slowly into the livery to find Freddie with her hands on her waist, being fitted for the gun harness and chattering away with Mrs. Boswell.

If the constable and the doctor had agreed that Mrs. Moss had slipped and fallen, and no crime had occurred, then how on earth were the absent friends to obtain justice for their dead?

CHAPTER 22

1:45 p.m.

aisy, please tell me what is going on," Freddie begged, nearly running to keep up as they left the smithy. "Your face—something dreadful happened in there. In heaven's name, what is wrong?"

"I cannot. Not out in the open. I promise, you will know all in only a few minutes."

It took all the strength Daisy had to walk up to Casa Gallina and ring the bell.

When Richard Pender himself swung it open, her knees went weak with the shock. Freddie, wearing her brand new gun harness, clung to her arm as though to hold her up, though she did not yet know the awful truth.

"Why, it's the Miss Lindens," he said, twinkling at them as pleasantly as ever. "I see you've been to see Mrs. Lorraine Boswell, Miss Freddie. Do you find the harness comfortable?"

"I do, thank you, Mr. Pender," Freddie said shyly. "It was a little more expensive than I would have liked. I may need to wash dishes for Mrs. Boswell to pay for it."

Had she been expected to speak, Daisy would have been incapable of more than a whimper. What a good thing she had not yet told Freddie what had happened. Her sister released her arm and proudly smoothed the narrow leather straps that depended from her waist and encircled her narrow hips. From the right side hung a beautifully worked holster in which the Colt now reposed. A small, square pouch at the waist would hold six bullets, with a little room left for whatever else Freddie chose to conceal there.

It was a lucky thing the Colt was not loaded; otherwise Daisy would have been tempted to pull it out and shoot him in sheer terror. What a mess they would be in then, committing murder in broad daylight!

"Is Mrs. Boswell in?" Daisy asked.

"Why, yes, I imagine so. I'm surprised you bothered to ring —you are as much at home here as I, surely."

When he stood aside to let them in, Daisy forced herself to say, "Mr. Pender, the smith gave me a message for you."

The twinkle faded from his eyes. "Oh?"

"He wishes to know what material you would like him to replace the grips of your Colt with. Apparently they were sadly damaged."

"Did he tell you that?" He frowned. "I'm not sure I like a man spouting my business all over town."

Fear fluttered along Daisy's veins. Good heavens. He might murder the smith next.

"I am sure he has not," she assured him, wishing her mouth were not quite so dry. "But he knew we had been staying here, so felt it appropriate to charge us with the message."

"Did you see the gun?" he asked.

The truth sprang to her lips and she swallowed it back. "Indeed not." With a smile at Freddie that she hoped communicated an urgent need for silence, she added, "It is hardly necessary, since it is practically a twin of Freddie's. I am sorry now that I did not examine it closely, or I would have had it repaired myself before I gave it to you. Good day, sir." Taking Freddie by the sleeve, she passed along the hall to the kitchen, feeling every moment as though he might strike her from behind.

"What are you doing, Daisy?" Freddie whispered. "Why did you spin him such a tale?"

"In a moment." She must not break down, in case he was still watching. And listening.

They found Mrs. Boswell at the stove, stirring stew. "Here you are again, girls. May I offer you some stew? It's yesterday's, but this recipe only seems to improve with age."

Daisy could not have forced a morsel down had she been held at gunpoint. Her face chilled at her mind's own terrible turn of phrase. "Thank you, ma'am, but no." She lowered her voice to a whisper. "We need an urgent meeting with as many of the absent friends as you can gather in the next quarter of an hour."

Mrs. Boswell's kindly face slowly paled, too, as she studied Daisy's eyes. Without a word, she removed the cast iron pot from the stove with a towel about the handle. "Go to Selena's house and we will meet you there."

Thank heaven for women who did not waste time with questions and helpless flutterings of handkerchiefs. Thank heaven for women who *acted*.

Not for worlds would Daisy walk back to the front door

245

and risk meeting Mr. Pender again. She and Freddie slipped out the kitchen door and around by Detective Hayes's deserted steam-powered velocipede, still leaning against the side of the house. If only he were here. He would know what to do. But he was goodness knew where, after calling upon Beth Selkirk this morning.

Never mind. *He* had not commissioned them to find the murderer of Mrs. Moss. The absent friends had done so. It was only right that they should know first.

Mrs. Chang let them in, startled at their grim faces. "Girls, whatever is the matter?"

"Mrs. Boswell is rounding up the absent friends," Daisy said. "As many as can be reached on short notice. I have news."

"Are you engaged?"

Daisy stared at her, completely unable to parse such a question in the horror and urgency of the moment.

"She is not," Freddie said, and Daisy realized Mrs. Chang thought she wanted to share the news of some man's proposal. She would have given in to hysterical laughter had not Freddie spoken again. "I believe this must be connected with Mrs. Moss," her sister said. "She has not told me, either, and has been behaving in a most peculiar fashion for the last half hour."

Mrs. Chang made a pale, astringent tea and forced Daisy to drink a cup, before going out to collect the neighboring ladies. Tea was all that kept Daisy from breaking down—in tears, in laughter, in teeth-chattering fear. Soon the little parlor began to fill—Mrs. Manning, Mrs. Porter, and a few minutes later several more ladies whose names Daisy did not catch. Mrs. Boswell came in last with a woman wearing a red zinnia upon her collar, gasping for breath in a way that told

Daisy the poor lady had dispensed with a messenger boy and had run nearly the length of Bodie to fetch her in person.

The room was full—of ladies, of whispers, of speculation. Daisy put her teacup down, its tiny clink acting like the sound of a judge's gavel. The room fell silent as she rose to her feet, gripping the ladder back of Freddie's chair.

"The man who killed Clarissa Moss is Richard Pender, presently staying at Casa Gallina," she said without preamble.

Freddie cried out. Mrs. Boswell gasped, and keeled over in a dead faint.

In the ensuing pandemonium, one of the ladies waved smelling salts under Mrs. Boswell's nose. Another offered the vial to Freddie. Half the room implored the other half to be quiet and listen, but it was not until Mrs. Boswell came to herself that Daisy was able to make herself heard once more.

"I have practically this minute learned of it," she told them all. "You see, we have not been able to determine a motive for the attack on she who was a friend to us all. Those who might have had a grudge against her were proven to be elsewhere at the time of her death." Her heart pounded so hard she had to pause to take a deep breath. "But there are other reasons to commit murder. Love. Fear. Greed. Two men cared for her and the attentions of both were declined. According to the papers, one was hundreds of miles away, and the other … well, no one seems to believe the other could have done it, and the point is moot in any case. Even the one man who might have acted out of greed—Mr. Moss—was seen in conversation in the ballroom during the crucial minutes when she was killed."

"But …?" Mrs. Chang prompted, the single word startling in the silence.

"But thanks to Mrs. Boswell—" Daisy smiled at that lady, who looked mystified, but whose color was coming back. "— we had reason to pay a visit to the smithy a little while ago, and saw the weapon used to end our friend's life."

Freddie took a long breath of realization. "The Army hogleg! That's why you lied to Mr. Pender. You did not want him to know you had seen it."

Daisy nodded. "Mr. Boswell said that Mr. Pender brought in his gun for repairs just before Mrs. Moss's funeral on Monday. Mr. Boswell had to clean a fair amount of … material … out of the grips and saw that they were damaged."

"What kind of … material?" Mrs. Manning's eyes were full of trepidation.

"Dried blood and hairs," Daisy said. Mrs. Porter covered her mouth with her hand. "He thought Mr. Pender had defended himself against an animal. The impact had caused a piece of the walnut grip—a hard, dark wood—to splinter away. I found such a piece of wood in Mrs. Moss's hair when we were preparing her for burial, and saved it in my handkerchief."

"The only link," Mrs. Chang breathed. "That and Clarissa's red zinnia."

"We have not solved that little mystery yet," Freddie said. "Go on, Daisy."

"With a moment alone in the smithy, I laid the fragment of wood from her hair into the grip, and it fit perfectly. It proved that this was the weapon that had killed her. I knew who owned it, though he has kept it concealed from everyone." She took another deep breath. "But what I do not know is *why* Mr. Pender killed her. Or what we are to do now."

"I do not care why!" snapped Mrs. Manning. "I am half tempted to march over there and shoot him myself."

Mrs. Porter laid a hand on her sister's arm. "I feel the same way. But then we would be murderers just as he is."

"It would be worth it, though I were to be hanged afterward. Poor Clarissa!" Mrs. Manning's face crumpled. She pulled a handkerchief from her sleeve and turned away.

"As for what we are to do," Mrs. Chang said, "we cannot exactly call up the six-oh-one. We must take this information to Constable Lynch at once."

Whatever was the six-oh-one? A train? "But the constable has already agreed with the doctor that no crime was committed," Daisy objected. "Will he be likely to change his mind?"

"He must," Mrs. Chang said crisply. "When he sees the proof, Mr. Pender will be in gaol before sunset."

"He had better be there before that," Mrs. Boswell declared. "Six-oh-one notwithstanding, I am not returning to that house until he is out of it. He can sing for his supper, as far as I am concerned."

3:10 p.m.

Constable Lynch gazed in some perplexity at the splinter of walnut nestled in the handkerchief in Daisy's palm. He blew out a breath, his walrus moustache lifting and falling over his upper lip. "This is your proof? A sliver of wood?"

Freddie and Mrs. Chang shifted uneasily as Daisy spoke. "It fits perfectly into the grip of his gun, sir. If you will allow me, my sister and I will demonstrate how he committed the crime."

He looked amused, and a little perplexed. "You think I have

time right now for amateur theatricals? Three men died in a bar fight last night, yet every man Jack who was there swears the bullets flew wide. There is a desert flower dead this morning down in Maiden Lane, and Mr. Parsons to be buried tomorrow with me no closer to finding his killer."

"Please," Daisy begged, tears springing to her eyes.

After a moment he implored patience of the books of poetry on the rough-hewn wooden shelf above his head. "Very well. Get on with it."

"He came upon her in the kitchen, and they must have had words," Daisy began.

"About what?"

"We do not know."

"You don't know?" He threw up his hands. "Why am I wasting my time?"

"Please. This will only take a moment. She may have turned to go out the kitchen door. In any case, her back was toward him. Freddie?"

Freddie came to stand in front of her, and handed her the unloaded Colt from her own harness.

"Imagine that this is a Colt Army Model 1860, if you would, sir."

"A hogleg? Nice piece. Wish I had one. Might have more order in this town."

"Yes, well, to avoid the loud sound of the report that would give him away, he struck her with the butt, here, just above the left ear." Daisy demonstrated, holding her sister's revolver by the barrel, like a club. "Mr. Pender, you will recall, is left handed. But the first blow did not kill her. He struck at least once more—possibly twice, given the blood on the wall."

"Arterial blood, I believe we told you, young lady."

"None of her arteries were severed, sir."

"And how would a gently bred young woman know that, if you please?"

Mrs. Chang said, "I have some medical training. It is as she says. We washed our friend's body together, and prepared it for burial. Her head possessed the only injury."

If the poisonous look he shot her had been a bullet, Mrs. Chang would have fallen dead on the spot.

"You can see that blood would have flown up in an arc on to the kitchen wall," Daisy went on steadily. "And the oval butt of the hogleg is the same size and shape as the broken area of her skull. I saw the gun at the smithy this morning, and this sliver of wood I took from Mrs. Moss's hair fits neatly into the grip from which it was broken."

He gazed at her in disgust. "You are a ghoulish little thing, aren't you?"

Ghouls dig up the dead, she might have corrected him. *And yes, I have seen that done, too, in the service of those who can no longer defend themselves.*

"Please, Constable, we beg you to reconsider your decision that there was no crime. Mr. Pender is clearly guilty, on the basis of this proof."

"I ask again, what proof?" His moustache retreated up under his nose as though a bad smell had wafted through it. "A sliver? Some playacting? The circuit judge would laugh at you—and worse, at me, for bringing a fine man like Richard Pender up on a charge of murder on so little."

"But—" Daisy began.

"You listen to me, missy." His thick finger wagged under her nose, and Daisy took a step back. "An investigator needs three things to solve a murder—motive, means, and opportunity. Without all three things, you don't have a case, and without a case, you can't stand before a judge and expect to win. I am not the six-oh-one."

"Sir, what is that?" Freddie asked. "We have heard it mentioned before."

"You'll stay in the house and bar the windows if you do more than hear it. That means six men, no judge, one rope." When they stared at him without comprehension, he roared, "It's a vigilante posse, for Pete's sake! Now, may I be left in peace to solve the cases already on my plate?"

"We have brought the opportunity and the means before you, sir," Mrs. Chang said, before he could get up to show them the door. "Will you not put him in gaol on the basis of that?"

"What do you think I am, some Canton kangaroo court?" he spat. "Get out of my sight, woman, and back to your laundry."

Mrs. Chang gasped, clapped a hand to her mouth, and fled, the whirl of her skirts sending up a skiff of dust from the floorboards. As the door banged shut behind her, Constable Lynch rose from behind the table which did duty as a desk. It was piled high with papers. Bulwer-Lytton, Daisy noticed, acted as a paperweight, holding down a pile on the right side. Behind him, prisoners in the two cells laughed and jeered.

All Daisy wanted to do was curl up and weep, but she could not. Would not, in front of this whiskered excuse for a lawman. At least General Van Ness in Santa Fe had had the courtesy to remain polite while he told her she was a fool.

"One last question, if I may, sir," she said, her voice quavering.

"No. Out."

"If we can discover Mr. Pender's motive for the crime, will you reconsider and arrest him?"

He took a deep breath and stood. Both Daisy and Freddie took a prudent step toward the door.

"For the last time, you will find no motive, because he didn't do it. I've known Richard Pender for years. He comes here regularly, on the trail of one story or another, keeping the public informed about everything from funerals to gold prices to society balls. He and I have toasted Elizabeth Barrett Browning with the Imperial Saloon's best whiskey, and let me tell you, you'll go a long way before you'll find a man as educated and fine as he. If I hear one more word out of you about his being a murderer—and, heaven help you, if any of this gets out and destroys his reputation—it'll be you two and your Canton laundress in gaol, do you hear me?" His face reddened with rage.

Of course Richard Pender had befriended the poor, deluded fool. What better place to tease out a news story than on the barstool next to the town constable? He had probably never read Barrett Browning in his life. But that was neither here nor there.

"Yes, sir," Daisy said, and pulled Freddie out the door before he lost his temper altogether, and made good on his threat.

CHAPTER 23

SATURDAY, SEPTEMBER 14, 1895

8:10 a.m.

The note came the next morning, just before breakfast. On the gangway, which bobbed gently as *Iris* tugged at her ropes, Daisy gave the messenger boy a penny and walked back up into the ship. She unfolded the sheet of paper bearing the masthead of the *Bodie Barker*.

To whom it may concern,

The article in the paper said you were looking for Prof. Linden. I believe I have information you will like to hear. We'd become friends over the week or so he was here, and he told me where he was bound.

Parsons' funeral is at 11 o'clock. The stamp is shut down for one hour so the men can pay their respects. Meet me there and I will tell you all I know.

Respectfully,

Wade Rivers, miner

Freddie peered crossly at the crabbed handwriting. "He couldn't simply have written down Papa's destination, could he? Why does it always have to be so difficult?"

"I expect he wants to be paid," Daisy said with a sigh. "I have one fifty-cent piece left. That will have to be the worth of one or two words."

Peony read the note swiftly. "Mr. Rivers seems to be a fairly well educated miner," she remarked. "He has included an apostrophe after the name Parsons."

"Men of all walks of life have abandoned said walks to come here hoping to make their fortunes." Detective Hayes took the note from her and looked it over, too. "Even men who know their way around apostrophes. That does not mean that Daisy should meet him alone, however."

"I shall go with her," Freddie said. "If he has information about Papa, I want to be there to hear it."

"But Freddie—" Daisy searched her sister's face, hoping her eyes could communicate what her tongue could not in present company. "The mine—the crowds." *The dead.*

"There will be no crowds, from this account," Detective Hayes said, looking from one to the other. "The men will be at the funeral. The writer must not have been a friend of the deceased."

"If there are crowds, I shall brave them for Papa's sake," Freddie said steadily for Daisy's ears only, and Daisy could do nothing but accept that she knew herself well enough to brave a possible onslaught of desperate souls.

Accordingly, she and Freddie pinned on their hats at half past ten. "Shall I wear my new harness?" Freddie held up the leather equipage from which dangled the Colt in its holster.

"It is up to you, but for my part, the Thaxton ought to be

enough to keep a man at bay should he want to offer marriage as well as information," Daisy said. "It should only be a matter of ten minutes to get the name of a city or town, no longer."

Detective Hayes was waiting at the bottom of the gangway. "I shall accompany you," he said in tones that brooked no argument, standing upright as though they might not notice his sling under his coat.

He had not been himself since the evening before, when they had returned from the constable's office in a state of complete upset, and told him, Peony, and her crew everything that had happened. This morning, he looked as though he had spent a white night, with shadows under his eyes and a face leached of its usual hearty color.

Or perhaps she only thought so because of her own white night, spent tossing and turning in the comfortable sleeping cabinet as she cudgeled her brain for a reason Richard Pender might have turned to murder. And more, what they were going to do if they could not bring him to justice.

They had not even reached the bottom of the hill when Detective Hayes blurted, "Daisy—Freddie—I am so ashamed."

"Why should you be?" Daisy asked gently, somehow knowing that the river of his thoughts was running in tandem with hers. "Richard Pender fooled us all. You cannot blame yourself for that."

"But I am a man in the business of capturing those who play sleight of hand with the law. I should have seen the signs. Been more alert. Living in the same house, for heaven's sake— had I been paying attention, that lovely woman might still be alive."

Freddie's laugh was short and without humor. "We had no idea either. He had every opportunity to kill us both up there in that empty field. He could have buried our bodies and told everyone we had left town."

"He had no reason to kill us," Daisy reminded her. "Even now, he does not know that we know. And it is driving me mad trying to imagine what reason he would have had to harm Mrs. Moss. For revenge, love, and greed do not apply."

"You forgot fear," Freddie pointed out.

"What would a respected journalist have to fear from a matchmaker fifty pounds lighter than he, whom he had known for years without incident?"

There was no answer to a question she had been asking herself since yesterday.

"I am going to have to get out of the detection business," Detective Hayes grumbled, clearly not ready to leave the confessional.

"Detective Hayes, you have been shot," Daisy said. "Be a little kinder to yourself. You have undergone the sort of trauma that knocks all sense from a person's head. You have been of immense help to us as we tried to help the absent friends. Your experience has taught us to pursue lines of inquiry that would not have occurred to us alone."

"For all the good it did you or the absent friends," he said. "Running all over town on a wild goose chase when the culprit was sleeping right upstairs the whole time."

They were fighting their way up Main Street now, going against the current of the men streaming down the hill toward the Miners' Union Hall. Detective Hayes swore as someone jostled his injured shoulder, and his face turned even more pale. "Blast it, Daisy—I do not think I can go any further. The pain—I cannot catch my breath. Yet another sign of my weakness and unsuitability."

The last thing they needed was for his recovery to be impeded by something as nonsensical as insisting on being their escort. If only Captain Boyle had come, too! Never mind. Perhaps he might do some good yet, without risking further injury.

"Let us divide and conquer, then," she suggested swiftly. "We will interview this miner, and you might visit Constable Lynch. You are known to him, are you not?"

"We are not the chums he and Pender seem to be, but yes, we are acquainted. He believes me to be a newspaper man, of course."

"But he does not know that you and I and Freddie are acquainted. Perhaps you might draw him out. Discover something—anything—that might point to a motive for harming Mrs. Moss. For it is not likely he will attend the funeral."

"Quote Byron to him," Freddie suggested. "You will become kindred spirits instantly."

Detective Hayes made a face, but Daisy could not tell if it was because he did not enjoy poetry, or if his shoulder had given him a spasm. "All right," he said. "Forgive me for letting you down."

"Not at all," Daisy told him. Poor man. No one enjoyed feeling inadequate—she should know. "You can be much more useful than we if you unearth even the smallest of possibilities."

With a nod, he took his leave, heading toward the constable's claustrophobic office, while they took a deep breath and plunged into the stream of humanity, fighting their way up the hill like a pair of slender salmon swimming against the current.

By the time they reached the mine, with its buildings and

gantries towering overhead, the crowd had dwindled to nearly nothing. They asked directions from a man who appeared to be a watchman, climbed the high stairs up the side of a vast brick building to which he directed them, and found themselves without difficulty on a catwalk over the arena both he and Wade Rivers had called "the stamp."

"Now I know what has been bothering me." Freddie pointed at the great pair of dusty iron automatons, towering twenty feet high, staring sightlessly straight ahead. The catwalk ran level with what would have been their noses, had they had any. "They're silent."

So they were. How odd that they had grown so used to the subtle vibration in the ground that they only now noticed its absence. "I suppose that with everyone at the funeral, they cannot operate on their own. Goodness, how large their feet are. Do you suppose that when they are working, they look rather like men crushing grapes in a barrel?"

A heap of crushed stone—higher than Daisy could have seen over if she stood on Freddie's shoulders—lay under the enormous heavy blocks of iron that were the automatons' feet. She could just imagine what working in this vast expanse would be like—the noise, the thunder, the dust and flying chips of stone. What man in his right mind would work here voluntarily?

"It is rather like that," came a voice from the left, in the gloom made all the more stark because of the shafts of sunlight striking down through skylights far above. "They do look like men crushing grapes. From here the men look like ants, small and soft and helpless."

There was a gruesome thought. "Mr. Rivers?" Daisy called.

"We have come as you asked. We are the Miss Lindens, the professor's daughters. You have information for us?"

"Oh, yes. Quite a lot for you, in fact."

And Richard Pender stepped into the light, the Colt revolver that Daisy had traded to him held loosely in his left hand.

~

BARNABY HAYES HAD NOT MERELY BEEN FEELING sorry for himself when he had confessed to the young ladies that he ought to give up detective work. Since the night of the Autumn Ball—and the second time he had been shot in the line of duty—he had been giving his entire career serious thought.

Unlike the circumstances of his birth, his career had begun honorably enough, with a respectable series of promotions in the Royal Aeronautic Corps. Then he had been tempted away by the blandishments and the money of Gerald Meriwether-Astor, Gloria's megalomaniac father. The fact that he had been an agent of the Walsingham Office during his employ was no salve to his conscience. Honorable though his service was to Her Majesty in that capacity, people had died because of his actions under Meriwether-Astor's command.

And then the man himself had died, taking a propelled bullet meant for his daughter, and Barnaby had been released from his assignment by Her Majesty. She had dispatched him to the Texican Territories with orders concerning gold, and along the way he had picked up a job or two with the Rocky Mountain Detectives. Unfortunately, he had also been shanghaied into the service of the Royal

Kingdom of Spain and the Californias, which had slowed him down substantially, but which had brought him into the acquaintance of Professor Linden, Evan Douglas, and Joe. That the latter had turned out to be a woman and the half-sister of the Viceroy of the Royal Kingdom had been quite the surprise. Her Majesty had been delighted with that information, particularly since his own relationship with certain highly placed members of the cabinet was most cordial. Her correspondence had conveyed her expectations of his continued usefulness to her.

He agreed that he could be far more useful to Her Majesty on the far side of the mountains, in the Royal Kingdom, than on this side. Getting there, however, was problematic at the moment. Once he solved the troublesome matter of who had been busy devaluing the mine in which Her Majesty had so much interest, a visit to Evan would be in order. Perhaps he might persuade the lovely Miss Churchill to visit, too, since she and Evan had friends in common.

Honestly, he had no business thinking of Miss Churchill at all. Her mother was known to him, being in a similar line of work, and because of that he knew that the daughter was destined for some minor potentate in a rich country, or at the very least an earl in her own. A bastard son of a duke with only a small estate to his name was far too base a substitute for the glorious future Isobel Churchill had in mind for her only child.

Still, it was difficult not to think of Peony. And he had had several days now to do nothing but. She was an excellent nurse and a good companion, beating him at cards but not at chess. She never failed to make him laugh, and he had caught himself many a time going soft-eyed in her direction when she did so. There was nothing quite as lovely as Peony, laughing.

Fool.

With his good hand, he pushed open the door of Constable Lynch's office, to find the man writing a report, his spectacles on his nose. When he lifted his head, his eyes lit with recognition.

"Carnegey," he greeted him. "Not covering the funeral?"

"I believe Pender has that story," Barnaby said easily. "Everyone will be jostling to propose to the widow. Besides, with only one working arm, I can't manage both pad and pencil."

"It'll be a few weeks yet," the constable said, taking note of the competent construction of his sling and nodding wisely. "I've seen many a gunshot wound. You look like you've been well tended."

"I have indeed. Selena Chang at Sunrise House had medical training in her youth. Without her, I would probably be dead and you'd be writing up a report on me."

Constable Lynch stared at him. "This Chang woman is a doctor?"

"Close enough. At the very least, a competent and knowledgeable nurse."

"Not a laundress?"

"No indeed." Barnaby chuckled at the thought. "I'd trust her with my life—which I cannot say for the doctor in town, or the medics up at the mine."

He watched closely as Lynch revised his ugly opinions. Daisy had told him what the constable had said to Mrs. Chang, the dadburned fool. He would not like to bet on the man's chances if *he* were wounded in the line of duty and someone called the lady to tend him.

"I thought you might be at the funeral yourself," Barnaby said easily, "watching for someone revisiting the scene of the crime."

"Parsons was killed at his home." The constable was very literal, as well as literary. Barnaby frowned at Bulwer-Lytton, teetering on top of a stack of reports, forms, and newspapers.

"Yes, I know. Gunshot wound to the head."

"No, it wasn't."

Barnaby's eyebrows rose. "That's what the *Barker* said."

"Only because the dadblasted reporter—Claypool? Cookson?—never got a look at the body."

It was not Cookson. It had been Elizabeth, masquerading as himself. Now he would have to abandon his fledgling career as a journalist, if he could not even ensure that the facts under his byline were correct.

"Poor Parsons was bludgeoned to death," Lynch said grimly. "The mortuary had quite a time making his remains presentable enough for the funeral."

"Bludgeoned, you say?" The drawing in Daisy's sketchbook appeared in his mind's eye. "What with?"

The constable frowned at his report as though it contained something offensive. "Hard to say. A rock? Not a poker or a cane, that's certain."

"He had a bone to pick with Mrs. Moss, didn't he?"

The constable, who read the paper as much as anyone in town, nodded. Then his gaze became fixed upon his report, though Barnaby was fairly certain he was looking past it, at something in his memory. He lifted his head. "The wound.

Now that I think about it, it was similar in shape to the one that felled Mrs. Moss. Smaller, though."

Barnaby went very still.

Then he took a chance.

"There has been some suggestion that she was killed by a Colt Army Model 1860, used as a club."

Constable Lynch's eyes narrowed. "You've been talking to that little girl over at Casa Gallina?"

"I have, as it happens." He nodded as though this were quite acceptable to a sensible man. "And oddly, now that I think of it, there was a similar case in Georgetown last spring. One of the directors of the mine, found in the tunnel with his head bashed in. I saw the body myself. The wound was the same size and shape. Left side of the head."

"Left handed attacker?"

"It would seem so."

The constable shuffled through the stack under Bulwer-Lytton, finally pulling out a handwritten report three-quarters of the way down, this one beginning to yellow, and bearing a ring made by some kind of brown beverage. He smoothed it out. "Had a case, also last year. A woman passing through town found bludgeoned to death in Maiden Lane, though she was no desert flower. City woman, out of St. Louis. Never solved. Her family was notified, and they gave instructions to bury her here. Funeral home had the same problem as with Mr. Parsons."

"Did you observe the wound?"

He nodded. "Looked similar, though as you'll see here, the doc gave cause of death as misadventure. She was found near a stone house foundation with blood on it. But that could have been splashed there to throw us off the scent. Mr.

Carnegey, you might not be at the funeral, but you might have yourself a story all the same."

Four people, murdered in much the same way, with much the same weapon? Barnaby would say so. If it was the same person—Richard Pender—then they had a madman on their hands. "Constable, would you accompany me to the smithy? I believe Mr. Boswell is repairing that Colt, and you ought to have a look at it."

Under the walrus moustache, the lawman was chewing the inside of his lip. "Doesn't sit right. Richard Pender is a friend of mine."

The moment was delicate, the next few words he said all-important. "He is a friend of mine, too. But if he has fooled both of us, we must be the ones to prove it. Before—"

Before someone else gets hurt.

It was almost as if the constable were finishing the sentence in his head. He got to his feet, checked that his revolver was loaded, and pulled his Stetson off the coat tree where it hung.

"I'm not looking forward to apologizing to that little girl if we're right."

Barnaby preceded him out the door. "I'm not looking forward to apologizing to Richard Pender if we're wrong."

CHAPTER 24

SATURDAY, SEPTEMBER 14, 1895

11:10 a.m.

"Mr. Pender," Daisy said after a moment of stark incomprehension well salted with terror. "We thought you might be reporting on the funeral."

Goodness, Daisy, could you sound any more stupid?

"Are you acquainted with Mr. Wade Rivers?" Once again, Freddie's talents as an actress came to their aid. Why not act as though this were merely a social call? "We were to meet him here. This is the area they refer to as the stamp, is it not?"

"It is." He strolled along the catwalk, then stopped about ten feet off. "And I have never met him, because he does not exist."

They had been gulled. Lured here like a pair of pigeons by a very experienced cat. Oh, why had she insisted on parting ways with Detective Hayes? The ball of fear in the pit of Daisy's stomach began to spread outward, and it was all she could do to press her wrists against her stomach to still the trembling of her hands.

The Colt dangled from his fingers the way some men held a cigarillo—loosely, carelessly. His forefinger lay within the trigger guard, however. It could be spun up into use in a second. And probably would be.

He gazed at them, his eyes twinkling in such a familiar, unthreatening fashion that Daisy wondered who was the more mad—he, or herself for believing him to be a murderer. But of course he was. "Please, have the goodness to holster that Colt," she said breathlessly. "I promise we are no danger to you."

"Oh, but you are. You with your little sketchbook and your nosy habits and your gossip. You are quite an acute danger to me. As were Clarissa and that Parsons fellow."

"How, sir? A matchmaker? An accountant? I should not bet on either of them matched against you." Freddie sounded as innocent as a child, her voice even straying into childlike registers. But that was likely from fear.

Fear.

His motive, it seemed, for murder.

"They were no threat physically, of course," he said dismissively. "But a few facts knocking about in their empty heads certainly were. There is nothing I dislike more than a snoop. I came upon Clarissa in my room. Cleaning, she said. But I know she found my latest article for the New York financial papers. It had been moved. My fault, really. I was in a hurry and did not hide it carefully enough."

"Your article…" Daisy's breath hitched. "Do your articles serve to make the men who finance mines anxious? And would speculation in the papers cause the value of the Bodie Consolidated shares to drop?"

He smiled at her. "Not simply empty air in that skull of

yours, is there?"

He comes here regularly, on the trail of one story or another, keeping the public informed about everything from funerals to gold prices to society balls.

Constable Lynch's voice echoed in her memory. "Do you correspond with Constable Lynch when you are not in town?"

"Occasionally. The man is a buffoon, but he has his uses." His face contorted. "Anyone who believes Bulwer-Lytton is a real poet is too stupid to know when he is being pumped for information."

Daisy might have remarked that they were pumping him at this very moment, but that would not be helpful in this volatile situation.

"So you killed her," she whispered through a throat tight with apprehension. "The night of the Autumn Ball. However did you get her to abandon the cake walk and return to the house?"

He smirked. "I merely scribbled a note from a certain Miss LeVesque that they had arrived to find the door locked, and were standing in the street with a mountain of luggage. I handed it to her as though it had been given to me. She went straight home, and did not even notice that I followed."

Freddie was nodding thoughtfully. "It is probably the only thing that would have drawn her away. I wonder whatever happened to those young ladies?"

"I do not know," he said, "but the two in present company have been dashed inconvenient. What possessed you to up and move your lodgings?"

"We were invited," Daisy said simply. Now was not the time to explain about the ghosts.

He rolled his eyes to heaven, shaking his head. "As soon as

you gave me that message from Boswell the smith, I knew you knew. But so much for strangling you quietly in your beds. I had to get creative."

"I congratulate you," Daisy said. "We did not suspect a thing. Though I will warn you that we are expected back on *Iris* for lunch in a very few minutes. If we do not turn up, the entire crew knows our errand. They will no doubt come looking."

"But they will not find you," he said easily. "At least, not in a form they recognize." He leaned over the railing, looking down into the stamp as though curious about the automatons. "There will be very little left to identify once their boilers are ignited and the stamps begin their work. If I shoot you up here, you will likely fall close to their feet, and I will not have the inconvenience of dragging your bodies up that slag heap."

It was all Daisy could do to draw her next breath. Her lungs were trying to seize up in sheer panic.

"I have only one question, sir, before you take action." Freddie's voice was high and thready. "How did Clarissa's red enamel pin come to be in the laundry?"

He gazed at her a moment, clearly perplexed at such a peculiar question. The gun, which he had spun into his grip, lowered an inch or two. "The laundry?"

"Yes. It was found by a laundress in one of the flower houses. She … well, I must tell you that she stole it. I hope that does not warrant her being killed, too. She seemed a harmless little thing."

"I wondered where it went. I took it from Clarissa's body. A keepsake, if you will. I have one or two other things to remember people by. A watch chain. A stock pin. That sort of thing. Bless me. It must have fallen off the dresser when I made up my wash bundle. The shirt I wore that night was ruined—I burned it when I burned Clarissa's dress. But a gentleman has more than one shirt, of course."

Goodness, he was so confident he was positively chatty. Daisy stopped herself with difficulty from looking toward the open door behind them. Could they keep him talking long enough for help to come? Would the watchman wonder why the two young ladies who had gone in had not come out again, and climb the iron stairs to investigate?

As though the same thought had occurred to him, he took a step forward. "As nice as it is visiting with you ladies, the men will be coming back to work soon." The gun rose, his arm straight.

Daisy stared into the iron eye of the Colt's barrel.

Freddie—run—

If I fling myself at him, then at least she can get to the door—

Oh, William—

Footsteps. Coming up the stairs outside.

Thank God.

The gun wavered. Daisy did not move. Did not breathe.

More footsteps, crunching in the crushed stone below.

Many, many footsteps. Had the miners all come back to work en masse?

Daisy did not dare turn. Her gaze was trapped on the forefinger of Richard Pender's left hand, which could squeeze the trigger at any second.

Under her boots, the catwalk vibrated as men walked out on it. This one, and the one on the other side, and the one that ran between the two automatons. And at last, over his shoulder, she saw them—men, filling the catwalks, some dressed in funereal black, some in work clothes, some just in pants and shirts, as though they had been interrupted at home by an emergency.

"Drop the gun, Pender," the man directly behind Freddie called.

"What in blazes are all of you doing here?" he demanded, looking wildly about him as the catwalks filled. Dozens of men, all staring at him, some with their own revolvers now trained upon him.

Surely he would not shoot them now. He would be hanged on the spot. Daisy did not dare retreat, though she heard a man's breathing directly behind her, for Pender had not relaxed his arm.

"Daisy? Freddie?" A woman called from the door. "Are you all right?"

She could not speak, frozen in a nightmare where she would surely be killed in front of so great a cloud of witnesses.

"Mrs. Manning?" Freddie's voice was a squeak of fear.

"Here," said the man behind Daisy. "Escort her back."

"But—but—no, I will not leave my sister! Let go of me!"

"Mr. Pender," Mrs. Manning called, "you are looking at a jury of your peers. A jury of all the single men in all the boarding-houses of this town who will never find a wife because you killed our matchmaker."

A rumble as threatening as any an enraged lion could make echoed in the empty reaches of the stamp. Richard Pender was now surrounded, but still he he did not lower his gun—or take his aim from Daisy.

"Drop the gun, Pender," the man behind Daisy said again. "If you shoot this girl, two dozen men will riddle you with bullets. You won't walk away."

Still he did not lower the revolver. Perhaps it was pride. Perhaps foolishness. But a sweat had broken out on Pender's face, and his eyes darted from one side of the catwalk to the other. Was he estimating his chances of survival should he leap?

"Have it your way," the man behind Daisy, who seemed to be their spokesman, said. "We the jury have examined the evidence presented to us, and we find you guilty of murder. Do you have any last words?"

"Is this an execution?" Pender demanded incredulously.

"Yes. The penalty for murder is death," the man said as though astonished that Pender did not seem to know this. "We aim to hang you from this very catwalk."

"Are you the six-oh-one?" Daisy whispered over her shoulder.

"More like sixty-oh-one, Miss Linden."

Good heavens, it was Alonso Gabriel!

And now an arm came around her waist, and quick as a polka step, Mr. Gabriel had swung her behind him and traded their places on the narrow catwalk. A revolver every bit as businesslike as the Colt now took aim at Richard Pender.

The men passed Daisy along the catwalk until she fell into Mrs. Manning's and Freddie's warm embraces. "Come, dears," the lady said in a whisper. "This is no place for young ladies."

"Will they really hang him?" Daisy croaked. Every part of her trembled uncontrollably.

"Oh, yes, dear," Mrs. Manning said. "It is the six-oh-one, multiplied many times. They are angry, and they have their man. Come away."

But before they could move, heavy footsteps pounded once more on the stairs outside and Constable Lynch burst through the doorway, followed closely by none other than Detective Hayes.

"Stop!" the constable roared, his voice amplified in the space so that it sounded like the bass horn in an orchestra. He pushed through the men on the catwalk. "I'll have no vigilantes in my town. Stop! Put your weapons down!"

No one moved. No one except Detective Hayes, who had a gun in his good hand and who planted himself firmly in front of Daisy and Freddie and Mrs. Manning.

Over his broad shoulder, she could still see Mr. Pender in the middle of the catwalk, now facing Constable Lynch.

"Richard Pender, I arrest you in the governor's name for the murders of Clarissa Moss, John Parsons, Clementine Gibbons, and George Apsley. You will be tried—*properly*—" He glared at the assembled single men of Bodie. "—in a court of law, and the circuit judge will decide your fate. Now, put that gun down and do the right thing for once in your life, sir!"

"The right thing!" Richard Pender laughed—a high, hysterical laugh full of derision. "You idiot, along with a decent poet, you wouldn't know the right thing if it shot you."

He swung up the Colt to take aim at Constable Lynch, and before Daisy could scream, or gasp, or even jerk in a breath, two dozen hammers were thumbed back.

That sound in the enormous space was a threat far more dangerous than any the constable could voice.

For the space of two seconds, Constable Lynch stared him down.

No one moved. No one breathed.

And then slowly, Richard Pender lowered his gun.

CHAPTER 25

SATURDAY, SEPTEMBER 21, 1895

Santa Fe, the Texican Territories
3:45 p.m.

A slender figure leading a horse bearing two people toiled up the zigzag path on the face of the red sandstone escarpment on which the Navapai village perched. They were not Navapai, by their Texican dress, and William Barnicott recognized none of them. But at least one of the three was causing a sensation in the village. A child appeared in the doorway and gabbled something too fast for William's knowledge of the Navapai tongue to catch. Alaia dropped her herbs on her workbench, hitched up her white wool dress, and ran for the square. Tobin snatched up the baby, his wife put their toddler on her hip, and they followed.

Lin and Davey gawked at one another, then as one dove out the adobe archway after their hostess at a dead run, Lin's cropped hair flying. William followed more slowly, though not by much, and emerged into the square to find Alaia weeping with joy, a young woman of about eighteen clasped in her arms. Alaia pressed a hand against the back of her head, holding her to her bosom as if she would never let her go, and tried to speak. "Atsa! Oh, Atsa, you are come back to us at last, back from the long path through the painted desert."

She must be a relative. Long away and much missed, from the look of it. William leaned against a warm adobe wall in the shade of a brilliant fuchsia bougainvillea, sharing the pleasure of the reunion from a distance. When Davey and Lin joined him, he watched with a smile as Tobin and the rest of the family greeted the stranger. Then the young woman indicated her companions, who had dismounted.

"Auntie, this is Senor and Senora Gabriel—the former Miss June Chu. They are newly married, and have come to live in Santa Fe. I have been their guide here, all the way from Bodie."

Bodie? Davey stood up straight, and glanced up at William.

While William was happy to put a name to these new faces, he found himself filled with urgency to know just how these people were connected. Daisy and Freddie were in Bodie—or had been, to the best of his knowledge. This could not be a coincidence. What were the odds that any one of them might have news of the Linden sisters?

"You are very welcome, Senor Gabriel, Senora Gabriel," Alaia said, one arm around Atsa's waist, as though she could not bear to let her out of reach. Atsa's dress was new, though subtly different from those of the ladies William had seen in Santa Fe. She wore a red enamel zinnia upon her collar, identical save in color to the one that had been given to Daisy. "Will you stay a little while? I believe my niece's return calls for a feast this evening, and you would be most welcome."

Senora Gabriel's dress was different, too. "She is a Canton

girl," Lin whispered. "Like me." The bride's traveling suit was of a Texican cut, but possessed scarlet trim on the jacket, and the intricate, delicate knots of silk rope that the Canton ladies favored as fasteners down the front.

Daisy would have loved to sketch her.

Blast it, could these new arrivals possibly know anything of her? How soon would it be polite to ask?

Senor Gabriel bowed respectfully to the most powerful shaman in the Wild West. "We would be most honored, senora," he said. "But before that, we have an errand that cannot wait. Tell me—do you know of a man called William Barnicott?"

Alaia's brows rose, and she turned her head to gaze at William. "I do. He is there."

William shoved off the wall and approached the young Texican man, his hand outstretched and Lin and Davey trailing in his wake. "I am William Barnicott. I am very pleased to make your acquaintance, sir. Ma'am." He bowed to Senora Gabriel, and smiled at Atsa, who had just persuaded her aunt to release her. "Senorita. Welcome home."

The girl smiled at him, and it was like looking into a mirror that reflected the past. She would be very similar to her aunt in a decade or two.

Senor Gabriel shook his hand firmly. "I have a letter for you from Miss Linden. I have been charged most specifically to give it to you and no other." From his inside jacket pocket, he withdrew a fat envelope with William's name on the front.

William's heart began to gallop like a wild horse racing the dusk to a safe valley. He took the packet and slipped it into his own coat. "Thank you. I had hoped you had news of the Miss Lindens. Do you know if they found their father in Bodie?"

He hadn't expected to feel so much disappointment as this when the man shook his head. "No, he had already gone by the time they reached the town."

"But I have seen him and spoken to him," Senora Gabriel said, clinging to her husband's arm. "I told the young ladies so. He told me he was going to the Barbary Coast, to work his passage on a ship. He was to have taken me, too, because I have lived in San Francisco and wanted to return." She gazed up into her husband's face, glowing with love. "But I am glad now that he forgot, and went without me."

"So Daisy and Freddie, then," Davey said. "They've gone to San Francisco after him?"

Senor Gabriel nodded, and William felt the impact deep in his solar plexus. "So far away," William said hoarsely.

"We tried to convince them not to do it." Senora Gabriel shook her head under its broad-brimmed, fashionable hat. "But at least they are in good company. Miss Churchill has taken them in the airship. They should be there already."

William had no idea who Miss Churchill was, and hardly cared. But San Francisco! It was a huge metropolis. William had never been there, but everyone had heard of it ... even his own *Tales of a Medicine Man* by An Educated Gentleman paled in comparison with the goings-on in the capital of the Royal Kingdom of Spain and the Californias. How on earth was he to find Daisy there?

You mean you are going after her?

He felt the substantial packet against his heart. Perhaps the answer lay inside.

"Thank you," he said to the couple. "For the news, and for bringing me Daisy's letter. You have taken considerable trouble, and I am very grateful."

"It is no trouble," Senora Gabriel said. "We wanted to see Atsa safely home to her family. Now it is our turn to find a home." She smiled up into her husband's eyes. "We are staying at the Comstock Hotel for now. I hope you will call upon us there."

He bowed, and Alaia and Atsa took them away to see that they had refreshments while the village prepared the feast.

"A letter from Daisy!" Davey and Lin followed William through the passage and out to the sun terrace overlooking the pinnacles where the village's balloons were moored. "Can we read it?"

"It's a *love* letter," Lin told him with the scorn of the elder by three years. "And it's addressed to him alone, not all of us."

William could only hope it was a love letter. Or at the very least, one that meant close friendship. Affection. He would settle for kind regard. Anything but a farewell. "I will share with you as much as I can, how's that?"

Lin sniffed, but she seated herself on one of the broad steps with Davey to hear the news all the same.

William ran a thumb under the flap and unfolded the contents. A bit of thick paper the size of his hand fell into his lap. It was a watercolour painting of the prettiest airship he had ever seen, bearing the name *Iris* on her bow. She floated at the ends of her mooring lines, and in the distance was a tumble of houses and cabins.

Something hard was folded into a little paper purse. He handed it to Lin, who unwrapped it to find an enamel pin.

A zinnia, yellow as the sun. In the language of flowers, he remembered, the zinnia meant *thoughts of absent friends*. What did it mean? Was Daisy thinking of him? Did she intend to be absent for longer? Perhaps for the rest of his life?

Frowning, he set aside an article torn from a newspaper, written by one E. R. Selkirk—JOURNALIST HANGED FOR MURDER AND ESPIONAGE—to read in a moment. The letter was two pages, closely written on both sides. That was a good sign. Wasn't it?

Dear William,

I hope that Alonso and June Gabriel (and thereby this letter) find you well, and that Tobin's repairs and improvements to your conveyance are nearly completed. Mrs. Gabriel is an aeronautics engineer of some talent; I hope that she will be able to use her education and skills in their new life in Santa Fe. If she and Tobin were to go into partnership I'm certain Santa Fe would never be the same!

Be assured that Freddie and I are well. If you like, you may ask Mr. Gabriel about recent events here in Bodie. He was there at the denouement that resulted in the arrest of a murderer—

"Good heavens!"

"What?" Lin demanded, leaning over his arm to get a glimpse of the letter. "I don't care if it is a love letter, you must read it to us."

"Lin's right," Davey said. "Daisy and Freddie are our friends, too. Just leave out the spoony parts."

William sighed. "Very well." He started over, reading aloud this time.

—murderer, who had killed our landlady, one of the absent friends. You will find enclosed a zinnia pin, which will identify the bearer as either an absent friend or a trusted friend of one. You will always be assured of a place to lay your head, if a boarding-

house can be found and your conveyance is unable to serve that purpose.

We are the somewhat perplexed recipients of one hundred dollars in gold, which the absent friends have insisted that we take as a reward. You will read the particulars of the case in the enclosed article. We need no reward for doing the right thing, but the money is welcome for all that. I had wondered how we were to keep ourselves as we continued our journey to find Papa. I gave Atsa ten dollars of it so that she might return to Alaia and take up her training as the shaman to follow her aunt. I wonder what she will change her name to now.

You will remember Barnaby Hayes, the Rocky Mountain Detective who was so helpful in Georgetown? Imagine my surprise to find him a resident of the same boarding-house as we. He was shot—

"Good heavens!" Lin exclaimed.

"Quiet!" Davey ordered. "I want to hear about Barnaby. This is a much better letter than I thought."

He was shot, and though he is healing well, I suspect that he is reconsidering his choice of career. He and Peony Churchill both claim an acquaintance with one Evan Douglas, who is privy councilor to the Viceroy of the Royal Kingdom of Spain and the Californias, so we lift tomorrow for San Francisco to pay a call. I cannot express my emotions at this turn of events. Freddie says I must find calm, and is pressing upon me Mrs. Boyle's teacups to paint. Captain and Mrs. Boyle and their family crew Peony's ship, a sketch of which I enclose.

On the one hand, I shall see the glories of the Royal Kingdom, and learn something of Papa's sojourn there. But William, the thought of going so far—to the dangers of the Barbary Coast at that —fills me with fear. What fate might have befallen my father in that lawless place? Worse than being in gaol and forced to work on the dam before the Rose Rebellion? For he will not be paying calls at the royal palace. Will we ever find him—or will we perpetually wander the earth, always a step behind?

Never mind. Forgive my sniveling. I must take a lesson from Peony, who never admits defeat, but sails on into the wind dressed in the latest fashion and a hat to make one swoon.

I dare not hope that your feelings are unchanged since last we met, but—

"Here comes the spoony part," Davey groaned, and crossed the courtyard to climb the parapet, the little distance and the wind serving to block the reading of anything embarrassing.

Lin rolled her eyes to heaven and stayed put.

—but I have learned, for my part at least, that I would rather face these adventures with my hand in yours, and my heart in your keeping. Perhaps I am too blunt after all these weeks, too forward in my expressions, but I cannot help it. I have seen so much of the depths that humans are capable of that I long for the antidote of their heights. I long for close companionship, for safety, for the sharing of life's adventures.

In short, I long for you, William.

If you no longer feel as I do, then perhaps a letter saying so, care of Iris, would be best. But if you do, then I will keep one eye on the eastern horizon, watching for the familiar scarlet-and-buff stripes of your extraordinary conveyance bringing you to me once more.

I will close now, for we are to lift soon, and I still must get this

to Mr. Gabriel. Peony is to take us shopping in Reno for some new
clothes. We must not disgrace her in the royal palace.

> *Ever your own*
> *Daisy*

P.S. Give Lin and Davey hugs from Freddie and me. We miss them
both dreadfully.

William looked up, his gaze moving from Lin to Davey. "Well?" he said.

Lin rose. "Tobin finished his improvements to the conveyance days ago."

Davey jumped down from the sandstone wall. "I'll go pack our things. But can we stay for the feast?"

William laughed, his heart lighter than it had been in weeks. "I believe we have as much to celebrate as anyone in the village." He ruffled Davey's hair. "We'll lift at dawn."

THE END

AFTERWORD

Dear reader,

I hope you have enjoyed *The Matchmaker Wore Mars Yellow*, and our continuing adventures in the Magnificent Devices world via this mystery series. If this is your first visit to that world, I hope you will begin your adventure with Mysterious Devices Book One, *The Bride Wore Constant White*. You might even go back to where it all began, with Magnificent Devices Book One, *Lady of Devices.*

Daisy and Freddie's adventures will continue in Mysterious Devices Book Four, *The Engineer Wore Venetian Red.*

I invite you to visit shelleyadina.com to subscribe to my newsletter, browse my blog, and learn more about my books. Welcome to the flock!

Warmly,
Shelley

The Matchmaker Wore Mars Yellow

The Engineer Wore Venetian Red

The Judge Wore Lamp Black

The Professor Wore Prussian Blue

ROMANCE

Moonshell Bay

Call For Me

Dream of Me

Reach For Me

Caught You Looking

Caught You Hiding

Corsair's Cove

Kiss on the Beach (Corsair's Cove Chocolate Shop 3)

Secret Spring (Corsair's Cove Orchard 3)

PARANORMAL

Immortal Faith

ABOUT THE AUTHOR

Shelley Adina is the author of 24 novels published by Harlequin, Warner, and Hachette, and more than a dozen more published by Moonshell Books, Inc., her own independent press. She writes steampunk and contemporary romance as Shelley Adina; as Adina Senft, writes Amish women's fiction; and as Charlotte Henry, writes classic Regency romance. She holds an MFA in Writing Popular Fiction, and is currently working on her PhD in Creative Writing at Lancaster University in the UK. She won RWA's RITA Award® in 2005, and was a finalist in 2006. When she's not writing, Shelley is usually quilting, sewing historical costumes, or enjoying the garden with her flock of rescued chickens.

Shelley loves to talk with readers about books, chickens, and costuming!
www.shelleyadina.com
shelley@shelleyadina.com

Made in the USA
San Bernardino, CA
20 January 2020